*Tony looked (...) disreputable, (...) blue jeans and motorcycle boots, sunglasses obscuring his eyes, a five-o'clock shadow darkening his jaw.*

*Lethal* was the first word that popped into Maggie's mind.

Feeling suddenly very nervous, she folded her arms, swallowing against the crazy flutter in her throat. Her heart started to pound, her mouth went dry, and common sense warred with a fierce longing.

Tony glanced up then and caught her watching him, and his expression went very still. He stood with his back braced against the window frame, his arms folded, one foot flat against the wall. There was something in his stillness, in the steadiness of his gaze, that made her heart skip a beat.

She took a deep breath and turned away.

Lord, he was driving her to distraction....

Dear Reader,

We've got six drop-dead-gorgeous and utterly irresistible heroes for you this month, starting with Marilyn Pappano's latest contribution to our HEARTBREAKERS program. Dillon Boone, in *Survive the Night,* is a man on the run—right into Ashley Benedict's arms. The only problem is, will they survive long enough to fulfill their promises of forever?

Our ROMANTIC TRADITIONS title is Judith Duncan's *Driven to Distraction,* a sexy take on the younger man/older woman theme. I promise you that Tony Parnelli will drive right into your heart. *A Cowboy's Heart,* Doreen Roberts' newest, features a one-time rodeo rider who's just come face-to-face with a woman—and a secret—from his past. Kay David's *Baby of the Bride* is a marriage-of-convenience story with an adorable little girl at its center—and a groom you'll fall for in a big, bad way. *Blackwood's Woman,* by Beverly Barton, is the last in her miniseries, THE PROTECTORS. And in J.T. Blackwood she's created yet another hero to remember. Finally, Margaret Watson returns with her second book, *An Honorable Man.* Watch as hero Luke McKinley is forced to confront the one woman he would like never to see again—the one woman who is fated to be his.

Enjoy them all, and come back next month for more great romantic reading—here in Silhouette Intimate Moments.

Yours,

*Leslie Wainger*

Leslie Wainger
Senior Editor and Editorial Coordinator

Please address questions and book requests to:
Silhouette Reader Service
U.S.: 3010 Walden Ave., P.O. Box 1325, Buffalo, NY 14269
Canadian: P.O. Box 609, Fort Erie, Ont. L2A 5X3

# DRIVEN TO DISTRACTION

## JUDITH DUNCAN

Published by Silhouette Books

**America's Publisher of Contemporary Romance**

SILHOUETTE BOOKS

ISBN 0-373-07704-1

DRIVEN TO DISTRACTION

Copyright © 1996 by Judith Mulholland

**Books by Judith Duncan**

Silhouette Intimate Moments

*A Risk Worth Taking* #400
*Better Than Before* #421
*\*Beyond All Reason* #536
*\*That Same Old Feeling* #577
*\*The Return of Eden McCall* #651
*Driven to Distraction* #704

*Wide Open Spaces

Silhouette Books

*To Mother with Love* 1993
"A Special Request"

## JUDITH DUNCAN

is married and lives, along with two of her five children and her husband, in Calgary, Alberta, Canada. A staunch supporter of anyone wishing to become a published writer, she has lectured at several workshops for Alberta's Department of Culture and participated in conventions in both British Columbia and Oregon. After having served a term as 2nd Vice President for the Canadian Authors' Association, she is currently working with the Alberta Romance Writers' Association, which she helped to found.

To my good fairy, Marlene Dunn,
for doing what she does best. I couldn't
have done it without you, Marlene.

# Chapter 1

Maggie Burrows felt as if her eyes were being sucked out of her head as she stared at the computer screen, a pencil clenched between her teeth, aggravation making her jaws ache. She entered the final numbers from the stack of checks clipped together on her desk, aware that a headache—a very big headache—was only moments away. Taking the pencil out of her mouth, she tossed it in the shoe box of receipts on her desk, then hit the Return key. The numbers froze on the screen as the figures compiled, then a total appeared. Frustration, blood and raw adrenaline rushed to her head, and she clenched her fists in her hair. "*Aggghhh!* This is driving me nuts!"

Frank Lucciano poked his head around the door, then rested his hand on the frame and studied his employee. The round, stocky businessman was totally bald on top, with dark, curly hair from the crown down. With his thin mustache, narrow, intent eyes and short stubby fingers, he looked like an overweight gangster. In one sense, Maggie supposed he was. He regularly robbed Revenue Canada of expected tax dollars.

And that was because Frank Lucciano was one of the shrewdest accountants around. His customers loved him, government auditors hated him and most of the time Maggie would have sold her soul for him—except right now. Right now she wanted to strangle him, along with her client.

He moved farther into the doorway. "You still fighting with the Macinrow account?"

He even sounded like a gangster. Maggie glared at him, resisting the urge to smash her brand-new keyboard over her brand-new computer. "Yes," she snapped, "I'm still fighting with the Macinrow account!"

He shifted his hand higher on the door frame, and sunlight glinted off his obscenely large diamond pinky ring. "I tolt you," he said, in something that sounded like a Bronx scold, "not to bail him out. This is the third year in a row he's been late with his corporate tax return. Then he comes in here with three shoe boxes full of receipts? Let them Revenue guys take a bite outta him. Next time he'll hop a little quicker."

Maggie glared at him. "Thanks *so* much for your support, Frank. As if you'd let 'them Revenue guys' take a bite out of anyone."

There was something that looked suspiciously like amusement lurking around his mouth. "Him I would. He's always late getting his books in and he never pays on time. Him they could have."

She shot him a hostile look. "This is Calgary, Frank, so cut the Capone act. I'm not in the mood. If I had a match right now, I'd torch the whole damned mess."

He straightened and lumbered over to her work station, leaning over her shoulder as he studied the screen. "So what's the problem?"

She let out a heavy sigh of exasperation. "I can't get a damned thing to balance. I've checked it so many times, I don't know what I'm doing anymore."

He straightened and flapped his hands at her in a shooing motion. "Move."

She compressed her jaw into a stubborn line. "I'm not—"

He gave her a long level look and flapped his hands again. "Just move it, Burrows. Let me see what that old bugger's done this time."

Relenting with another sigh, Maggie got up, and Frank settled his heavy frame in her chair. He adjusted the slant of the monitor, then hunched his shoulders. "Go home," he said to the screen. "Have a shot of gin or a Valium or something. If anybody's going to torch Macinrow's box of crap, it's going to be me."

Maggie released another heavy sigh. "I can't leave you with this. Especially when I'm taking holidays next week."

Frank scrolled through the entries. "Go home, Burrows," he reiterated firmly. "If this old bugger kept decent records, he wouldn't end up in these damned messes. Besides, who in hell in their right mind would have set a corporate year-end for the end of May? Doesn't he know when personal income taxes are due in this country?" Maggie's boss gave a disgusted snort. "He probably never filed those, either."

"Frank—"

"Go home, Maggie." A grin worked its way around his mouth. "Hell, you're over forty—what can you expect? Miracles?" His grin broadened. "Maybe it's menopause."

Narrowing her eyes at him, Maggie bit back a humorous retort and considered slugging him with the complete volume of the Income Tax Act. Instead, she picked up a shoe box of receipts and dumped it from shoulder height onto the desk. "Then go to it, Lucciano." She reached out and grabbed her handbag from the top shelf of her computer station. "And I hope this mess gives you hives and ulcers."

Frank Lucciano chuckled. "Women," was all he said.

Maggie had her hand on the door when she stopped and turned, guilt and gratitude warring within her as the spring sunshine taunted her. "Thanks, Frank."

His gaze was riveted on the screen as he waved off her comment. "Yeah, yeah."

She stared at him a moment, then responded, the guilt giving way to amusement. "If you decide to murder him, let me know. I'll raise bail."

The older man chuckled again. "You're all heart, Burrows."

Hooking the strap of her bag over her shoulders, she pulled open the door. "See you next week."

"Yeah, yeah. Don't slam the door on your way out. And don't take any wooden nickels."

She grinned at him. "Yes, Mother."

"Just go home, will you?" he said, scrolling through the figures on the screen. "You're getting on my nerves."

Maggie gave him a rude salute and left, making darned sure she slammed the door after her.

If she hadn't been forty-three years old and somewhat sane, she would have immediately jumped up and down on the accounting firm's steps and shouted hallelujah. Tax season was over, it was spring and she had a week off. The feeling of freedom left her feeling almost giddy.

Straightening her shoulders, she took a big, cleansing breath and started walking down the street toward home, humming "Spring Is in the Air." Lord, it was a relief to get out of there. And today she was going to enjoy the walk home.

Every step was as familiar as her own face. She'd grown up in Calgary, in this neighborhood. And though there was "big city" all around it, the Marda Loop district somehow managed to maintain a small-town feel, even through a major revitalization. Trendy new businesses were now mixed in with the old, and a significant number of young, upwardly mobile professionals had moved in, restoring old homes or building sleek new in-fills.

But in spite of the changing complexion, the small-town feeling had remained. Named for an old city transit stop and tucked into a hilly southwest corner of the city, Marda Loop had all the energy of renovation, but it also had the history and flavor of an old, established area, and Maggie loved every square inch of it.

After her divorce twelve years ago, she had moved back to raise her three kids. Her mother had died years before and her father was alone, and he had wanted her to come home. So she had, and she'd never once regretted it.

Heaving a deep, contented sigh, she turned down a side street, the sunshine and scent of spring filling her up, putting a bounce in her step. She was simply going to enjoy the day and the rare feeling of freedom. And she was not going to think about all the things she had to do on her week off— things like paint. Nope, she wasn't going to think about that.

She didn't feel this lighthearted very often, so she was going to revel in it as long as she could.

She crossed the street, relishing the smell of new leaves and green grass, all laced with the scent of fresh bread coming from the bakery a block over. Skirting the storm grate, she stepped up on the sidewalk and snapped off a single bud from a lilac bush as she passed, twirling the stem between her fingers. Once she got the living room painted, she'd pick herself a big bouquet.

She looked up and immediately tripped over a crack in the sidewalk, stumbling a few steps before catching her balance. Then she stopped and stared, horror paralyzing her as she stared at the no-longer-vacant tire shop next door to her home. The two-story building, for sale for the past year, ever since her neighbors, the Millers, had retired and moved to Arizona, was set back from the street. On the cement apron in front, four sinister, black Harley Davidson motorcycles were parked, their heavy chrome glinting ominously in the sun. The two bay doors were open, and as Maggie stood there, trying to assimilate the sight before her, a blare of rock-and-roll music came from one of the bays. Her heart lurched in her chest, and icy alarm washed through her.

A motorcycle gang. Oh, God, the Millers had sold out to a motorcycle gang. Oh, lord! Clasping her hand against her chest to try to stop the wild pounding of her heart, Maggie stared at the nightmare before her. She knew about this. About gangs buying houses in older neighborhoods. Bringing crime. Terrorizing the residents. But she couldn't believe it was happening here. Not in this quiet corner of the neighborhood. Not next door to her!

Feeling as if there was a race horse loose in her chest, she dragged her gaze away and stared numbly down her once-peaceful street, too stunned to move. She was living next door to a nest of Devil's Angels.

A fresh shot of alarm slithered up the back of her neck, and she started walking, a hard little ball of fear taking shape in her belly. Her gaze fixed straight ahead, she hurried past the property and turned up her sidewalk, feeling as if the dogs of hell were hot on her heels. Devil's Angels. Right next door.

Fumbling with her keys, she unlocked her front door and practically fell into the glassed-in porch, her heart still beating a wild tattoo in her chest. Extracting the key, she pushed the door shut, threw the dead bolt and leaned back against the heavy wood panel, her knees suddenly shaky. Taking a steadying breath, she opened her eyes and stared at the brass knocker on the inside door. *Now* what in hell was she going to do?

Determined to draw on her usual common sense, she tried to will away the panic in her abdomen. Okay, maybe she was overreacting. Maybe it wasn't a gang. Maybe whoever had bought it was going to open a motorcycle shop next door. Not a great addition to the street, but definitely better than a Devil's Angels' fortress. In any case, the first thing tomorrow, she was definitely going to call Johnson's Securities and get them to install new dead bolts, and security bars on the basement windows. And outside lights and—

The inside door opened abruptly, and Maggie jumped and clamped her hand to her chest, her heart going into overdrive.

Her fifteen-year-old daughter stood staring at her as if Maggie had lost her mind. "What are you doing home? It's only 3:30."

Certain that if she got one more bad scare today, she'd be needing a cemetery plot instead of security bars, Maggie managed a weak smile. "Frank gave me the afternoon off."

A frown appearing, Kelly studied her mother. "What's the matter? You look weird."

Determined not to alarm her daughter until she had a chance to find out what was going on next door, she put more effort into her smile. "I spent all morning working on Mr. Macinrow's taxes."

"He's the guy that always brings in his receipts in shoe boxes, right?"

"Right."

Kelly grinned and opened the door wider. "Well, this must be your day, Ma, because there's also a letter from Dad in the mail. Which means he's delivering one of his lectures. I wonder what's ticked him off this time."

Digesting this piece of news, Maggie stared at her daughter, then released a long sigh. Just what she needed. Devil's Angels next door and a letter from Bruce on the same day. If she had a choice, she'd rather have the Devil's Angels. Expelling another heavy sigh, she followed her daughter into the house and tossed her purse onto the easy chair just inside the living room. Then she went into the kitchen, experiencing 'a twist of distaste when she saw the stack of mail on the kitchen table. It wasn't that she and her ex-husband had an unpleasant relationship. In fact, for the most part, it was quite civil. As long as he kept his opinions to himself.

With not an ounce of well-being left, Maggie stared at the pile of mail. She knew darned well what the letter was about. Haley, their twenty-year-old daughter, who was attending university in eastern Canada, had landed a summer job on a cruise ship. Bruce had wanted her to spend the summer in Vancouver, working for him. Haley and her father had got into a battle royal over that, and she had finally phoned her mother, asking her opinion. Haley was on the dean's list at university, held down a part-time job, managed her money like John Paul Getty and still found time to volunteer at a women's shelter. She was one of the most levelheaded, sensible, independent kids around. She was also nobody's doormat.

Maggie was well aware that her daughter would make more money working in the accounting firm for her father, and she also knew that Haley's expenses in Vancouver would be next to nothing. After all, Bruce had made a point of informing her that he and Jennifer had fixed up the guest room just for Haley, so she could have a "decent, suitable" place to live— insinuating, of course, that Maggie had never provided such accommodation for their children. In spite of Bruce's pointed little dig, she had bit her tongue and kept out of the battle— until Haley phoned her.

Knowing full well that her daughter's practical side was warring with her thirst for adventure, Maggie had advised her not to let her father talk her into doing what *he* wanted, and that maybe this once she should forgo a better paycheck and take the job that was going to be fun. It was the opportunity of a lifetime. If Haley was short of money when she went back to university in the fall, they'd work it out somehow. But Maggie did not want her daughter to give up an opportunity like this. She didn't want Haley making the same mistakes she had.

Consequently, this letter had come from Bruce, probably reprimanding her for not supporting him in his attempt to do the best thing for his daughter. Maggie sighed again and raked her hair back from her face with both hands, wanting to scream. Instead, she turned toward the kitchen counter. Picking up the electric teakettle, she filled it under the tap and plugged it in. If she'd been smart, she would have walked the other way when she'd left work this afternoon.

"Jeez, there's never anything to eat in here."

Folding her arms, Maggie turned and leaned back against the counter, watching her youngest child rummage through the fridge. Her light brown hair was slipping loose from its French braid, giving her a gamine, almost-fragile look. But Kelly Lynn was no porcelain doll, much to her father's and stepmother's distress. There was a big grass-and-dirt stain along one hip of her worn blue jeans, the neckband and cuffs of her sweatshirt looked like a dog had chewed on them and her sports socks, which were also grass stained, each had different-color trim. The kid did not look like a doll; she looked like an orphan.

Amusement lifted one corner of Maggie's mouth. "Were you playing baseball with the guys again?"

Kelly turned and looked at her mother, a telltale tint creeping up her cheeks. "Yeah." She lifted her chin in a slightly belligerent way. "How'd you know? Did Mr. Casson call again?"

Mr. Casson was the phys-ed coordinator at the high school Kelly attended, and he'd phoned Maggie several times, upset that Kelly didn't seem to want to participate in the girls' programs. Maggie knew that Kelly was desperately unhappy at high school, and that her daughter never made new friends easily. She'd had the same best friend since kindergarten — Scott Anderson, who lived four houses down the street. And there were a couple of girls on her swim team who had become pals. But if she hung around after school at all, it was with Scott.

Maggie gestured toward her sweatshirt. "You've got grass stains all down your back. It was either baseball or you got dragged home by a bus."

Kelly's expression relaxed into a sheepish grin. "I tried to steal home."

The kettle started to boil, and Maggie turned to the counter and unplugged it, then opened the cupboard and got down her favorite mug. Dropping in a bag of herbal tea, she poured the boiling water. "So what do you have planned for the weekend?"

Kelly closed the fridge door. "We swim at six tomorrow morning—the swim club is bringing in a sports therapist to talk to us. And we have pool time again on Sunday."

"Will you need a ride tomorrow morning?"

"No. Scott and I are going to bike over. We thought we'd go down to Prince's Island after."

Not yet ready to deal with Bruce's letter, Maggie pushed aside the pile of mail on the table, then pulled out a chair and sat facing the kitchen window. Bracing her chin in her hand, she stared out, wishing she could regain that happy, bubbly feeling she'd had when she'd left work. With a small grimace, she looked down and began sloshing the tea bag up and down in her mug, watching the amber color swirl through the hot water. Okay, so maybe life wasn't a bowl of cherries; she still had a lot to be thankful for. She had a good job close to home. She hadn't had one shred of trouble with any of her kids. And she had a very comfortable home with no debts. It was just that her life was so darned humdrum and dull. She'd trained herself not to think about it, because if she did, she could put herself in a real funk.

"I forgot to tell you," Kelly said as she washed two apples under the tap. "Shawn left a message on the answering machine. Said he was heading out to a new site, but he'd call home as soon as he could."

Her chin still propped on her hand, Maggie turned and looked at her daughter, feeling suddenly very depressed. Shawn was her twenty-two-year-old son, who was also attending university down east. He was spending his summer working with a reforestation project on Vancouver Island;

Maggie had hoped he would come home this year. He'd been ten when things had unraveled between her and Bruce, and Shawn had stuck by her like glue. He'd always been grown-up and responsible, but after his dad left, he'd become even more so. He had become the man in the family—and Maggie still felt guilty about the responsibility he had shouldered when she'd gone back to work. And this was the second time in a row she'd missed him when he called.

Her throat suddenly tight, she glanced at her daughter. "Did he say when he'd be back out?"

The two apples and a baseball hat clutched in one hand, Kelly paused at the entryway to the back door. "Nope. But he did say he'd be in touch again as soon as he got a chance." Sticking the cap on backward, Kelly glanced at her mother. "Scott and I are going to bike around the reservoir, okay?"

Her chin still propped in her hand, Maggie tipped her head, experiencing a sharp rush of aloneness. "Okay. But be home by six for dinner, okay?"

"I will. I've got a lot of homework to do." Tossing one apple in the air, Kelly disappeared into the entryway.

When the screen door slammed behind her, the house suddenly felt too quiet, too empty to Maggie. Maybe Frank was right. Maybe menopause was creeping up on her.

The back step faced north, but it offered an unobstructed view of the western sky, and Maggie sat with a sweater draped over her shoulders, her back braced against the aluminum siding. With her arms locked around her knees, she watched the last of the color fade from the sky, trying not to think at all. It was after ten, and Kelly was in bed because of her early morning swim, but Maggie still hadn't been able to shake the downer she was on. She had finally read the letter from Bruce, which was basically another lecture. He was upset that Haley had taken the cruise job, and Maggie suspected that writing to her was his way of venting his hurt feelings that his daughter had selected four months at sea instead of four months with him and his family.

Maggie smiled to herself. If you could call one uptight, superorganized wife, a permanent housekeeper and two

Pekingese dogs a family. She rested her chin on her upraised knees, wondering for the trillionth time what had happened to the Bruce she had married. It was as if something had occurred twelve years ago to change him into a different person—maybe the fact that he'd been approaching forty and hadn't accomplished half the things he'd wanted to. Maybe he had woken up one day and realized he was married to the wrong woman, or that he was plain dissatisfied with his life. Whatever the reason, he had changed, turned into a man obsessed. Obsessed with Registered Retirement Savings Plans, with investing for his retirement, and fervently obsessed with planning what was best for his kids.

Bruce had been an accountant with a major Calgary accounting firm, and one day he had come home and told Maggie he was leaving her. Leaving her for a workaholic, RRSP-endowed CPA with mutual funds. He had moved out that night, and a month later, he and Miss Compound Interest had both taken jobs with an even bigger accounting firm in Vancouver. The day he'd left Calgary was the day that Maggie had dug out her accounting certificate and applied at Frank's for a job.

Her head still resting on her knees, Maggie continued to watch the darkening sky, thinking about her ex-husband and his wife. In many ways, Bruce and Jennifer deserved each other, and Maggie was certain they had a wonderful time hoarding their money, calculating their accumulating interest and slavering over their blue-chip shares. Their idea of a good time, she was sure, was watching their bonds mature.

Which, she supposed, was more than she had. She didn't even know what her personal idea of a good time was. She went to work, came home, and the only outside interest she had, if she wanted to call it that, was her volunteer involvement with Kelly's swim club. If she was being honest with herself, she would have to admit her life was pretty damned dull. And she'd also have to admit that she and Bruce had developed a weird relationship over the past few years. Her ex-husband had been very upset when her father had died, and he'd flown back to Calgary immediately. He had been the one who had taken care of everything. And when her car had conked out last year and she had decided she couldn't really afford to buy a new one, he'd had one delivered within days. And a couple of times, when there had been trouble between himself and Jennifer over the kids, he had come to Maggie to talk about their problems. She also had to admit he did his damnedest to be a good father. He had been the one who had insisted they start an education account when each child was born, and he had continued to contribute toward them after the divorce.

Realizing that thinking about her ex-husband was driving her deeper into a depression, Maggie shifted her head and stared at the back alley. It was in almost total darkness again. Which meant there was another problem with the electricity. Ever since the city had installed underground cable, the alley lights were off more than they were on. She supposed they were going to have to dig the whole mess up again and start all over. She wondered what *that* would do to her taxes.

Releasing a despondent sigh, she tightened her arms around her knees. She was feeling sorry for herself, and she knew it. Her life was drab, and so was she. It was pretty damned pathetic when the big thrill of a week's vacation was that she was going to have time to paint her living room.

A light across the alley went off, and she heaved another sigh. Obviously La Goddess and Le God were heading out for the evening. But then, no forty-three-year-old woman should have to face Stephanie—otherwise known as Stevie—Coombs on a regular basis. Maggie's across-the-alley neighbor was tall, gorgeous and had a figure to die for, and she also owned a tanning salon and fitness center on the main drag of Marda Loop. Maggie got depressed every time she saw her. Stevie's housemate and significant other was as equally depressing. Tall, blond and handsome, Mitch had the build of a Greek god, drove a Porsche and was some kind of hotshot advertising executive. He took Stevie on incredible vacations to incredible places. Together they were enough to make Maggie want to stick her head in a brown bag. They were the beautiful people. She wanted to hate 'em, but she couldn't. Stevie was just too damned nice.

Giving herself a mental shake, Maggie sighed and straightened her legs. Not only was she was thoroughly depressed, she had herself feeling as dull as dishwater at the same time. She was really batting zero tonight. Stripping off her sweater, she drew up her legs to stand, but just then heard the crunch of gravel in the back alley. Only there was no sound of a motor, no illumination from headlights. It was as if a vehicle was coasting down the steep incline that ran past her house. Going dead still, she moved back in the shadows, an uneasy feeling making the hair on her neck rise. She had just about convinced herself she was imagining things when a dark shape drifted past—the shape of a man on a motorcycle.

Alarm making her stomach churn, she remained absolutely motionless, her heart suddenly jammed in her chest. The bike slid into the shadows behind the old tire store, and her alarm mounted as she watched the rider dismount, then soundlessly start toward the stairs leading to the second story. Unable to see him from that point on, Maggie flattened her back against the house, her heart suddenly too big for her chest. Oh, God, there was a drug-crazy biker next door, and she was out here alone. Tomorrow she was going to go buy a big, mean dog.

A softly muttered curse sent another jolt of alarm through her and she held her breath, certain she'd been spotted. But instead of a roar of rage, there was the sound of glass shattering, and her heart did another panicky barrel roll. Envisioning someone with long greasy hair, tattoos on his arms and big black boots with chains on them, she clenched her hands into fists and pressed herself tighter against the wall, thinking about Kelly asleep in the house. No one would lay a hand on her baby. No one. Not even Attila himself.

The sound of a door being closed released the tight muscles in her body, and she got to her feet, her knees trembling. Trying not to make a sound, she eased open the aluminum screen door just wide enough for her to slip into the house. Once inside, she eased it shut with a soft click, then closed the heavy wooden door, shaking so badly she could barely slide the dead bolt into place.

Stumbling against a chair in the dark, she grabbed the portable telephone and went into the hallway. A mindless prayer circulated in her head and her fingers trembled as she pressed the buttons for 911.

The dispatcher answered on the first ring, and with her back pressed against the wall, Maggie slid to the floor. "I'd like to report a break-in," she whispered unevenly.

Five minutes later, she was standing at her front-room window anxiously watching through the crack in her drapes. Her pulse was still pumping pure adrenaline, her legs felt like strands of spaghetti and her heart was hammering so hard she felt as if someone was dribbling a basketball in her chest. She should have asked. She should have asked if she should get Kelly out of the house. She should have asked if they would be safe inside. But she hadn't. And now it was too late.

She was considering the wisdom of crawling downstairs to wake her daughter when three police cruisers appeared, lights off and sirens silent as they converged on the old tire shop. Nearly undone by the surge of relief, Maggie watched as five officers slipped from their vehicles, leaving the car doors open, their guns drawn. Gripping a fold of the drape, she closed her eyes and weakly rested her head against the cool windowpane, her insides trembling. She didn't give a damn what her taxes cost. It was worth every red cent to have those uniforms surrounding that building right now. Every red cent.

The sound of male laughter jerked her out of her reverie and she yanked open the curtains and looked out. The headlights of one cruiser had been turned on, illuminating the cement pad at the front of the shop, and she stared at it, trying to assimilate what she was seeing. Three cops were escorting a man dressed in blue jeans and a white T-shirt to the front of the building, his arms handcuffed behind him. That part of the picture tabulated, but the rest did not. The two other officers were standing with their arms hooked over the open vehicles doors, and they were laughing. As if it was some big joke.

Wondering if they'd all lost their marbles or if she had, she opened the curtains wider, totally confused. No doubt about it. They were all laughing. Feeling as if she'd just stumbled into a really bad movie, Maggie numbly watched as one officer, sporting a huge grin, broke away from the others and started toward her property. It took a minute for comprehension to kick in, but it finally dawned on her that he was, in fact, heading toward her front door.

Her insides still trembling like jelly, she girded herself and made her way across the darkened living room, pinching her thumb when she unlocked the dead bolt. Swearing under her breath, she turned on the outside light and the light in the sun porch, trying to erect at least a semblance of composure as she opened the outer side door.

The cop was big—no, immense. At least six foot four, he had shoulders that made her think of the Incredible Hulk. He looked as if he was pushing fifty, and he wore sergeant stripes. With a reassuring smile, he presented his ID, then braced one arm on the railing of the front steps. "Sergeant Cooper, ma'am. We're here in response to a 911 call. Are you Ms. Burrows?"

Folding her arms against the night breeze, Maggie leaned against the door frame, partly to play out her false calm, partly to keep from collapsing in a heap at his feet. She glanced at the scene on the garage pad, unable to make any sense out of the taunting catcalls and the laughter.

Confusion leaving her bemused, she turned her attention back to the giant in front of her, who was clearly enjoying himself. Clearing her throat, she spoke, hoping that her voice didn't crack. "Yes, Officer. I'm Maggie Burrows."

He took off his hat, grinning broadly as he glanced back at the men in front of the tire shop; then he turned back to her, his eyes twinkling. "We appreciate your call, ma'am. Prompt public response makes our jobs that much easier."

Another burst of laughter erupted from next door, and Maggie glanced over, again feeling as if she was in the middle of a massive practical joke when she saw one of the uniforms slap his thigh in merriment. A different kind of flutter taking off in her chest, she glanced back at the sergeant. His eyes were twinkling as he drew his thumb across his mouth, as if to erase his broad grin.

Not liking the feeling unfolding in her stomach, Maggie tightened her arms, her tone one she used on Kelly when she wanted an answer, and wanted it *now*. "What's going on, Officer?"

He chewed on his bottom lip and looked away, obviously trying to refrain from laughing. Finally he turned to her, his amusement under control. His tone was almost officerlike when he finally answered, "Well, ma'am, it's like this. The owner of the property inadvertently locked himself out, and he, um…" He stalled, again fighting to restrain another grin. "He accessed his property with his usual disregard for locked doors."

With none of this making any sense at all, Maggie looked back at the small parking lot, confirming that, yes, the man in the white T-shirt was handcuffed. She glanced back at the sergeant, who was also watching the scene in front of the tire store, obviously enjoying what was going on.

Maggie suddenly wanted to shake somebody. As if sensing her frustration, Sergeant Cooper looked up at her, cleared his throat and indicated the handcuffed man. "Um, it's like this, ma'am. The gentleman next door is an ex-cop by the name of Tony Parnelli. And, um, and since he had the habit of giving us sleepless nights when he worked undercover, the, um, the boys figure he deserves something of a hard time."

Maggie gave a stunned squeak. "He's a *cop?*"

Sergeant Cooper's voice was definitely choked with laughter. "Ex-cop, ma'am. But we know him pretty well."

Her own voice rose in horror. "You mean I called 911 on an ex-cop?"

Her tone wiped the grin from Sergant Cooper's face, and he looked up at her with real concern. "No, ma'am. You called because you thought someone was breaking in next door. And that was absolutely the right thing to do." A fresh glint appeared in his eyes, and the corner of his mouth lifted with barely contained amusement. "And off the record, ma'am, you've pretty much made the boys' night. It isn't often they have a chance to even the score, especially after the fact."

Feeling like a complete fool, Maggie tried to stammer an apology. "Oh, lord. I'm sorry. I had no idea that—"

"Now, ma'am," interjected Sergeant Cooper, his tone again serious, "you have no need to apologize. You did the right thing. Believe me. We had no idea who it was in there until two of my men brought him outside." The grin reappeared. "This is just sorta a bonus, so to speak."

Closing her eyes in a rush of feeling, Maggie berated herself for letting her imagination get the best of her. She had imagined a drug-crazed biker with tattoos and boots with chains on them, but what she had was an ex-cop who was now the butt of a big practical joke. Resigned to permanent mortification over her new neighbor, she heaved a sigh and glanced at the parking lot. Tony What's-his-name was standing in front of one of the squad cars, and it was apparent, even from this distance, that his hands were still secured behind him. She looked back at the sergeant, indignation on his behalf surfacing. "Then how come he's still handcuffed? You aren't taking him downtown, are you?"

Sergeant Cooper cleared his throat again and looked at her. "Well," he said, fighting another grin. "The boys are considering their options right now."

Maggie knew that cops had a reputation for being a bunch of practical jokers, but this was going a little too far. Especially when she was to blame. She opened her mouth to speak her mind, but was interrupted by a commotion next door. She looked over. Unencumbered by handcuffs, her new neighbor was now standing above one cop, who was sprawled on the ground in front of the squad car. The man was rubbing his wrists and grinning.

Suppressing the urge to go inside and never come out, Maggie numbly nodded when Sergeant Cooper took his leave, the effects of too much adrenaline making her light-headed. She rubbed her forehead, feeling as if she'd just gone three rounds with Alice in Wonderland. Deciding it was time for her to melt into the woodwork, she started to go back into the house, but heard a commotion behind her. She turned just in time to see the police officers pile into their cars and peel away, their blue and red lights flashing. Off to the doughnut shop, no doubt, she thought with a certain amount of cynicism.

Picking up the doormat she had draped over the railing to dry after yesterday's shower, she dropped it on the step, then turned to enter her house. Except ex-detective Tony Whatever-his-name-was was heading her way. Maggie considered ducking into the house and bolting the door, but hesitated. Then she heaved another weary sigh, resigning herself to a nasty confrontation. And in all honesty, she couldn't blame him one darned bit. Handcuffed and hauled out of his house in the dead of night, he had every reason to be ticked off. Refolding her arms, she watched him approach, wondering how good she was at eating humble pie. As he stepped into the sphere of light coming from her porch light, her heart went dead still, then started to hammer in her chest. Lord, he was attractive.

Wide shouldered and slim hipped, he moved with the athletic, cocky swagger of a man who knew he was every inch a man. But if his body was perfect poster material, his face was enough to stop every female heart from the North Pole to Texas. He had a square chin with a deep cleft, a straight nose and dark, Mediterranean eyes, with lashes so long and thick she could see them from ten feet away and in bad light. His hair was short on the sides and on top, long at the back, and there was a day-old stubble darkening his jaw. His looks were startling, but it was the aura around him that kicked off a storm of awareness in her middle—a woman's awareness. He simply oozed sensuality, and she knew—*knew*—that this man had full carnal knowledge of what a bedroom was all about.

Badly unnerved by that thought, Maggie swallowed and wet her lips, reminding herself that she was responsible for having this man hauled out of his home in handcuffs. Suddenly conscious of her sagging bum and the thighs God had allocated to keep her humble, she folded her arms, trying to still the frantic pounding in her chest.

Just then he looked up, and a startled look crossed his face. Maggie realized he hadn't seen her there, standing in the nook created by the climbing honeysuckle that clung to the wrought-iron trellis. Expecting a blast, she was caught completely off guard by his lopsided grin. ''Margaret Burrows, I assume?''

If his body and face were a fantasy come true, his husky voice sent shivers of awareness racing up and down her spine. Somehow she managed to make her mouth move. ''Maggie. It's Maggie Burrows.''

Pausing on the bottom step, he stared at her a moment, something in his eyes making her heart want to climb out of her chest. There was a brief pause, then he smiled, and Maggie's lungs ceased to function. It was a smile that would have had her dentist writhing in ecstasy. He stretched out his hand toward her. "Tony Parnelli. I'm your new neighbor."

Oddly reluctant to touch him, Maggie forced herself to descend one step and take his hand, her pulse running completely amok. He was younger than she'd originally thought—probably not much over thirty—and she experienced a sudden hollow feeling in her chest. It took everything she had to tighten her fingers around his. "I'm sorry," she began, her voice catching a little. "I had no idea that—"

He closed his hand around hers and looked up at her, his gaze suddenly intent. He didn't shake her hand, he just held it, and Maggie had to fight the sudden urge to sit down and bury her head in her knees. He didn't say anything for a moment; then he gave her a slow, lopsided smile. "Hey, no apologies, okay? I really appreciate the fact that I've got a neighbor who's watching out for me."

Realizing that he was still holding her hand, Maggie shivered, loosened her grip and pulled away. Resisting the urge to rub her palm against her slacks, she affected a semblance of a smile. "Well, it had to be pretty unpleasant, getting hauled outside like that."

He chuckled and draped his arm over the newel post at the bottom of the steps. "Don't worry about it. I got my revenge."

Remembering the cop sprawled on his back in front of the cruiser, Maggie allowed a small smile, keenly aware that her palm was still tingling. "So it seemed." Sticking her hands in the pockets of her slacks, she leaned back and braced her weight against the wrought-iron railing, wishing her legs didn't feel so shaky. "I hadn't realized the Millers had found a buyer for the shop."

His arms still draped over the newel post, Tony Parnelli glanced back at his property. "Signed the papers day before yesterday." Then he glanced back at her, a twinkle in his eyes.

"I guess I could have spared myself a lot of grief if I'd ripped down the For Sale sign right away."

Trying to forget her biker-gang scenario, Maggie hunched her shoulders and smiled a little. "I *am* sorry."

He straightened, sticking his hands in the back pockets of his jeans. "Don't be." He grinned, holy hell in his eyes. "Maybe someday I can return the favor."

"I'll forgo that kind of favor, Mr. Parnelli," she responded dryly.

Tony Parnelli grinned again, then made a motion with one hand. "I guess I'd better get going. I have to find something to stick over the window."

Still feeling a little foolish, Maggie opened her door. "Well, welcome to the neighborhood."

He nodded and started down the sidewalk, then stopped and turned to face her. "By the way, it's Tony."

"Welcome to the neighborhood, *Tony.*"

He grinned, raised his hand in a farewell salute and jogged off across her yard. Maggie watched him, then resolutely turned and entered her sun porch, firmly closing the door behind her. Just what she needed. A virile Italian hunk living right next door.

## Chapter 2

Sunlight streamed in through the naked front-room window and splashed across the wrinkled, paint-spattered canvas covering part of the hardwood floor, leaving the bare walls in stark relief. The spring breeze wafting in through the open casements rattled the plastic sheets that were taped up to protect the windows and woodwork from splattering paint. Maggie, hot and sticky from her labors, pulled her T-shirt out of the waistband of her jeans. Cans of paint, extra paintbrushes, a paint tray and several rollers lay piled in one corner, ready for the redecorating assault. The drapes had been hung out on the clothesline to air, the pictures, books and knickknacks had been moved to the master bedroom and the plants were in the bathroom.

The room had been stripped of everything Maggie had been able to move, and all that remained were a few pieces of furniture.

Checking to make sure the coasters were in place under the sofa so as not to mark the hardwood floor, she put her weight behind it, shoving it to the center of the room. She covered it with an old sheet, then surveyed her morning's work. This room and the hallway were the last of her major overhaul.

Kelly had moved downstairs to the big bedroom in the basement right after Christmas, and Maggie had been yanking the
house apart ever since. The kitchen and bathroom had been
completely remodeled the year before, and the woodwork and
hardwood floors refinished. And now she was determined to
get a grip on the remainder of the place.

One upstairs bedroom had been turned into a guest room,
for when one of the other kids was home, and the third bedroom had been turned into an office for her, complete with a
computer station, bookshelves and two new oak-veneer file
cabinets. Maggie had wallpapered the dining room over the
Christmas holidays, and now all that was left to do was apply
a fresh coat of paint in the hallway and living room.

She had started the redecorating frenzy two years ago,
shortly after her father had died. It had been her way of
working through the shock and awful sense of loss. Maybe, in
some ways, she was still working through it; his death had left
a terrible hole in her life.

"Mom!"

Jarred by her daughter's yell, Maggie tucked a loose strand
of hair under the scarf covering her head, then shouted over
her shoulder, "In here."

Kelly came hopping into the living room on one bare foot,
trying to pull off her remaining sneaker at the same time. With
her hair scraped back in a tight knot, still wet from swimming, the teenager caught her balance at the archway, tugging
at her shoe. She had on cycling shorts and her swim-team
jacket, and excitement radiated from her face. Wondering
what this was all about, Maggie folded her arms, leaned back
against the sofa and waited. Kelly was the one who looked
most like her—with honeyed, light brown hair, wide hazel eyes
and a full mouth that wasn't completely dead center in her
face. But there was an effervescence in her daughter that
Maggie didn't think she'd ever had. Or maybe she simply
didn't remember ever feeling that full of life.

Kelly finally managed to yank off her shoe, and she tossed
it down the hallway. Her eyes alight with a frenzy of enthusiasm, she flung her swim bag onto one of the easy chairs,
throwing her arms up in jubilation. "You'll *never* guess what

I just saw next door. Never. The ultimate Mustang—a 1969 Boss 429. It rolled out of one of the bays just as I was coming down the street. I couldn't believe it—I nearly drove my bike into a tree. In mint condition, Mom. A classic! Black with tinted windows—I nearly died. Do you know what a car like that is worth? Do you know what it'll *do?* Wow! I can't *believe* it! Right next door."

Her arms still folded, Maggie studied her daughter, a twist of humor pulling at one corner of her mouth. "This is not a horse, I take it."

Kelly looked at her mother, obviously appalled by her lack of knowledge. "It's a *car,* Mom. A classic. A classic! It was one of the hottest cars ever built, and they're so rare, I never, ever expected to even *see* one for real."

As her daughter continued to reel off statistics about the miracle car living next door, Maggie sent up a silent rebuke to her father. This was all his fault. He had taken Kelly to a car show when she was six years old, and ever since, her daughter had been obsessed with cars. Most teenage girls had posters of teen idols in macho poses pinned up on their bedroom walls, but not Kelly Lynn. She had posters of cars. Other girls had pinups of rock stars. Kelly Lynn had production stats and speed records. Other girls wanted to be doctors or lawyers. Her daughter wanted to design the ultimate prototype. Releasing a resigned sigh, Maggie let her wind down, then tacked on a polite smile. "That's nice, Kelly. Now, how about cutting the grass?"

Kelly cast her a totally exasperated look and snatched up her swim bag. "Jeez, Mother. A car like that right next door. Aren't you even the least bit impressed?"

Not wanting to be reminded about anything "right next door," she crossed her ankles. "I'm very impressed," she lied. "But that doesn't change the fact that the grass needs to be cut."

Her daughter grumbled something under her breath and slung the strap of her bag over her shoulder, her expression rife with disgust.

Deciding to salve her daughter's indignation, Maggie flicked a piece of lint off the back of the sofa, adding slyly, "That way, if you're working outside, you might get a chance to talk to the owner."

Pumped up by that idea, Kelly didn't even realize she'd just been had. Her face lit up again, and she headed toward the kitchen. "Wow. That's a great idea! A Boss 429—wait till I tell Scott."

Maggie watched her go, her smile lingering. She should feel like a louse for that stunt. But she didn't. Kelly would be high for days if she got to talk cars with someone.

An image of Tony Parnelli coming up the walk took shape in her mind, and Maggie abruptly straightened. She was not going to think about next door. Period. Or her stupid mental lapse over Tony Parnelli. She was a grown woman, for heaven's sake. And she had better things to do. Like getting the living room and hallway painted.

The long extension on the paint roller was greasy with wet paint, and Maggie squinted up at the ceiling, carefully working her way across it. Her arms felt like lead and the small of her back felt as if it was broken, but she gritted her teeth and kept at it. She never should have tackled the damned ceiling on her own. Loaded with paint and accumulated loose plaster, the thick sheepskin roller weighed a ton, and with every pass, bits of the stippled surface rained down on her. She was covered in it, especially her face. Thank God she'd protected her hair with a scarf, or she'd be picking paint and plaster out of it for next the three weeks. But her face was such a mess that it was getting to the point that when she looked up, her eyelids stuck. But damn it, she had only a four-foot-square corner left to do; then she'd be finished. Finished. She'd probably be blind and broken, but she would be finished. And she was never going to do this again. Ever.

Running the roller through the paint tray for another load of paint, she gritted her teeth and lifted the apparatus to the ceiling, her arms, shoulders and neck screaming in protest. The extension was supposed to make things easier, so she wouldn't have to work from a ladder. But at this point, she was sure it made it worse. It felt as if she was lifting a barn over her head. Just four more square feet . . .

Maggie had narrowed the amount down to two when Kelly came bursting in the back door, shouting for her.

Her daughter, dressed in shorts and a ratty old T-shirt, her face awash with excitement, came bounding into the living room, nearly incoherent in her haste. "Guess what, Mom? Guess what? I was putting my bike in the garage when the new owner from next door came jogging down the back alley, and he saw Grandpa's car in the garage."

Not giving a damn about anything but getting through this mess, Maggie opened her eyes wide to unstick her eyelashes, then continued to carefully work the roller back and forth. Right then, she wanted to toss the roller, the pricey extension handle and every can of paint she had out the front-room window. Her shoulders felt as if there were hot knives embedded in them, and she was certain she'd never be able to straighten her neck again.

She locked her teeth together and kept working. She didn't want to hear one more word about that damned car. It was an old Golden Hawk Studebaker her father had purchased in the late fifties, claiming it was going to be a hot collector's item one day. But for nearly forty years, it had been nothing but a coddled garage queen. Her father had fussed over it constantly and taken it out on the road rarely, and it had driven her mother nuts. And now it was driving her nuts, because her father had given it to Kelly.

"He couldn't believe it, Mom. Especially the low mileage and the shape it's in. He wanted to know if we could park it outside for a minute. He wants to take a picture."

Aggravated no end by the mess around her and by how her eyelids kept sticking, and further aggravated by the little lurch her heart gave at the mention of Tony Parnelli's name, Maggie tightened her grip on the handle. "Mr. Parnelli," she muttered through clenched teeth, "can take that damned car and park it somewhere dark and painful, for all I care."

"Well, now," said an amused male voice directly behind her. "If you sell me that damned car, I'll park it anywhere you want."

Horror radiating through her, Maggie froze. Unable to handle the strain, her muscles let go in a rush, and she staggered backward, the roller skidding down the full length of the wall. Her feet tangled in the canvas covering the floor, and she threw out her arm to try to catch her balance. A strong hand gripped her upper arm, stopping her from plunging into the stack of paint cans.

Feeling like an utter fool, she managed to get loose from the canvas twisted around one ankle, fervently wishing the floor would open up and swallow her whole. Inanely grateful for the off-white paint covering her red face, she took a deep breath and forced herself to brazen it out.

Wiping her paint-speckled hands on her jeans, she lifted her chin and turned to face one Tony Parnelli. A wicked grin on his face, he folded his arms and rested his weight against the archway. He had on a very expensive pair of sneakers, faded cutoffs and a bright red tank top that displayed an upper-body muscle development that put Le God to shame.

Aware that one of her eyelids was stuck open, she gave him a rueful smile. "If revenge is sweet, you should go into sugar overload any minute now."

He continued to watch her for a moment, his dark eyes flashing with laughter, then he glanced at the paint cans and back at her. The grin broadened, revealing his perfect white teeth. His gaze fixed on her, he spoke, his voice underscored with barely contained amusement. "Mrs. Benjamin Moore, I presume."

His reference to the brand of paint she was using made her laugh in spite of herself. "Very cute, but I don't think so. She probably made her husband do all the painting."

Disconcerted by the way he was watching her and aware that Kelly was taking this all in with a speculative look, Maggie picked up a solvent-soaked rag from the top of a paint can, wiping the worst of the paint from her hands. "As for the car, you have to work that out with my daughter. She inherited that hunk of metal from her grandfather."

"Astute man, her grandfather."

She shot him a pithy glance, then wiped a blob of paint from between her fingers. "That, Mr. Parnelli, depends on your point of view."

He was still standing with his arms folded and his shoulder resting against the archway, but he'd angled his head to one side, as if he was studying her. "Tony. The name is Tony, Maggie."

Experiencing a funny rush of heat to her face, Maggie folded the rag to expose a clean area, then wiped it across her cheek. Before she got in a second swipe, he grabbed her wrist and snatched the cloth out of her hand. "Hey! Don't use that on your face. You shouldn't be using something that dangerous so close to your eyes. I have some special cleaner over in the shop."

Still holding Maggie's wrist, Tony looked at Kelly. "It's in a gray-and-black pump container by the sink in the first bay. How about getting it for your mother?"

Kelly, who was nobody's fool, licked her lips in pure greed. "Can I check out the Boss after?"

A small smile lifted one corner of Tony's mouth. "Yeah, you can check out the Boss after. And," he added, glancing at Maggie, "I'll even take you for a ride later if it's okay with your mom."

Kelly's eyes lit up and she was out the door so fast Maggie didn't even have time to take a breath.

She glanced back at Tony, about to make a comment about her daughter's obsession with cars, but the words lodged in her throat. He was watching her with an odd, assessing look, as if he was seeing something no one else could see. Maggie swallowed and dropped her gaze, a funny flutter of awareness unfolding in her chest. Withdrawing her wrist from his grasp, she pulled the scarf from her hair and began wiping the remaining paint from her hands.

Determined not to fall victim to such silliness, she glanced up at him, forcing a smile. "That container you sent for isn't Super Glue, is it?"

He was still watching her, and he smiled, but it was an odd, distracted smile, as if his thoughts were focused on something else. Faltering under his intense scrutiny, Maggie tossed the rag on the stack of paint cans and said the first thing that came into her head. "I think I need a coffee. Would you like a cup?"

The huskiness in his response sent a shiver down the full length of her spine. "I thought you'd never ask."

Shaken by her response, Maggie couldn't get into the kitchen quickly enough.

By the time Kelly came back with the cleaner then dashed off for a look at the car, Maggie had given herself a get-a-grip lecture, erected a barrier of basic common sense, made a fresh pot of coffee and defrosted some homemade cinnamon buns, the whole time kicking herself for blurting out the invitation. The last thing she needed was Tony Parnelli in her kitchen.

But by the time she'd cleaned her face, had the cinnamon buns on the table and coffee poured, the knot in her belly had relaxed, and she was able to act normal. Partly because her new neighbor had the ability to make people feel very much at ease with him, and because he also had the sneaky, underhanded ability to make her laugh.

In fact, it was almost scary how natural it felt to have him at her kitchen table, scarfing down a startling number of cinnamon buns and drinking his way through a whole pot of coffee. Mindful that her paint roller was drying into a hard lump, Maggie told him about her dad's old car. Then Tony told her about buying the shop.

"So," he said, licking a blob of cream-cheese icing off his thumb, "after I handed in my notice with the force, my brother and I decided to get into the car business. Nick used to drive the NASCAR circuit, but he was in a bad crash a couple of years ago and wrecked one leg. We'd always talked about going into business building high-performance engines for the track, so we decided to go for it." His head bent, he folded his arms on the table, revealing the well-defined muscles in his shoulders.

Stroking the side of the earthenware mug with his thumb, he shrugged and looked up at her, his gaze serious. "We're set up in another location for that, but we'd had a lot of inquires about blueprinting engines for street use. We figured it was worth a crack, so we bought this shop, and I moved into the apartment upstairs." He gave her a lopsided grin, a slightly sheepish glint in his eyes. "And scared the hell out of the neighbors in the process."

Knowing she owed him some kind of an explanation, Maggie wadded up her napkin and tossed it on the plate in front of her, a rueful smile appearing. "The neighbors saw four Harleys parked in front and immediately got a little paranoid."

He held her gaze, the glimmer in his dark brown eyes intensifying. "Paranoid, huh? So what do the neighbors think now, Maggie Burrows?"

Not wanting to acknowledge the sudden tightness in her midriff, Maggie indicated the cinnamon-bun crumbs on his plate. "I think you've been away from a doughnut shop too long, Officer Parnelli."

He grinned and touched the back of her hand with one finger. "You're pretty cute, Ms. Burrows."

Wishing he'd quit using that husky, familiar tone of voice—as if they were old friends and they'd done this a thousand times before—she quickly shoved both hands in her lap. Needing to define her situation for her own benefit as much as for his, she gave him a wry smile. "Don't try to charm me, Parnelli. I have two grown children and one nearly ready to launch. And I know cute when I see it. The next time I make cinnamon buns, I'll make an extra dozen for you."

His expression suddenly unreadable, Tony Parnelli continued to stare at her, and for an instant, she thought she saw a flash of annoyance in his eyes. His arms still folded on the table, he didn't say anything for a minute; then he leaned back. After a moment, one corner of his mouth lifted and he pushed his chair back and stood up, still watching her. "You do that, *Maggie,*" he said, and Maggie could have sworn there was a subtle challenge in his voice. Picking up the container of cleaner, he gave her a casual salute and turned toward the door. "Thanks for the treat. See you around."

Experiencing a nasty little clutch in her stomach, Maggie remained in her chair. She heard the back door slam behind him; then she watched as he cut across her back yard and effortlessly vaulted over her four-foot-high fence and disappeared from view. Shifting her gaze, she rubbed a film of dried paint off her index finger with her thumb, her insides unaccountably heavy, as if she'd done something wrong. She sat there for a moment, then sighed and collected the empty mugs.

Now she had to go back and deal with the dried mess on the damned paint roller.

It was not a good weekend. The paint for the hallway and living room turned out to be the wrong color, which meant she had to get cleaned up and return it to the paint store. Kelly cut the garden hose in half when she was mowing the backyard, and the smell of paint had given Maggie a persistent headache. And that awful feeling in her middle would not go away.

Maggie didn't kid herself. She knew what that feeling in her middle was all about. It was about Tony Parnelli, which was absolute foolishness on her part. First of all, he had to be ten years younger than she was. Second, even after a twenty-minute coffee break, it was pretty obvious their life-styles were light-years apart. And thirdly, it was *her* hormones that were running amok. Besides, she did not want to be attracted to him. Not in a million years. Any woman with half a brain could see he had *trouble* written all over him.

But in spite of her long, tedious and brutally frank self-lectures, disturbing feelings kept sneaking in—and equally disturbing dreams. It probably wouldn't have been so bad if she could have sent her daughter to live with her father. But Kelly had found a hero, and every conversation was peppered with Tony this and Tony that. Tony and his car. Tony and his cool bike. After two days of stories about Tony Parnelli, it was obvious to Maggie that this man thrived on living life on the very edge—fast cars, faster bikes, skydiving, snowboarding—anything with an element of danger and speed kick-started his engine. And Kelly, darn her, thought all this was the best thing that had happened to her since her braces had come off. Maggie wanted to strangle her.

Then, as if all this wasn't enough, Bruce made an unexpected visit to Calgary. He said he was there because he had some business transactions with a big law firm; Maggie was sure he'd come with the sole purpose of delivering a lecture in person.

She'd had such a headache by the time he left Sunday afternoon that she wanted to decapitate herself. But in spite of everything, she had two accomplishments under her belt. One was that she had gotten the living room and hallway painted. The second was that she had gotten even with Bruce for inflicting another lecture on her.

Lifting the roast chicken out of the oven for their Sunday dinner, Maggie smiled to herself in spite of her blinding headache. It wasn't often that she scored on her ex-husband, but she had scored this time.

There had been a lottery ticket stuck on her fridge with a magnet, and he had demanded to know if she was in the habit of wasting money on that sort of nonsense. Fed up and tired, with her shoulders and neck still feeling as if someone had driven over her with a tank, and a headache that was trying to suck her eyes out of her head, she had retorted that it was not nonsense, it was her long-range financial plan. Her tart response had sent him into acute throes of vein-bulging apoplexy, and his reaction had done more for her headache than any painkiller. It had almost made up for the aggravation he'd inflicted on her.

"Do you want me to do anything?"

Maggie set the chicken onto a platter, then glanced over her shoulder at her daughter. "No, I don't think so. There's a salad in the fridge you could put on the table. And you'll need to get yourself a glass of milk."

Some of Kelly's silky hair had pulled loose from her braid, subtly accentuating her high cheekbones and wide eyes. Her cheeks showed signs of a sunburn, and there was a new crop of freckles on her nose. She smelled of sunshine and soap, with a faint hint of chlorine still lingering from her morning swim. Her woman child. God, to be that young, that fit, that full of energy. The thought made Maggie's throat close up a little.

Retrieving the salad and a container of milk from the fridge, Kelly pushed the door shut with her elbow. "Please, please, please tell me you made mashed potatoes."

In spite of the funny little clog in her throat, Maggie had to smile to herself as she added flour to the roaster for gravy. Mashed potatoes and gravy, her daughter would live on them, given a choice—one of the advantages of swimming God-only-knew how many lengths and burning up thousands of calories in a week. "Yes, I made mashed potatoes."

"Can I carve the chicken? I'm starved."

Maggie added the potato water to the gravy mix, then bent down to check the flame as she adjusted the setting on the gas burner. "The good knife is in the sink. But be careful. I just sharpened it."

Standing shoulder-to-shoulder with her mother at the counter, Kelly turned the platter to give her better access, then carved a slice off the breast. "Scott and I saw Tony at the corner store this afternoon. He said he has some pit passes for next season's races for us, if it was okay with you." She stopped carving and looked at her mother, her expression anxious. "You'll let us go, won't you, Mom? He said he'd come with us, so you wouldn't need to worry."

Tamping down a peculiar flutter in her middle at the mention of Tony Parnelli's name, Maggie added salt to the gravy, keeping her expression even. She may as well get used to the fact that her daughter had found a real live hero. She just wished this hero didn't live right next door. Replacing the salt container on the back of the stove, she stirred in the seasoning, deliberately stalling. Going to the track would be such a thrill for Kelly. Restraining a sigh, she answered, "You'll have to check it out with Scott's parents, Kell. I don't want him sneaking off without their approval."

Kelly gave a little squeal. "Then I can go?"

"Yes," Maggie answered, trying to keep the resignation out of her voice. "You can go."

"Right on!"

Repressing the urge to give her daughter a little lecture about not shortchanging any of her responsibilities, like homework and the swim team, Maggie opened the cupboard door and got down a bowl for the gravy. She was definitely feeling her age.

"He's so neat, Mom," Kelly exclaimed. "He showed us around the shop, and he told us about some of the engines they're working on. And how they rebuild them." Encouraged by her mother's silence, she babbled on. "He's got a weight room where the Millers used to store the extra tires—some really great equipment. We told him about our training program with the swim club, and he said we could use his stuff whenever we want, as long as there's someone there to spot for us." Kelly broke off a drumstick and placed it on the platter, then gave an excited little shiver. "Scott asked him all about the police force, and Tony told him exactly what he'd have to do if he wants to join up when he graduates. Tony joined when he was twenty-one, and he was in thirteen years. He didn't say why he got out, though."

Maggie's brain computed the figures before she could stop herself, and a heavy feeling slid through her stomach. She was losing it—really losing it. Attracted to a man who was nine years younger than she was. It must be some sort of aberration. Maybe Frank was right—maybe she was going through a midlife crisis and didn't even know it. Kind of like a case of emotional shingles. Maybe what she needed was a damned hobby.

By Tuesday, Maggie had the house put back together and the windows washed. She had even cleaned the oven. With everything caught up inside, she decided to start on the yard. She never put her bedding plants out until the long weekend in May, but she had other things she wanted to do. Like move some perennials in the backyard. And plant her dahlias. But the yard wasn't work for Maggie. It was pure relaxation. After her mother's death, the yard had been let go, and it had become a thistle-infested disaster when she and the kids had moved back with her father. She took smug pride in the fact that she had the prettiest yard on the block.

Going to the garage, she got her plastic tool caddie filled with garden implements, then unwound the hose and settled down for a few hours of digging in the dirt. Humming to herself, she knelt by the bed along the garage, the one she always planted sweet peas in, and began working the soil, relishing the feel of warm sun on her back. After a weekend of paint fumes, she needed this.

She was halfway down the flower bed when she caught a flash of black out of the corner of her eye, and she looked up just in time to see Captain Hook dart under the back step. Sitting back on her haunches, she was thinking she should put some food out for the neighborhood stray cat when she saw traces of fresh blood on the sidewalk. Alarmed, she dropped

her trowel, got up and crossed the yard. The step itself was cement, but her father had built a two-tier deck around it. There
was, however, a hole under the step, where the ground had
caved in a little. Getting down on her hands and knees, she
peered under. "Hey, Captain," she said softly. "What happened? Did that big German shepherd get you again?"

The cat responded with a hostile hiss, and Maggie sat back,
considering what she should do. The Captain had been hanging around the neighborhood for nearly five years. Haley had
named him Captain Hook because his tail was broken and had
a permanent crook in it. He was an independent renegade of
the first order and, in spite of numerous attempts, had refused to be adopted by anybody. A few conscientious neighbors had made repeated attempts to catch him and take him to
the SPCA. They'd even succeeded a couple of times, but
within days, Captain Hook had, without fail, reappeared in
the alley. It was as if this alley was his, and nothing or nobody was going to change that.

Staring across the yard, Maggie chewed her bottom lip. She
and Stevie, the blond bombshell who lived directly across the
alley, had more or less taken joint custody of the big, black,
battle-scarred cat. But right now Stevie was at her fitness spa,
no doubt busy sculpting dumpy, high-cholesterol businessmen into fit, sleek gods. Maggie grinned to herself. She wished
she could have found it in her heart to really hate the woman,
but La Goddess was as sweet and friendly and funny as she was
perfect and gorgeous.

Expelling a long breath, Maggie braced her arms on her bare
thighs, staring at the streaks of blood on her sidewalk. She just
couldn't leave him like that. And besides, she was the only one
on the whole block who could get within ten feet of the cat.
She had no choice—the rescue operation was up to her.

Getting to her feet, she went into the house.

Five minutes later, she was back with a can of sardines, a
ball of twine, a broom handle, an old blanket and some heavy
leather gloves. Getting an empty garbage can from behind the
garage, she put the blanket in the garbage can. Then, tugging
down the back of her shorts, she knelt on the sidewalk, putting together her strategy.

She opened the can of sardines, tied a long length of twine around it and pulled on the gloves. Stretching out on her stomach on the sidewalk, she shoved the sardines under the step with the broom handle until it was about a foot from the cat, then settled in for a long haul. Catching Captain Hook would take some doing. It would likely take her an hour to coax him out.

Using her best here-kitty-kitty voice, she started talking to the cat. "Come on, sweetie. Come on. You like sardines. I got them especially for you." She pushed the can a little closer, then withdrew the broom handle and threw it on the grass behind her. "Come on, Captain. Here kitty, kitty, kitty. Come on. I know you like them."

"I gotta tell you. I don't know about sardines, but *I'd* be in there if it was anchovies."

Horror racing through, Maggie swiveled her head around, her heart colliding with the sidewalk beneath her chest when she saw Tony Parnelli standing on the other side of her four-foot-high fence, his arms looped over the top. He was grinning a grin he hadn't acquired from being an altar boy.

Aware that her thighs were spread out like two baby whales beneath her paint-spattered cutoffs, she had to suppress a nearly overpowering urge to bang her head against the cement sidewalk. Mentally resigning herself to humiliation, she lifted her chin a notch, trying to maintain some dignity. "I am trying to rescue a wounded cat," she said, her tone tart. "Not amuse the neighbors."

His grin broadened and he held his hands up in a gesture of surrender. "Hey," he said with fake seriousness, "I'm not amused."

Maggie watched him, a wry smile threatening to break out on her face. "Like hell you're not."

He gave her a wide-eyed, innocent look. "I'm not."

She stared at him a minute, then rolled her eyes. "Haven't you got a carburetor to rebuild? I could do without a peanut gallery."

He frowned, barely hiding his grin. "Just what does that mean, Ms. Burrows? What *is* a peanut gallery?"

Not wanting him to see that he'd made her smile, she rested her head on her outstretched arm. "It means go away. He'll never come out with someone else around."

There was the creak of wood under strain, then all of a sudden, Tony was on his stomach beside her. She looked from him to her fence, then drew a deep breath. She was going to have to speak to him about that—about using the wooden barrier as some sort of free-standing gymnastic apparatus.

She was about say so when he spoke, his tone full of amazement. "That's one damned big cat. What is he? Part panther?"

"No," she said, giving the string a little tug, "he's pure alley cat. And he's hurt. I'm trying to coax him out."

Propping his head on his hand, he looked at her, that bad-boy smile back in full force. "I don't think he wants to come out, Miss Maggie. I think he's planning on hanging out in there for a long time."

"Thank you for your opinion," she said, her tone sarcastic.

"You're welcome." He levered himself up a bit and pulled his T-shirt off over his head, then reached behind him and retrieved the broom handle. He nudged her to move over, then slid the handle under the step. "The way he's hunkered down in there, this could take all day. Let's see what happens if we give a little poke from behind."

Maggie was about to yell a warning, but the instant he touched the cat, Captain Hook shot out from under the step like he'd been fired from a cannon. Before she had time to move, Tony had the cat trapped in his T-shirt, a blaze of red scratches running from his collarbone to his midriff. Holding the cat's head so he couldn't bite him, the ex-cop rolled to his feet, swearing under his breath. "Damn it! That smarts." He swore again and did a little dance of pain, still holding the cat immobilized against his rib cage.

Maggie scrambled to her feet, horrified by the claw marks. "Oh, God. I'm sorry. I should have told you how wild he is."

Readjusting his grip on the struggling cat, he gave her a pained smile. "It's a little late for that now. Just tell me what in hell I'm supposed to do with him."

She grabbed the lid off the steel garbage can. "Dump him in here. And do it quick. He's faster than lightning."

Wrestling with the thrashing cat, he staggered over to the metal container. "I noticed." Tightening his hold, he looked at her. "Ready?"

"Ready."

Tony thrust the hissing cat into the garbage can, yanking his arms and T-shirt free as Maggie slammed on the lid. The racket inside the garbage can sounded as if someone had unleashed a wild tiger. Clamping the lid closed, Maggie dragged the can onto the sidewalk, then turned back to where Tony was swearing and swabbing at the slashes on his chest with his T-shirt. At least she thought he was swearing. There was a litany of rapid Italian coming out of his mouth.

Feeling absolutely awful, she reached out and touched the undamaged flesh next to the wounds. "You'd better come inside so we can clean that. Old Hook isn't big on personal hygiene."

Tony grabbed her hand and held it against his warm flesh, surprising her with a husky chuckle. "If you think I'm going to let you pour antiseptic on this, you're out of your ever-loving mind."

Keenly aware of his grip on her wrist, of the heat radiating from his body, Maggie eased in a deep breath past the sudden flutter in her own chest. Lapses. She was having middle-aged lapses again. Clearing her throat, she took another breath and made herself look up at him. "It'll get infected and—"

"Nah," he said, watching her steadily, a small, somehow intimate smile appearing. "I never get infections." He rubbed his thumb against the frantic pulse in her wrist, still watching her with that steady, mesmerizing stare. "Maggie?" he said softly.

Her heart doing a series of loops and stalls, she stared up at him, her mouth suddenly very, very dry. "What?"

"I should have your can for trying to do this by yourself," he said quietly, rebuke in his tone. "He could have ripped you to shreds."

Trying to make her lungs function like they were supposed to, Maggie forced a smile, attempting to release her wrist. "He was just scared."

Continuing to stroke her skin with his thumb, Tony looked directly into her eyes, his gaze oddly sober. Then, as if realizing what he was doing, he grinned, giving her wrist a squeeze. "That makes two of us. For a minute I thought he was going to turn me into dog meat."

Her gaze drifted to his chest—his very naked, very tanned, very muscled chest—and Maggie's mouth went dry all over again. Trying to convince herself she was just in the throes of some crazy hormone thing, she swallowed hard. Maybe the paint fumes had fried her brain.

Releasing his grip on her wrist, Tony slid his hand up her bare arm, then turned away. He switched on the hose and washed off his chest, then pulled on his T-shirt over his wet skin. Suddenly very businesslike, but somehow very chummy, he said, "Now what, Burrows? What's the plan?"

Feeling as if she'd just come through a revolving door, Maggie wiped her hands on her shorts, then squared her shoulders. "I'm going to take him to the vet."

Turning to face her, Tony rested his hands on his hips and stared at her, silently responding with a shake of his head.

Lifting her chin, she stared right back at him. "What?"

"Oh, no, you aren't. You aren't transporting that animal by yourself."

He was standing in the middle of her yard, his hands on his hips, blood oozing through the wet spots on the front of his white T-shirt. His hair was standing on end, he had grease stains on his jeans and he was clearly aching for a fight. For some reason, it made her smile. "Look," she said, suppressing a grin and using her most rational tone. "This cat is not your problem. In fact, he's nobody's problem. I'm going to change my clothes, then I'm going to put that garbage can in the back of my car and take him to the vet." On the verge of laughing and not even sure why, she turned and started toward the house. "Thank you for your help. And if you get an infection, that's *your* problem."

Without a shred of warning, an ice-cold jet of water hit her square in the back, and she let out a shriek and tried to twist away. "Wrong answer," he called after her, holding the hose on her. "This was a team effort, Burrows. You're not cutting me out of the action now."

Flailing under the cold spray and soaked to the skin, Maggie beat a retreat into the house, laughing and out of breath, wondering what in hell had happened to her common sense.

The trip to the vet was actually pretty routine. Dr. Swainson, having gone a few rounds with the Captain in the past, had him restrained, muzzled and sedated without acquiring a scratch. He did, however, compare Captain claw marks with Tony, showing Maggie's neighbor old scars on the back of his hands and up his arms. He gave Tony some antibiotic cream and told him to get a tetanus shot. The cat did, in fact, need stitches—twenty to be exact. Being a prudent man, Dr. Swainson used dissolving sutures so they wouldn't have to go through this a second time, then discharged the cat. The Captain was so anesthetized that Maggie was able to hold him all the way home. Discounting all his scars—his torn ear, his tail and now the clipped and sutured area on his back haunch—he was a gorgeous cat. Maggie had a special fondness for old Hook—maybe because he was such a survivor. She gently stroked his head, watching him sleep on her lap. "You're a pretty kitty, aren't you, Hook?"

Braking for the turn down their alley, Tony shot her an amused look. "Kitty? That cat's a killer, Burrows."

"No, he isn't. He's just an old alley cat, aren't you, Captain?"

Tony parked on Maggie's driveway, then got out and came around to her side of the car. He opened the door and helped her out, the cat still cradled in her arms. "So now what?"

"I'm going to put him in the garage. He'll be safe in there, but he can get in and out whenever he wants."

She made a bed for the cat in a cardboard box and was just settling Hook in it when Tony reappeared through the side door, carrying the can of sardines and a dish of water. He set them both down beside Maggie, then began circling the

Studebaker, running his hand along the back fin. "This is a hell of a car, Mag. She's worth a small fortune, you know."

Maggie glanced up at him, a small smile appearing, then went back to tending the cat. "You sound just like my father."

Tony began covering the car with the special tarp that Kelly had obviously forgot to put back on. "Kelly's mentioned her grandfather quite a few times. Sounds like they were pretty close."

Maggie smiled as she covered Captain Hook up with an old towel. "They were. They were thicker than thieves." She stroked the cat's head and turned, sitting cross-legged on the floor by the makeshift shelter. A funny feeling unfolded in her middle as she watched him straighten the tarp and stroke out the wrinkles. Trying not to acknowledge the disturbing flutter, she slid her hands under her thighs. "Tony?"

He looked up from the far side of the car, one hand resting on top of the vehicle. She hesitated a moment, then spoke, her voice not quite steady. "Thank you for offering the tickets to Kelly. It really means a lot to her."

Resting his other hand on his hip, he stared across the ill-lit garage at her, then tipped his head in acknowledgment. He continued to watch her for a minute, then he went around to the back of the car, hooking the elastic binding under the back bumper. "She told me she wants to design cars."

Picking up a rusty bolt from the floor, Maggie rolled it between her fingers. "Since she was six years old."

"How do you feel about that?"

Maggie tossed the bolt into a box of garbage sitting under the dust-covered workbench. "I just hope she can make it happen. It's all she's ever wanted."

Tony moved up the near side of the car, then folded his arms and leaned against the front bumper. He didn't say anything for a moment. He just studied her, as if he was considering something. Then he spoke, his voice oddly clipped. "There was something I wanted to ask Kell, but I didn't. I thought it only right I ask you."

She looked up at him, frowning slightly. "What's that?"

His head tipped to one side and he continued to stare at her. "What's the deal on Mr. Burrows?"

A strange, shivery feeling went from the top of Maggie's head to the tip of her toes, leaving her feeling out of breath. She stared up at him for a moment, then withdrew her hands and began folding the old rags she had dug out for Hook's box. "Mr. Burrows is living in Vancouver with the new Mrs. Burrows," she answered, her tone even. "He left twelve years ago."

"And the wedding ring you wear on your right hand?"

Maggie spread her hand and looked at the wide, worn ring, warmed by fond memories. "It was my grandmother's," she answered softly.

There was a funny silence; then he reached down and caught her wrist, pulling her to her feet. The edge was gone from his voice when he spoke. "Why don't we leave old Hook to sleep it off. At the very least, you owe me a coffee, Burrows."

Feeling as if she'd just been thrown completely off balance, Maggie brushed the dust from the seat of her pants. She had to get a grip. All he was trying to do was be a good neighbor. And here she was, having a midlife crisis.

# Chapter 3

Maggie didn't want to face Wednesday. She awakened at dawn, feeling as if she had a rock sitting in her chest. Knowing she wasn't going to be able to go back to sleep, she got up, slipped on an old, fleece-lined sweatsuit, then went out to the kitchen and put on the coffee. The house, filled with the blue twilight of early morning, was unnaturally quiet, the stillness adding to the hollow feeling in her chest. Folding her arms against the chill, she rested her hip against the cupboard and watched the dark brew trickle into the carafe, the burble of the coffee maker unnaturally loud in the perfect stillness.

She felt like crying, and she didn't even know why. Maybe it was nothing. Or maybe, some traitorous little voice in her head whispered, it was because she was feeling as if life had passed her by.

Yanking open the cupboard door, Maggie got out a mug, slammed it on the cupboard, then reached for the half-full carafe. She poured herself a cup, shoved the coffeepot back on the element, then picked up her cup and headed for the living room. She was feeling sorry for herself, and damn it, she was going to stop it right now. This was ridiculous. Just because some great-looking guy moved in next door didn't mean she had to fall apart at the seams. She was a grown woman, for heaven's sake. Not some dewy-eyed adolescent.

The smell of fresh paint greeted her, and for some reason, that made her want to slam her cup down and kick the wall. Curling up in one corner of the sofa, Maggie took a sip of coffee and stared out the window, trying to squelch the feelings churning around inside her.

Okay. So it was time for a little honesty here. She *was* reacting like some dewy-eyed adolescent, but that didn't mean she had to let it continue. So some gorgeous hunk from next door had unearthed some basic feelings she'd thought she had buried a long time ago. That was to be expected. She was just middle-aged, not dead. Something like this was bound to happen. So what if she'd spent the past several years dodging her own suppressed sensuality. That didn't mean it wasn't there.

Slamming her cup on the coffee table, she drew up her legs and locked her arms around them, pressing her forehead to her knees. This was just some crazy time warp she had to get through. The fact that Tony made her spine collapse and her pulse race every time he touched her was just another problem she'd have to deal with. She'd stopped reading romantic novels and going to hot steamy movies for that very reason. Now what she had to do was make sure he stayed on his side of the fence and she stayed on hers. Maggie closed her eyes, making herself focus on something else. Like rearranging the back flower garden in her mind.

It was the sound of Kelly's voice that snapped her awake. "What are you doing up? I thought you said you were going to sleep in all week."

Her forehead still against her knees, Maggie answered, "I lied."

"Does this mean you're going to give me a ride to school?"

"No." Feeling like a dog in the manger, Maggie lifted her head, squinting against the brightness in the room as she looked at her daughter. "Are you late? Do you need a ride?"

Standing in the archway dressed in faded blue leggings and a baggy sweater that reached her knees, Kelly had her arms up, French-braiding her hair. She gave her mother a slightly sheepish look, a rueful smile appearing. "No. I was just bugging you. You looked kinda dorky, asleep like that." Kelly secured her braid with a piece of scrunched-up fabric, then dropped her arms. "Scott's mom has an appointment downtown this morning, so she said she'd give us a ride to school."

"Have you had breakfast?"

"Yep. I made porridge. There's some left if you want it."

Maggie suppressed a shudder. Her daughter's swim coaches were heavily into nutrition, stressing a low-fat, high-carbohydrate diet for their athletes. But Maggie thought porridge for breakfast was taking things a little too far. She gave her daughter a fixed smile. "No, thank you."

Kelly grinned, flashing a big dimple. "I *know* how much you love it, Mom. So I made extra."

Resting her cheek on her knees, Maggie narrowed her eyes at her daughter. "You're a loathsome child, Kelly Lynn. I hope your porridge gets weevils in it."

Her eyes dancing, Kelly smacked her lips and put on a big show of approval. "Yum, yum. I *love* weevils."

Maggie shivered and made a face of utter distaste. Kelly grinned at her mother's reaction, tucking back a strand of hair that had slipped from her braid. "So what are you going to do with all this free time on your hands, Mother?" She got a sly gleam in her eyes. "You could make some peanut-butter cookies if you got *really* bored."

Suppressing a smile, Maggie stared straight-faced at her daughter. "I couldn't do that. That would be in violation of Coach Bronson's training program. I'm going to work in the yard instead."

Her hands on her hips, Kelly gave her mother a disgruntled look. "Not fair, Mom."

Maggie gave her a wry smile. "Life's not fair, Kelly Lynn."

A car horn sounded outside, and Kelly grimaced and grabbed her canvas backpack, heading toward the front door. "Oops. That's probably the Gordons. I told them I'd meet them outside." She opened the door, then looked back at her mother. "See you later, Mom."

"See you later, babe."

Maggie watched her daughter climb in the back seat of the dark blue minivan parked outside, a funny cramp forming in her throat. It wouldn't be long before Kelly was gone, just like Shawn and Haley.

Realizing she was doing a first-class job of depressing herself, Maggie released a sigh and unwound her legs. She would vacuum the downstairs and catch up on the laundry; then she was going to go outside and dig up the back flower bed like it had never been dug up before. Maybe some hard physical work would put things in perspective.

Frank phoned just before lunch, needing some information. After spending fifteen minutes on the phone with him, she could not dredge up one more ounce of enthusiasm for any more work. Her house had never been so clean. Nor had she ever been such a coward. Her cleaning frenzy, she finally admitted, had nothing to do with cleanliness; it had everything to do with her new neighbor next door. Disgusted with herself and her adolescent behavior, she resolutely put on a pair of shorts that did nothing for her thighs, and headed outside. Enough was enough. This nonsense had to stop. And besides, she should have checked on that darned cat as soon as she got up.

Captain Hook was not in his box; in fact, there wasn't a trace of him anywhere. The food and water dishes were both empty, which salved her conscience a little. Still feeling guilty about the Captain, Maggie untangled the pitchfork from the jumble of garden tools in the corner and stomped outside. Surely she could dig up one lousy flower garden without making a big deal out of it.

The garden was a big one, and by the time Maggie had finished digging it up, she had blisters on both hands and her shoulders, still sore from painting, felt as if they had spikes driven into them. Perspiration dampened her T-shirt and trickled down her temple, and she knew her face was red and sweaty from hard work. Feeling slightly weak in the knees, she washed her face and hands under the hose, relishing the coldness against her heated skin. She was going to need a twenty-minute soak in the tub to get all the sweat and grime off.

Attaching the sprinkler head to the hose, she set it in the center of the yard, then turned it on, making sure the fine spray hit the corners of the newly tilled garden. Wiping her hair off her face with her arm, she headed back to the house, experiencing some real satisfaction. All she had left to do in the yard was set out the bedding plants, and then she'd be finished with the most labor-intensive part of her spring work. The rest was just day-to-day upkeep, and that she enjoyed. Stopping on the deck, she hooked the heel of one battered shoe on the step and pulled it off, then did the same with the other. A bath. And then she'd make a batch of peanut-butter cookies for Kell. She looked up, pausing to survey her afternoon's work, her gaze snagging on the sun deck of the trendy new infill directly across from her.

La Goddess and Le God were out on Stevie's deck tanning, their perfectly honed bodies gleaming with a fine film of oil, both of them lazy and catlike in the sun. Stevie, wearing a bright red bikini, was stretched out on her back on a padded tubular lounger, her blond hair wrapped in a towel, her arms extended above her head. Mitch was lying on his stomach in another lounger right beside her, his head turned toward his companion as he slowly stroked his hand up and down her body. When his fingers slipped under her bikini top, Stevie arched her back and stretched like a cat, pressing against his hand.

A half-forgotten need coursed through Maggie and she whirled around and closed her eyes, pressing her forehead against the glass in the back door. An image of Tony Parnelli peeling off his T-shirt took shape in her mind, and her breath suddenly jammed in her chest. As if it were happening all over again, she remembered how it had felt when he'd gripped her wrist, trapping her hand against his rib cage when she had reacted to the claw marks on his chest. He had been so close. So close that she had felt the heat from his body. So close that she had seen the tiny flecks of gold in his eyes. So close.

Her breasts suddenly tight and the lower part of her body heavy and throbbing, Maggie stifled a groan and pressed her head more firmly against the glass pane, trying to force some sense into it. She didn't need this. And she damned well didn't deserve it. She had kept anything the least bit erotic out of her life. She went to church once in a while. Her underwear was plain and practical. She hadn't even looked at the firemen's calendar that had all the mothers at the swim club running fevers. She'd been the model of discretion, damn it, and now this. She did not deserve this!

Grinding her teeth, she straightened and yanked open the door. Damn Stevie and Mitch. Damn Tony Parnelli. Damn her own paranoia. It served her right for letting her imagination run wild and calling the cops.

Slamming the door behind her, she turned and went downstairs to the game room. Yanking the cover off the competition-size pool table and tossing it on the floor, she banged the rack on the table and began jamming balls into it. She was going to deal with this insanity, one way or another.

Removing the rack, she picked up the custom-made cue her father had given her for her sixteenth birthday and began roughly chalking the tip. Stuffing the chalk cube in her back pocket, she bent over, imagining her ex-husband's face on each and every ball as she lined up for the break.

The crack of the cue ball splintered the silence, and the colored balls exploded across the green baize surface. This was not going to be her usual game of strategy, form and finesse; this was going to be a billiards-style demolition derby. She hadn't done a demolition run in a very, very long time.

Maggie sat on the back deck, her arms locked around her upraised knees, her back braced against the aluminum siding. Hidden from view by the big honeysuckle bush at the west corner, she tried to concentrate on the vivid colors fading from the evening sky. Playing demolition derby hadn't worked. A long hot soak in the tub hadn't worked. Making peanut-butter cookies for Kell hadn't worked. A terrible feeling of despair had swept over her halfway through the billiards thing, and she'd finally gone upstairs and had a damned good cry, which usually worked. Fifteen minutes of that kind of venting, and she could usually pick herself up and get on with it. But it wasn't working this time. Not one damned bit. All she'd got out of it was a vicious headache, a plugged nose and puffy bags under her eyes.

Wiping away another flood with a wadded-up tissue, she blew her nose and straightened her spine. Okay. This was it. She was being a big baby for letting this kind of self-pity take hold. She was going to stop it, and she was going to stop it right now. So what if there was no excitement in her humdrum existence. So what if she was feeling all alone. All right, so she had once thought maybe she'd get lucky and someone special would turn up in her life. That it hadn't happened was not the end of world. Maybe she needed a hobby. Maybe she should take some course—like Spanish. She'd always wanted to learn Spanish. Maybe she should start doing things, like going to the museum, to art shows, to movies.

The thought of trotting off by herself brought on another bout of tears, and she clamped her jaw against the brand-new ache in her throat, determined to put a stop to this foolishness. Kelly would probably be home from her baby-sitting job in a couple of hours, and Maggie was going to have herself back together by then or die trying.

Tipping her head against the wall, she stared up at the sky, concentrating on the slashes of color on the undersides of the clouds. Maybe she was going about this all wrong. Maybe what she needed to get out from under the Class A downer was to face up to the feelings she'd stuffed away years before. Maybe she needed to lick her wounds, grieve a little for her lost youth and acknowledge the fact that life was not perfect. Maybe facing all those feelings would clear her system; it was damned obvious that trying to set them aside hadn't worked.

Maggie banged her head against the wall and took a deep, hopefully stabilizing breath. Okay. That's what she would do. She'd join a self-help group. There had to be other forty-plus women who were in the same situation she was. Now *there* was something to really look forward to....

Her eyes blurred again, and Maggie angrily ripped apart the tissue, looking for a dry spot, then wiped her eyes and blew her nose. Maybe she should go find her father's bottle of Scotch, which was stuffed in the back of a cupboard somewhere, and just get drunk. That would really give Kelly a new level of maturity to shoot for.

"Hey, cat woman. How would you feel about sharing a pizza and some cold beer?"

Shock snapped Maggie back to the real world, the rush making her stomach drop away to nothing. Tony Parnelli was standing on his side of the fence watching her, one elbow hooked over the wooden structure, a pizza box and a six-pack of beer resting on the cross beam. Horrified that he might have witnessed her pity party, Maggie found it was all she could do to drag up a weak smile.

Hooking both elbows over the fence, he watched her through the gloom, then gave her a small, off-center grin. "Is that a yes or a no?"

There was something about that smile that went straight to her heart, as if he expected her to brush him off. She'd always been a sucker for strays, and there was something about Tony Parnelli that was just a little too much like Captain Hook. Fighting the funny flutter in her chest and hoping he couldn't see the shape her face was in, she put a little more energy into her smile. Determined to get this good-neighbor thing off on the right foot, she rested her elbow on her upraised knee, propping her head in her hand. "Do you even know the meaning of the word *no?*"

His grin broadened, and before she could say anything he'd vaulted over the fence, sweeping up the pizza and beer as he landed on the other side. He walked toward her with that cocky swagger, grinning that grin that probably had landed him in all kinds of trouble. "Not nice, Burrows. You could hurt my feelings with comments like that. This is just a neighborly little fence crossing, that's all."

Her head still propped in her hand, she watched him come up the deck steps, the fence-crossing comment lifting one corner of her mouth. "I think you and I need to have a talk about that fence, Parnelli," she said, her tone pointed.

He came over and sat down beside her, then stretched out his legs. Placing the beer on the decking beside him, he rested the pizza box on his lap. He shot her an amused glance, then opened the flap on the box, the hot, cheesy aroma making

Maggie's mouth water. He held the box toward her, giving her a bad-boy grin. There was an odd, provocative timbre in his voice when he spoke, almost as if he were offering a challenge. "You aren't going to *scold* me, are you, Mag?"

She held his gaze a moment, then took a piece of pizza, the funny flutter moving to her middle. Deciding she could easily get in over her head if she pursued the fence thing, she lifted the piece out, stretching the strings of cheese. Fighting a smile, she glanced at him. "You were never a good little altar boy, were you?"

He chuckled and glanced at her, then helped himself to a slice. "You must play baseball, Burrows. You throw one hell of a curve ball."

Her mouth full, she restrained a grin. She was going to have to stay on her toes with this one. He threw a few curve balls himself.

They ate in silence, sitting shoulder-to-shoulder, and Maggie reevaluated the sky. She hadn't noticed before what a truly beautiful sunset it was. Licking her fingers, she was about to wipe her hands on her jeans when Tony fished some paper napkins out of the back pocket of his jeans, handing her one. He gave her another wicked grin. "I always come prepared."

Maggie took the napkin from him, fighting another smile. She wasn't going to touch *that* comment with a ten-foot pole. Wiping her fingers, she deliberately switched gears. "So tell me about your shop, Parnelli."

He set the pizza box on the deck and lifted up the six pack, then pulled one can free of the plastic rings, cracked the tab and handed it to her. He shrugged, opening a can for himself. "Not much to tell. My brother and I have been into cars since we were kids. I raced stock cars before I decided to get a real life and join the force." He took a long swallow, then wedged the beer can between his thighs, leaning his head back against the side of the house. "I did it for the hell of it. Mario raced because it was inside him." He shrugged again and looked down, running his thumb around the rim of the can. "He was good," he said, his voice suddenly husky. "Damned good."

Watching his profile, Maggie spoke. "I told Kelly your brother used to race on the NASCAR circuit. She knew all about him. Said he was one of the top drivers."

Tony took another drink from the can, then wedged it back between his thighs. His face somber, he broke off the tab. "He was. But he was in a hell of a crash two years ago—a five-car pile-up. Another driver was killed, and it was touch and go with him for a while. He nearly lost one leg, and now he has to wear a brace on it, so that finished his career. But he'd socked away a stack of cash, so when I bailed out of the force, we started the business." He lifted his head and looked at her, his expression unsmiling. "We've been pretty lucky—built a few winning engines for the track—so we decided to expand."

Sensing that he didn't really want to talk about the business with his brother, Maggie gave him a rueful smile. "You had me putting bars on my windows and big locks on the doors."

He shot her a startled look. "What?"

The rueful smile remained. "When I came home and saw four black Harleys parked in front of your shop, I was certain the Devil's Angels had moved in next door. That's why I called the cops that night—I saw you coast down the back alley with no lights on, and I was certain some hard-case biker was breaking in."

He stared at her for a second, then tipped his head back and started to laugh. She was on the verge of getting exasperated when he finally stopped, releasing the last of his amusement with a long sigh. He looked at her, his eyes still dancing. "You're going to owe me for a long, long time, Burrows. I get permanently disfigured helping you rescue a renegade cat. I bring you pizza and cold beer. And now I find out you tried to have me thrown in the clink because you thought I was some bad-assed biker dude."

Experiencing a rush of heat to her scalp, Maggie tried to brazen it out. "You should have put up a sign."

Still watching her with a glint in his eyes, he shook his head. "You owe me, lady."

Pursing her mouth against the desire to smile, she narrowed her eyes at him. "You should have a sign, Parnelli."

His expression altering into a soft smile, he continued to study her. Finally he spoke, a husky quality in his voice. "It goes up on Saturday."

Unnerved by the steadiness of his gaze, by the sudden clamor in her chest, Maggie drew a deep, uneven breath and made herself respond, her tone deliberately chastising. "And 'permanently disfigured' is a bit extreme, don't you think? Four little scratches aren't going to qualify you for handicap parking."

Still smiling that funny, distracted smile, he continued to study her. "You don't give an inch, do you?" he said softly, a hint of amusement in his tone.

Feeling as if the air was suddenly too thin to breathe, she stuck a smile on her face. "Inches turn into miles, Parnelli. You've been around the track enough times to know that."

The twinkle reappeared in his eyes, and he grinned at her. "Obviously not often enough. You're miles ahead of me."

Amused by his response, Maggie took a drink from the chilled can of beer. Tony drew up one leg and draped his arm across it, resting his head back against the wall. "So, Maggie Burrows. What's the scoop on you?"

Setting the can in her lap, she laced both hands around it. "Not much."

"You mentioned other kids that day in your living room. I take it Kelly is the youngest."

Crossing her ankles, Maggie stared out across the yard. "She has an older brother and sister. They're both away at university." She paused, then realized that was really misinformation. "Well, they're on summer break right now. Haley has a summer job working on a cruise ship, and Shawn is planting trees in a reforestation project on Vancouver Island."

Maggie felt his gaze on her. "How old are they?"

A nervous disturbance churned in Maggie's stomach. "Shawn's twenty-two and Haley's twenty." She paused, the butterflies in her middle getting bigger as she waited for him to make some comment about her having kids that old. She held her breath.

As if the ages of the kids hadn't even registered, he asked another question. "You raised them on your own?"

Experiencing a flutter that was closely related to relief, she shrugged again. "Not really. My mother died right after Shawn was born, so my father was alone for quite a few years. After the divorce, he wanted me to move back home so he could help with the kids, so I did. The kids adored him, and I didn't want to have to dump them off at baby-sitters. Actually, it worked out really well."

"Kelly told me he died a couple of years ago."

Maggie heaved a sigh and nodded. "Yes, he did. They were as thick as thieves, and she really misses him."

"Where do you work?"

"At FL Accounting."

"You mean the one over in the Loop?"

Maggie looked at him, the growing darkness almost obscuring his face. "Yes."

There was genuine surprise in his voice when he spoke. "Well, I'll be damned. You work for Frank Lucciano?"

"You know him?"

Tony grinned and shook his head. "Know him? Hell, he and my father have been playing chess every Thursday night for the past twenty years." He gave a little laugh. "We wanted to hire him when we started the business, but he said he never did business with friends."

Maggie's smile was wry. "If you ever saw him throw one of his temper tantrums, you'd know why."

An evening breeze wafted across the sun deck, raising goose bumps on Maggie's arms, and she shivered.

Checking his watch, Tony turned his wrist to pick up the light from the street lamp in the alley. She heard him mutter an oath under his breath. "Hell, I didn't realize it was so late." With the ease of an athlete, he got to his feet, then reached down and caught her wrist, pulling her up beside him. He gave her a small smile. "You could have said something, you know."

Folding her arms and hunching her shoulders against the sudden coolness, she resisted the urge to step away from him.

"I *have* been known to stay up past midnight," she said, her tone dry.

He grinned again and turned away. "I'll remember that."

As he started down the steps, Maggie looked at the beer and leftover pizza. "Hey. You're forgetting something."

He turned, and she indicated the stuff he had brought with him. Tony shook his head. "My treat, Burrows. Have it for breakfast."

Maggie went over to stand at the railing, rubbing her upper arms. "Beer and cold pizza aren't my idea of breakfast, Parnelli."

Totally ignoring her, he headed down the steps, then stopped with his back to her. Turning, he gazed up at her, his expression oddly intent. "You're right," he said, his voice very quiet, very serious. "I did forget something."

He came back to where she was standing, then stopped, his gaze locked on her. He stared at her a moment, then, before she had an inkling of what he intended, he framed her face with his hands, tipped her head back and covered her mouth in a full, searching kiss. The instant his lips touched hers, Maggie's heart dropped, setting off a frantic, breathless flutter in her chest that made her knees want to buckle. Her whole body flooded with a sudden weakness, and she closed her eyes and gripped his arms. Tony tightened his grip on her face, making a low, approving sound. Holding her immobile, he shifted the angle of his head, realigning his mouth against hers in a slow, deep, wet kiss that set off an explosion of colored lights behind her eyelids. Electric sensations coursed through her, and Maggie opened her mouth beneath his, the taste of him sending another flood of weakness through her.

He took his time, as if he were drinking in a thousand sensations, as if he couldn't get enough of the taste of her. Maggie was out of breath and trembling when he finally dragged his lips away. Roughly pressing her face against the curve of his neck, he wrapped her in a tight, fierce embrace, his chest heaving.

Shaken and weak, with her heart hammering so hard that she could not catch her breath, Maggie nestled her face tighter against him, her whole body quivering. Oh, God. She had wondered what it would be like. And now she knew. Not even in her wildest imagination had she ever dreamt that she could feel like this.

Brushing her hair aside, Tony tucked his head against hers, then cradled her tighter against him. He didn't say anything. He just held on to her, his breathing still uneven against her ear.

He held her like that for a long time, until the trembling stopped and she was able to relax her grip around his waist. Then he brushed her mouth with one last, soft kiss and loosened his hold. "Go to bed, Maggie Burrows," he whispered unevenly. With one final glance, he went down the steps and disappeared into the darkness. Maggie closed her eyes and hugged herself, still shaken and unsteady. She felt as if she'd just been shoved out of a fast-moving train.

It was a feeling that did not go away. It was as if that one single kiss had pulled the plug on her safe little world, leaving everything out of focus. The entire next day, Maggie wandered around the house in a daze, trying to reassemble herself. Part of the problem was pure, simple exhaustion. Every time she closed her eyes, the same sensations piled in on her, making her restless and tense. It was almost as if her skin was too tight, leaving every nerve stretched and oversensitized.

It got so bad that she considered going back to work, but she knew that would be courting disaster. So she spent the day pacing around her house, feeling either too cold or too hot, experiencing the most unnerving lapses. Lapses in concentration. Lapses in memory. And most of all, big gaping lapses in rationality. And she didn't dare stop moving, because every time she did, she'd get lost in the memory of that kiss, and she'd experience the weakening sensations all over again.

Kelly was convinced her mother was coming down with something. Maggie was convinced she'd simply lost her mind. By Friday morning, she was practically staggering around the house. She honestly didn't realize just how strung out she was until she more or less passed out in her cornflakes. Kelly had already left for school, and Maggie was at the kitchen table, trying to make herself eat. In a wave of despair over her lapse in pure common sense, she'd put her head down on the table. She woke up six hours later, at two in the afternoon, with the weave of her placemat pressed into her face.

It was at that point that she realized she had to get a grip; if she didn't she was going to end up in a white rubber room. So she spent the day giving herself a hard, cold reality check. She was forty-three years old. And according to the information Kelly had passed on, he was thirty-four. That was nine years difference—or sixty-three in dog years. She had two grown children and one who was getting there. He had a freewheeling life-style that was eons away from her own. And, she told herself hard-heartedly, one kiss—no matter how earth-shattering it was—did not mean anything. It was only a kiss. Maybe he'd just been lonely that night. Maybe she'd just been handy. He was Italian, for heaven's sake; he probably kissed everyone that way. An image of him with some tall, gorgeous Stevie prototype took shape in her mind, and Maggie put her head down on the table again. Maybe she should just sell her house and move.

One thing about hard cold reality—it definitely put things back into focus. Painfully so. She *was* in the middle of some midlife crisis. And she was just going to have to get over it. But oh lord, she thought, pressing her head into folded arms, he had made her feel things she hadn't thought she was capable of feeling.

It started to rain late Friday afternoon, and it was still raining when Maggie got up Saturday morning. She found the heavy gray, overcast sky somehow comforting, as if it insulated her from the rest of the world. She spent most of the morning standing at the kitchen window watching the rain, thinking about how she'd let herself slip into the rut she was in. There was no one to blame but herself. When she and Bruce got married, she had arranged her life around his. And after the kids were born, they'd always had top priority. But now she had reached a point in her life where she had to take charge of her own well-being—attend some classes, find a hobby, learn another language—something that would expand her dull day-to-day existence. The thought of spending the rest of her life like this was just too damned depressing.

Sighing heavily, she turned from the window, running her one thumb along the chrome edge of the kitchen table. She wondered why she hadn't seen all this earlier.

"Hey, Mom. I'm home."

Startled by the sound of her daughter's voice, she checked her watch. It was one o'clock, for Pete's sake.

She went toward the living room. "What are you doing home so early?"

Bracing her weight against the frame of the front door, Kelly pried one shoe off against the other, then shot her mother a peculiar look. "I told you this morning. The coach is out of town so he cut the practice short."

Maggie watched her daughter, trying to recall the conversation. She drew a complete blank. "Oh."

Shrugging her backpack off her shoulder, Kelly dropped it by the door, then grinned. "Guess what?"

Folding her arms and resting against the wall, Maggie managed a small smile. "What?"

"I stopped at Tony's on the way home. They were just getting their sign put up—Parnellis' Auto Shop. It looks really nifty. Anyhow, he said they decided this morning to throw a big open-house party tonight." She gave a little shiver of excitement, her eyes bright. "And he asked us to come."

Experiencing an awful, hollow sensation in her middle, Maggie looked down, running the toe of her shoe along the seam where the hardwood and kitchen tile met. She didn't know what to say. The last place on earth she wanted to be was at the Parnelli brothers' open house. Finally she raised her head and looked at her daughter, her expression unsmiling. "Honey," she said, her tone quiet and placating, "I don't think that would be a good idea. Something like that is for his customers and the suppliers he deals with. It's not like a neighborhood block party."

Partway out of her jacket, Kelly stopped and stared at her, defiance in her eyes. "It is not. He said Frank and Nancy were going to be there, and he asked the Popoloposes. Mrs. Popolopos told me when I stopped in to get the strap on my backpack fixed."

A funny nervous flutter developed in Maggie's throat, and she shifted uncomfortably. The Popoloposes ran the little shop on the corner, and they had been repairing shoes there for as long as Maggie could remember. She dredged up a small smile, trying to reason with her daughter. "Then he probably invited some of the Loop businesspeople, Kell. And I don't think it would be appropriate for us to go."

Her hazel eyes flashing, Kelly snatched up her backpack, slinging it over one shoulder. "Well, if that's the case, how come we went to Stevie's open house when she started the fitness center? Tony wouldn't have invited us if he hadn't wanted us to come. He's not like that." She gave her mother a heated look, then pushed past her. "You always make such a big deal out of everything. It's just a stupid open house—it's not an invitation to have tea with the Queen or anything."

"Kelly—"

The teenager turned around, a stubborn look on her face. "Just drop it, okay?" Her chin started to quiver, and Maggie knew she was close to tears. "I just wanted a chance to meet his brother. But never mind. It isn't *appropriate.*"

Not giving Maggie a chance to say anything more, she stormed off into the back entryway, and Maggie heard her thunder down the stairs. A second later, there was a loud slam.

Dragging her hair back off her face with both hands, Maggie closed her eyes. Kelly never stormed off. That kind of display was something Maggie would expect from Haley, but not Kelly. Feeling suddenly very tired, she went into the living room and flopped down on the sofa. She put her feet on the coffee table, rested her head against the padded back and stared at the ceiling, feeling like something that had crawled in under the door.

Kelly had her dead to rights, and Maggie knew it. They *had* gone to Stevie's open house, and she hadn't thought a thing about it. And she knew Kelly would give anything to meet Mario Parnelli. Folding her arms, she shifted her gaze and stared out the window. She had said no for all the wrong reasons. It had nothing to do with who was going to be at the open house or whether it was appropriate or not. It was because of one Tony Parnelli. And one damned kiss that had nearly knocked her socks off. She didn't know why he had done it and wasn't sure she wanted to know. She did know she got a flock of butterflies in her stomach every time she thought about coming face-to-face with him again. And that was the real reason she didn't want to go. Which was hardly fair to her daughter.

Slamming her head against the padded back of the sofa, she closed her eyes again. God, she hated it when she was wrong.

# Chapter 4

Maggie gave herself an hour to get her backbone together, then she bit the bullet, drove to the supermarket and picked up everything she needed to make a big tray of nachos.

The house was dead silent when she returned, and she felt like a total rat. After setting the bags of groceries on the kitchen table, she stripped off her rain jacket, then smoothed down her slacks. She wouldn't blame the kid if she didn't speak to her for a week.

Bracing herself for a chilly rebuff, she went downstairs, a combination of nerves and guilt making her insides quaver. Taking a deep breath, she knocked on Kelly's door. "Can I talk to you for a minute?" she said, her voice scratchy.

There was no response for a moment, then Kelly opened the door. Without looking at her mother, she turned around and went back into her room, leaving the door open. The teenager sat down at her desk, her back to her mother, hooking her feet on the base of the chair.

The air practically crackled with tension. Sensing that no pat little apology was going to placate her daughter, Maggie realized she would have to make at least a partial explanation. Her voice was not quite steady when she began, "The reason I said what I did was because I did something really stupid." Then, as briefly as possible, she told her daughter about the police raid the night she'd called 911.

Partway through the recounting, Kelly turned around, a look of wide-eyed disbelief on her face. When Maggie got to the part about the cops bringing him out in handcuffs, the stunned look turned into a slow, amazed grin. "You're kidding!"

Recalling her own discomfort, Maggie gave her daughter a rueful smile. "No, I'm not kidding. And I still feel pretty dumb about it." Kelly started to say something, and Maggie held up her hand, wanting to finish. "And you were right, Kell. We did go to Stevie's open house, and there's no reason we can't go to this one." She managed another rueful smile. "It's my problem, not yours."

Kelly nearly knocked her chair over when she stood up. "Really?"

With wry amusement still pulling at her mouth, Maggie tipped her head. "Really. But we should take something over. I went out and got everything we need for nachos, so if you feel like grating a couple of pounds of cheese . . ."

Kelly flew across the room and hugged her mother, then did a little dance of elation. "I can't believe it. I'm going to get to meet Mario Parnelli." She looked at her mother, the wisps of hair that had slid from her French braid framing her face, her eyes sparkling. "He's so hot, Mom. Wait until you see him. You won't believe it."

Maggie didn't even want to think about it. His brother was more than she could handle.

The party was in full swing by the time Maggie and Kelly went over, which suited Maggie just fine. Both bays were open, with people milling around outside. Inside was a madhouse. Hundreds of helium-filled balloons clustered in the rafters in a kaleidoscope of color, with wall-to-wall people and wall-to-wall noise. Rock-and-roll music blared from a sound system set up on one workbench, and wildly gyrating bodies were dancing to the beat in the second bay. It was the closest thing to bedlam she'd seen in a long time. Taking a deep breath to quell the nervous flutter in her middle, Maggie entered the structure, heartily wishing she was somewhere else.

The music ended and someone shouted from the far bay, and she smiled a little, wondering how long it would be until old Mrs. Brown from down the street complained. Mrs. Brown and the noise-bylaw officer were on intimate terms. The elderly woman had once complained to Maggie because her lawn sprinkler was too loud.

Handing Kelly the huge tray of nachos with all the trimmings, she pointed to the table of food set up along one wall, then gave her daughter a little push, not even trying to talk above the din.

Frank Lucciano appeared at her side, his face flushed and damp with perspiration, a bottle of beer in his hand. He yelled into her ear. "Some party, huh?"

She looked at him and nodded, amused by his state. Obviously he had been dancing—Frank never broke into a sweat over anything else. He ranted and raved, but he did not sweat. A definite plus when dealing with Revenue Canada.

His hand on her shoulder, he pointed to one corner with his bottle of beer. There were some tables and chairs set up, and a whole contingency of people from the neighborhood were there—George Perkins, the butcher, and his wife; Mr. and Mrs. Popolopos; Big Bertha, who ran the coffee shop; the Gorskys, who owned the bakery.

Relieved to see some familiar faces, Maggie made her way through the crush of people. Nancy Lucciano spotted her, welcoming her with a big grin. "I hope you brought your earplugs. I think this bunch is trying to bring the roof down."

Dropping into an empty chair at the back of the table, Maggie shook her head when Frank held up his beer, his expression questioning. She released a pent-up breath, the knot of nerves finally letting go. This was going to be okay. She'd got herself in a panic over nothing.

Relaxing back in her chair, she studied the crowd. There was everything from biker types to grandmas, and they were all clearly having a good time. The music started up again, and she spotted Kelly with Scott in tow, heading toward the designated dance area. Maggie's heart gave a painful lurch when she caught a glimpse of dark hair in the crowd. The person turned, and she experienced an equally disturbing feeling when it wasn't Tony. She looked away, focusing her attention on Kelly and Scott, a sudden sense of aloneness sweeping over her. She shouldn't have come. Her instincts had told her this was a bad idea.

Maggie stuck it out for a half hour. Then someone put on a CD of old hits that had been popular when she was in high school, and the rush of nostalgia, on top of everything else, was just too much. She'd never felt so alone in her life. It was as if the music had scraped off some protective shell, exposing years of accumulated loneliness, and it had all come together in one big, aching lump. She knew she couldn't stay there one minute longer or she'd really make a fool of herself.

Pleading a headache, she excused herself from the group at the table, then slipped out through the milling crowd. She couldn't see Kelly anywhere, but Frank was standing outside the big bay door, another beer in his hand. He grinned at her. "Coming to keep me company?"

Suddenly cold, Maggie shivered in her light sweater. She shook her head, her whole face feeling unnaturally stiff. "No. I'm going home, Frank."

"What?" he demanded, looking totally scandalized. "You can't go home yet. You just got here."

She managed a small smile. "I'm getting a headache. I'm going home to bed."

He gave her an intent look. "You sure that's all? You don't look so hot, Mag."

She lifted one corner of her mouth. "I never look hot, Frank." She indicated the second bay. "I can't see Kelly, and I don't want to fight my way through that crowd. Would you mind letting her know I've gone home? And tell her I'll leave the back door unlocked for her."

He nodded brusquely and gave her shoulder a little shake. "Will do. You go on, and don't worry about her. I'll make sure she gets home all right."

She met his gaze. "Thanks, Frank," she said, her voice uneven.

Frank was watching her, a thoughtful expression in his eyes. "Something bothering you, Maggie?"

A tight lump formed in her throat, his gruff kindness making her feel even worse. Fighting against the constriction, she dredged up another small smile. "It's just a headache, Frank. Not the end of the world." There was a burst of laughter and a series of loud pops, as if someone was exploding balloons, and she glanced toward the shop. She caught a glimpse of Kelly in the crowd, but that wasn't what made her insides drop away. It was seeing Tony standing in a group of people, laughing at something happening outside her field of view. Feeling more alone than ever, she turned abruptly and started toward her house, wanting to crawl in a hole and never come out. What was wrong with her? She hadn't been this adolescent when she was an adolescent. It was as if that one single kiss had opened up the floodgates, and she was never going to be the same again.

She *was* never going to be the same again. Maggie sat on the sofa in total darkness, her legs drawn up, her arms folded around them, her head buried in her knees. She had been wallowing for the past three hours, and she could not make herself stop. She would just about get things under control when something would happen and she'd start all over again, until her nose was plugged, her eyes throbbing and her throat raw.

She'd headed straight to the bathroom when she got home and had taken a long shower with the water turned on full blast, mentally allowing herself one good, cleansing cry in the safety of her shower enclosure. She had stayed in there so long that she'd emptied the forty-gallon hot-water tank, but that therapy had only worked for a little while—until she got out of the shower. Then somebody had cranked up the volume on the stereo next door, and the sound of music seemed to echo in her silent, empty house, bringing on another wave of emotion. She'd finally shut the living room windows and closed the drapes, but that hadn't helped. Nothing helped.

Her chest feeling as raw as her throat, Maggie pressed her forehead against her knees. It was crazy. Some guy moves in next door—a hunk who has an overdose of sex appeal, a body like a Roman god and a smile with more wattage than Las Vegas—and she falls apart at the seams. She was having fantasies about him in her sleep, and she was terrified to go outside in case she ran into him in the back alley. Her body hummed every time she thought about him, and her suppressed sexuality was wound up like a clock.

What was wrong with her? Why couldn't she stuff all those feelings in a mental closet? She had done it once; why couldn't she do it this time? Maggie didn't know what was wrong with her. She was forty-three years old, for crying out loud, and she was daydreaming about being twenty-five with no stretch marks. It was nuts. One little emotional upheaval in her life and she was a mess. She was normally a levelheaded, practical person, wasn't she? Why was it that a simple pizza and beer had changed all that?

Okay. It wasn't just the pizza and beer. It was that one long, deep, devastating kiss that had thrown her into total chaos. Just remembering the feel of Tony's hands cradling her face was enough to put her heart into overdrive. Lord, one kiss—one unbelievable, bone-melting kiss—and he had turned her world upside down and given it a darned good shake. And now she was left with the consequences. And those consequences were pretty hard to deal with, especially for someone who truly believed she didn't have a shred of foolishness in her. What a joke. At the moment she didn't have an unfoolish thought in her head. She had developed an adolescent crush on a man who was nine years her junior.

"Mom?"

She kept her head down, heartily wishing she was somewhere else. Kelly could make more noise than a herd of elephants, but she could also move like a shadow when she wanted to. And she was the only person in the whole world who could miss the squeaky floorboard by the front door. Maggie prayed she would leave the light off.

The light came on, and Maggie heard her daughter kick off her shoes. Still resting her forehead against her knees, she made a stab at normalcy. "So did you have a good time?"

"How come you left without even saying hello to Tony?"

There was no mistaking the miffed tone in Kelly's voice, and Maggie released a tired sigh. It served her right for drilling her daughter in good manners—now she was going to get drilled herself. Determined not to let Kelly see the state her face was in, she kept her head down. "I didn't even see Tony," she responded.

"Well, he was looking for you. He seemed pretty ticked off when Frank told him you'd gone home."

Wondering why she felt compelled to defend herself, she mumbled. "It wasn't a deliberate insult, Kelly. I was getting a headache, so I came home." Which was no longer a lie. A dull pain was developing behind her eyes, and her head was beginning to pound.

"You were fine when we left home."

"Yes, I was. Then I wasn't. It's not a federal offense."

"Well, you should have at least thanked him for the invitation."

Maggie experienced a tiny flicker of amusement. She wondered what Kelly would say if she told her she was beginning to sound just like her father.

"Big Bertha said to give you these. They're the keys to the coffee shop, so you can pick up her books on the way to work Monday."

Knowing she couldn't hide any longer, Maggie released a long sigh and lifted her head. Without looking at Kelly, she took the keys her daughter was holding out to her, sticking them in the kangaroo pocket on her sweatsuit top.

"Mom?" Kelly crouched down in front of her and touched her hand. "What's the matter?"

Setting the keys on the end table, Maggie avoided her concerned gaze. "Nothing, honey. I've just got a bad headache, that's all."

"You've been crying."

The tone of quiet accusation in her daughter's voice made Maggie smile just a little, and she finally met Kelly's gaze. "That's not a federal offense, either, Muffy."

Kelly gave her a return smile, but it didn't reach her eyes. "Come on, Mom. You never cry. What's the matter?"

Reaching out, Maggie smoothed back some loose wisps of air that had slipped out of Kelly's braid, her throat cramping a little. "Nothing's the matter," she said, her voice husky. he tried to put a little lightness into her response, a tug of wry musement lifting one corner of her mouth. "Maybe my hormones have run just amok."

Kelly looked up at her, her eyes serious. "You aren't worried about anything, are you?"

Maggie smiled back. "No, I'm not worried about anything. It was just an off day."

"You're sure?"

"Yes. I'm sure."

The teenager stared at her mother, as if assessing her response. Finally she spoke. "Okay then." She got to her feet. Well, I guess I'd better go to bed. We swim at six-thirty tomorrow morning."

Maggie watched as she picked up her shoes. "Do you need ride?"

"No. Mr. Gordon is going to take us. Scott wants him to leotape us so we can see how we're doing." Kelly paused at e archway. "Go to bed, Mom."

Maggie gave her a small smile. "I will."

Stacking her arms on her knees, Maggie rested her chin on em, considering the room. She liked the results of her labor. She had painted the walls an eggshell color, and with the k woodwork and floors, it had given the room a clean, uncluttered look. One thing she had indulged in over the past few ars was artwork, all done by local artists, and she had spent ortune getting it all matted and framed. The frames were a x—wide, narrow, some with wide matting, some less dramatic—but the effect pleased her. There were some oils, several watercolors and some pen-and-ink sketches, and she had ent considerable time arranging them in groupings.

he sound of car doors slamming interrupted her mental anderings, and she realized it had finally grown quiet next r. Experiencing a funny let-down feeling, she raked her r back with one hand and got up. The party was over, in re ways than one. Going over to turn off the light, she

winced at the heavy pounding in her head. It served her right
for claiming she had a headache. Now she had one for real.

It was nearly nine when Maggie awoke the next morning.
Her first thought when she looked at the clock was that she'd
slept in and was late for work. The second thought, after she
waded through the grogginess and remembered it was Sunday, was that she felt like hell. She groaned and rolled over on
her stomach, the movement setting off a drum chorus in her
skull. Pulling the pillow over her head to block out the
brightness, she tried to swallow against the rawness in her
throat. Feeling hot, sweaty and kick-the-dog cranky, she
pushed off the covers. Too tired the night before to change into
one of the oversize T-shirts she used as nighties, she had gone
to bed in her sweatsuit. She felt as if she were strangling in it.
She tried to swallow again. Yep, no question about it. Her
throat was definitely sore.

Trying to scrape together enough energy to get up, she
pushed the pillow away and squinted at the clock again. Ten
o'clock? She was sure it had said nine. Or had she gone back
to sleep? She didn't know.

A loud knocking on the back door made her consider pulling the pillow over her head once more. But then she remembered that she had come home late on Wednesday and missed
paying David, her paperboy. Which meant he'd be back
sometime today. Since he delivered her paper in a neat little roll
and never dumped it in the hedge, unlike his predecessor, she
felt obliged to pull herself out of bed. Holding her head with
both hands, she staggered down the hallway, feeling decidedly off kilter, as if one leg had suddenly become shorter than
the other. This did not feel like the aftermath of three hours of
howling self-pity. This felt like something else altogether. The
other obvious answer did not fill her with joy. About once
every five or six years, she got nailed with a bout of bronchitis that made her feel like she had a forest fire raging in her
chest and that her throat had been put through a meat grinder.

Another knock sounded and she muttered a nasty comment under her breath as she unlocked the dead bolt. Shading

er eyes against the brightness, she pulled open the door, about
o give David a lecture on patience and prudence.

Only it wasn't David. His feet were definitely the wrong size.
A nasty little fizzle spreading through her, Maggie lifted her
aze, her eyes widening in alarm. It definitely wasn't David
anding there. It was Tony Parnelli, her tray hanging from one
and, his other hand braced on the door frame. He had on a
air of faded jeans with frayed rips in the knees and an un-
uttoned orange shirt that had one pocket torn off. His jaw
as dark with heavy stubble, his hair was standing on end as
he'd just got out of bed and his eyes were red rimmed and
oodshot. And from the grim set of his jaw and the glint in his
es, he was feeling cranky as well. "Here," he said, his tone
ostile. "Your name is on the bottom."

Grasping the tray, Maggie lifted her chin, taking exception
his tone. Her head felt as if it just might explode if she
oved too fast, her legs were telling her to sit down and now
e had to deal with Bozo the Bear.

"And a good, good morning to you, too," she said, her tone
rcastic.

He glared at her. "Don't start in with the good-morning
ap, lady. I'm returning your damned tray. That's all."

He turned and started for the steps, and pure, unadulter-
d annoyance sizzled through Maggie. "Thank you for
nging over such a nice tray of goodies, Mrs. Burrows," she
d, as if prompting a small, spoiled child.

Tony stopped. He didn't move for a moment; then he
ned. Jamming his hands on his hips, he stared at her, the
uscles in his jaw bunching. Then he came toward her, a
ngerous glimmer in his eyes. "Boy, did I have you figured
ong. I invited you over thinking you might have a good
e. But no. You toss some food on the table, then leave.
at's the matter, *Mrs*. Burrows? Wasn't the company good
ough for you?"

Gripped with the totally unexpected urge to laugh, Maggie
sed her eyes and rested her forehead against the door,
hing she didn't feel so darned dizzy. What was wrong with
? She should be absolutely indignant over his accusation;
ead she wanted to laugh. But the way her throat and head

were feeling, it would probably kill her. Making an effort to school her face, she raised her head and looked at him. "I didn't see you there."

Shifting his weight onto one hip, he narrowed his eyes. "I had to pick up some more beer. What was your excuse?"

"I had a headache."

One corner of his mouth lifted in a nasty smile. "Yeah. Right." He cast her one last look, then turned and went down the stairs.

Experiencing a rush of all the same feelings she'd had the night before, Maggie watched him go, suddenly on the verge of tears. On top of that, she had offended him, and that made her feel even worse. He had tried to be nice. Tried to be a good neighbor. If her female hormones were in full revolt, that was her problem, not his. He had got clawed up helping her with the Captain, and he'd brought her pizza and beer. *He also kissed you,* whispered a devious little voice in her mind, *like you have never been kissed before.*

A good dose of guilt mixed in with everything else she was feeling, and Maggie felt like pure slime. He was at the corner of the garage when she swallowed hard and called out to him.

"Tony?"

He turned, his expression set.

Feeling as if she was either going to throw up or cry, she tried to dredge up a smile. "Thank you for the invitation," she said, her voice raw and scratchy. "It was nice of you to ask. And I was rude not to stay until you showed up." He started to say something, but she stepped inside, shoved the door closed and rested her head against it. Closing her eyes, she waited for the painful cramp in her throat to ease; then she turned and stumbled back to her room. Crawling into bed, she pulled the pillow over her head, tears leaking out. Damn it. She had cried more in the past two days than she had in the past twelve years. Maybe Frank was right—maybe she was menopausal. She pressed her face against the mattress, blotting up the tears. But if that was the case, why did she feel as if she'd just shot Bambi?

By Sunday night she was running a fever, her chest was starting to get tight and her throat was so sore it made her eyes water every time she tried to swallow. Her head still feeling as if it might explode any minute, she did all the home-remedy things—gargled with saltwater, breathed in mentholated steam, loaded up on vitamin C. She had to make it to work on Monday. Frank would be ready to rip out what was left of his hair over the Macinrow account, and she felt bone-deep obligated to rescue him from Mr. Macinrow and vice versa.

By Monday morning, she knew she was in big trouble. Sometimes she was able to head off a case of bronchitis with some treatment, but this time it hadn't worked. She breathed very carefully, partly because of her raw throat and partly because she knew if she coughed, her chest was going to hurt like the dickens. She felt a little better after she took a hot shower and cautiously, very cautiously inhaled the steam. But she still felt like hell. Knowing her legs wouldn't hold out for four blocks, she drove to work. She was halfway there when she remembered she was supposed to pick up Big Bertha's books, and she had to turn around and go back for the key, then stop at the coffee shop. Bertha had closed up for a week to do some renovating, and the smell of fresh, oil-based paint was like breathing in fire. After a coughing spell that just about killed her, Maggie arrived at work feeling as if she had a troupe of acrobats loose in her head.

Frank took one look at her, then grabbed her by the shoulders and firmly turned her toward the door. "Get out of here. Go home, go to bed and take a bottle of rum with you."

She locked her knees and braced her legs. "I'm just going to finish the Macinrow—"

"No," he said, pushing her toward the door. "I don't want your big red nose and hacky cough in here. You look like hell and you sound like hell. Which means you probably feel like hell." He opened the door and tried to push her out. "Go."

Grabbing either side of the door frame, she resisted. "Frank," she whispered, her voice so hoarse that it sounded like gravel. "Just a minute."

He quit shoving her, and she turned, pressing her fists against her chest to stifle another cough. The burning tightness made her eyes water, and she remained motionless, praying the seizure would pass. Swallowing hard, she looked up at him, her eyes tearing in the bright lights. "Would you phone Dr. Donaldson and see if I can get an appointment?" she whispered, her voice gone almost completely.

He shook his head, as if despairing for her; then he walked to her desk and picked up the phone, raising his eyebrows in a silent query. She went over and wrote the number on a note-pad, and he shook his head again and punched in the number. Maggie went outside and leaned against the door frame. Frank's establishment was really an old house that he'd bought and renovated twenty years before. It was situated on a corner lot, with big trees in the yard, a cotoneaster hedge and a single-car garage in back. The only thing that indicated it was a business was the big, old-fashioned sign hanging from a post by the front walk.

Maggie leaned her head back and closed her eyes, trying to endure the waves of heat washing through her. She had been cold when she got dressed, so she'd put on a sweater. Now she wanted to rip it off. God, she wanted to lay down and die.

Frank came outside. "The doc was just leaving for ar emergency at the hospital, but he said it sounded like the usual He's phoning in a prescription. He said to go home, go to bed and if you don't feel any better in twenty-four hours, to come in and see him."

Hooking his big beefy arm around her neck, her boss guided her down the walk to her car. He opened the door, practically stuffed her inside, then shut it. Then he waggled one finger a her. "I don't want to see you back here for another week Mary Margaret. You got that?"

Gripping the wheel, she looked up at him. "But, Frank—'

"No buts," he said, scolding her. "You go home. And yo take care of yourself." His voice became gruff. "If you nee anything—anything at all—you call me, you hear?"

Wanting to put her head down on the steering wheel and nc move for a week, she dredged up a weak smile. "I hear."

He stood there until she pulled away, and Maggie focused a her attention on getting from Frank's to the neighborhoo pharmacy without crashing into anybody.

Jack, the pharmacist, had gone for coffee. Would Maggie like to sit down and wait until he got back? the salesclerk asked.

No, Maggie didn't want to sit down and wait. Jack's coffee breaks were like minivacations. Would it be all right if Kelly came by later to pick it up?

Yes, that would be fine.

Not really caring about anything anymore, Maggie drove home at half the speed limit, both hands on the wheel and her eyes never wavering from the road. She felt like she was a hundred and five.

Downing some over-the-counter decongestant medication and a few aspirins, she stumbled into her room. She peeled off her clothes and immediately began to shiver. Cold. God, she was so cold. She put on a pair of socks and a huge knee-length, fleecey T-shirt and crawled into bed, huddling under the covers. She truly did want to die.

By the time Kelly came home from school, Maggie had lost her voice completely and had been sweltering hot and freezing cold so many times that she'd lost count. She was back to freezing again when her daughter entered the room, carrying a mug of hot lemon and honey. Knowing she hadn't taken in nearly enough liquids, Maggie dragged herself up against the pillows Kelly stacked behind her, huddling in her comforter as she took the mug in both hands.

A worried look in her eyes, Kelly carefully combed her mother's hair back with her fingers. "Mom, you're really sick. I think I should call Dr. Donaldson."

Maggie shook her head and whispered painfully, "No. I just need the prescription."

Tucking the blankets more snugly around her shoulders, Kelly rose. "I'll ride down and get it right now." She set the portable phone on the bed beside Maggie. "I'll be back in fifteen minutes. Okay?"

Feeling like an orphan, she nodded, sipping greedily at the hot lemon. Lord, it felt wonderful on her sore throat.

She was still sitting there nursing the hot drink when her daughter returned. Her mind was so foggy that she had no sense of time. It seemed like Kelly had barely left before she was back, a white paper pharmacy bag in her hand.

Maggie got up and went to the bathroom, took a double dose of the foul-tasting medicine and some more aspirin, then staggered back to her room. Kelly had straightened the bed, and there was a thermal pitcher of ice water and her grandmother's antique dinner bell sitting on her bedside table. Feeling as weak as a kitten and as drunk as a lord, Maggie crawled back into bed, burying her face in the plumped-up pillow.

Kelly pulled the covers over her. "I'm going to do my homework in the kitchen. If you need anything, you ring the bell, okay?"

If Maggie hadn't felt so totally rotten she probably would have been a tiny bit amused. It was exactly what she'd done when the kids were sick. She moved her head and concentrated on not coughing. If she did, it would kill her for sure.

The sound of voices woke Maggie up. Dredging up what energy reserves she had left, she rolled onto her back, resting one arm across her eyes. The movement set off a burning pain in her chest. Why was the room so dark? The sun had been shining just a minute ago.

"Mom?"

Forcing herself to respond to her daughter's worried whisper, she shifted her arm onto her forehead and opened her eyes. Her first thought was that she was hallucinating. That couldn't be Tony Parnelli crouched down by her bed, his face solemn with concern, her daughter standing behind him. Sure she was seeing things, Maggie closed her eyes and tried to clear her mind; then she opened them again. She was not seeing things. It was definitely Tony Parnelli. His gaze serious, he reached up and smoothed the sweat-dampened hair back from her face, his touch confirming that she was definitely not seeing things. Maggie closed her eyes, her heart doing a clumsy barrel roll in her congested chest. She wasn't going to die from bronchial pneumonia, after all. She was going to die from cardiac arrest.

He slipped one hand under her head, then began stroking her cheek with his thumb. "Your daughter's pretty worried about you, Burrows," he said, his voice gruff. "And I agree. I think we should take you to the hospital."

Thrown into sensory overload by his soft caress against her hot, sensitive skin, Maggie swallowed hard and wet her chapped lips. It took a major effort to ease some air into her lungs. "What time is it?" she whispered unevenly.

"It's going on ten. Kell says it's time for your medicine."

Maggie tried to make her brain focus. Ten? It couldn't be ten. Marshaling her courage and her energy, she opened her eyes. Too miserable to care that she probably looked like something Captain Hook had dragged in, she tried for a smile. "I'm not dying," she whispered, her throat feeling as if it had been seared by a blowtorch. "I just feel like I am."

A tiny glint of amusement appeared in his eyes and the corners of his mouth lifted a little, but his expression was still filled with concern. "You're soaking wet, Mag," he chastised softly, smoothing his thumb across her cheek.

Suddenly far closer to tears than she wanted to be, Maggie closed her eyes, that soft, gentle touch doing something incredibly painful to her heart. She wanted to crawl into his arms, bury her face against his neck and stay like that for the next week. She waited for the awful spasm of longing to pass; then she eased in another very careful breath. "I've had this before," she said, her voice raw and gravelly. "The medicine just needs time to work."

There was a long pause; then he spoke, his tone still gruff. "Okay. We'll do it your way for now, but if you're no better in the morning, you're going to the hospital, Burrows."

Her throat closing up from sheer emotion, Maggie gave a barely perceptible nod.

Tony ran his thumb across her cheek one more time, then withdrew his hand. The sudden feeling of loss was so intense that Maggie wanted to roll onto her stomach and bury her face in the pillow, but she just didn't have the energy. She heard Tony say something to Kelly as she fumbled for the quilt. Her sweats had abruptly given way to a chill, and she was freezing again. Maggie huddled under the quilt, vaguely aware that both Tony and Kelly had left. God, she was so cold.

Someone entered the room, and she heard something being set down on the bedside table. The mattress shifted as someone sat down. "Come on, Tinkerbell," Tony said softly, sliding his arm under her shoulders and lifting her up so her head was nestled against the curve of his shoulder. "Let's get another shot of medicine and some more aspirin down you."

Feeling as if her eyelids weighed a ton, Maggie opened her eyes, squinting against the light from the lamp on the dresser. She took the medicine and the aspirins, the warmth of his body offering her more comfort than she thought possible. He held her for a minute, as if making sure she'd got everything down; then he eased her back onto the pillow. Maggie rolled to her side and closed her eyes, locking her fists against her chest so she wouldn't start coughing. Tony pulled the covers up and tucked them snugly around her shoulders, then smoothed her hair away from her face letting his hand rest against the back of her head.

"Thank you," she whispered thickly.

He tightened his hold, and Maggie could have sworn he brushed a soft kiss along her temple. She pressed her hands harder against her chest. She *was* having hallucinations. Her fever must be higher than she thought.

The clock on her bedside table said 1:00 a.m. when she awoke again. This time her lungs rebelled, determined to clear out the congestion, and she knew she wasn't going to be able to stifle the involuntary need to cough. Scrambling into a sitting position, she grabbed a pillow and held it against her chest. Lord, this was not going to work.

She was right; it didn't. She was nicely into a wrenching coughing spasm when the light on the other side of the bed came on. She got such a shock that her lungs seized up altogether. Tony Parnelli was there, and he rose up on one elbow, dragged one hand down his face as if to rid himself of sleep, then squinted at her. He looked tired cranky and totally groggy. "You're worse, aren't you," he said, his tone accusing.

So stunned was she to find him there, Maggie dazedly lay back down unable to answer. He leaned over her, a determined set to his jaw. Knowing what he was thinking and where he was planning on taking her, she shook her head. "No," she said, her voice barely a squeak. "Coughing is good." Well, it wasn't *good*. It made her chest feel like it was on fire, but it did serve a purpose.

Scowling at her, he muttered something and started to pull the covers over her, but his hand grazed her nightshirt. He swore, running his hand down her body. "Damn it, Maggie! You're soaking wet."

Before she knew what was happening, he had her sitting up. Muttering something about her not having the sense God gave a twit, he whipped her sweat-dampened T-shirt off over her head. Shock left her gaping, and she just sat there, her arms pressed against her breasts, unable to form a single sentence in her head. Then she grabbed the sheet, hot embarrassment shooting through her, sending her fever skyrocketing. Oh, lord. Maybe death really was a good option right now. Except Tony didn't seem to notice that she was sitting there stark naked. Looking as if he was still wonky with sleep, he grasped the fabric at the back of his own T-shirt and dragged it over his head. "Here," he said, still out of sorts from being awakened. "Put this on." Then, as if she was a small, recalcitrant child, he pulled it over her head.

Feeling absolutely dazed, Maggie sat there staring at him like some halfwit as he dressed her. She was shivering again, partly from the cool air against her damp skin, partly from shock. Yanking the comforter loose, he hauled her over to his dry side of the bed and flopped back down, locking her against his side. Then he dragged the quilt over her and stuffed it around her shoulders, pulling her head onto his shoulder. "Now go to sleep," he said, his tone irritable. "You get your next shot of medicine at two."

It had all happened so fast that Maggie wasn't sure it had happened at all. It couldn't be possible. She couldn't be lying in bed with Tony Parnelli, feeling as if she'd just gone into orbit. It had to be just another hallucination. But the wonderful warmth of his body enveloped her and she turned her face against his neck and closed her eyes, inhaling the male scent of him. Maybe she had died, after all. This certainly felt like heaven.

## Chapter 5

During the night, Maggie had the most amazing fever-induced dreams. Warm, comforting dreams. Sensual dreams. Dreams of being held by Tony Parnelli. Dreams of someone rubbing her shoulder.

Well, maybe not rubbing. More like shaking. Annoyed that this outside intrusion was spoiling her drifting sense of well-being, she tried to swat the annoyance away.

"Don't give me any grief, woman. It's time for your medicine."

Wait a minute. That voice did not come out of any dream. Her eyes flying open, Maggie found herself staring across an expanse of naked chest. And it certainly wasn't her own.

Jerking her head up, she clipped something above her head very hard. The voice swore, and a hand shoved her head back down. There was another muttered curse, then the voice said wryly, "You're not half as much fun to sleep with as I imagined, Burrows. You run hot, then cold, then you just about dislocate my jaw."

Maggie jerked her head back, her mind suddenly horribly clear, and she stared up at Tony Parnelli. He looked like a rumpled, tired desperado with that dark stubble and a bad-boy glint in his eyes. Oh, God. It hadn't been a dream, after all. Experiencing a rush of sheer mortification, she closed her eyes.

She remembered him being in her room last night. But how in hell had he gotten into her bed? Fuzzy memories slowly took shape, and she vaguely recalled him giving her her medicine. Another memory surfaced, this one embarrassingly clear, of him stripping off her damp nightshirt. She winced, knowing she had to get herself out of this mess.

Easing in a careful breath, she tried to brazen out the situation. "Dr. Livingston, I presume?"

He gave a gravelly laugh and tightened his arm around her shoulder in an approving squeeze. "You're a real piece of work, Burrows. You just don't give up, do you?"

Not sure if she wanted to laugh or cry, Maggie knew she had to face this situation head-on. Her heart suddenly pounding much too fast, she swallowed, immediately noticing that her throat was not quite so raw. Now if her heart would only smarten up... Taking another careful breath so as not to set off anything in her congested chest, she spoke, her voice still a little hoarse. "Don't you think maybe you're taking this good-neighbor thing a little too seriously?"

She felt him smile against her temple. "I don't know about that. I was just lying here thinking maybe I wasn't taking it seriously enough."

Not sure what he was driving at, and knowing she wasn't up to a battle of wits, she copped out. "Hmm," was all she said.

She felt him smile again as he rubbed her shoulder, then he carefully eased his arm out from under her. "Come on, Mag," he said, sitting up beside her. "The prescription says every four hours."

Feeling like her head was full of sawdust and twice as heavy, Maggie struggled to a sitting position. She drew up her knees under the covers, then hunched over and closed her eyes, stifling the need to cough. If she could just keep from coughing for the next few hours, until that searing pain in her lungs eased, maybe her chest wouldn't be torn to shreds. She heard Tony leave the bedroom, and she rested her head on her knees.

Feeling suddenly weak and shaky, she tried to convince herself it was because she was sick.

Tony reentered the room a few moments later, and she felt him sit down on the bed beside her; then she heard him open the bottle of medication. He poured the medicine into a teaspoon and offered it to her. Gathering what little energy she had, she lifted her head and swallowed it, shivering at the taste. Then she closed her eyes and weakly rested her head on her knees, being very careful not to breathe too deeply. She did not want to cough. It was going to hurt like hell if she did.

He rearranged the pillows behind her, then brushed back her hair. "Why don't you lay back," he said quietly, "and let me give you a sponge bath? It'll make you feel better."

The thought of him bathing her gave her a shot of adrenaline that had her sitting straight up, wide awake and staring at him. A sponge bath? From Tony Parnelli? Not a chance. Her heart tried to climb out of her red-hot chest. She had to get out of this somehow. "I want a shower, Tony. That would do me more good than anything."

He got a stubborn look in his eyes and shook his head. "No way."

"Please," she begged. "The steam will be good for my chest."

The laugh lines around his eyes creased, one corner of his mouth kicked up and a wicked glint appeared in his eyes. "I don't think we know each other well enough to discuss your chest, Maggie," he said, the glint intensifying.

She had the nearly uncontrollable urge to laugh, but she knew that would kill her for sure.

He grinned at her, then folded his arms. He studied her for a moment, then spoke, a sly look in his eyes. "Okay, Burrows. I'll agree to the shower, but you have to agree to a home remedy of my grandmother's."

She stared at him, weighing her options. She didn't like the sounds of Grandma's home remedy, but what she was trying to avoid here was a sponge bath. If it was one or the other, the home remedy won hands down. Feeling a little uneasy, she stared back him. Finally, her tone somewhat wary, she answered, "All right."

He grinned at her, and she was suddenly very dubious about what she'd let herself in for. But anything—*anything* was better than his giving her a sponge bath.

He got her housecoat for her, allowed her three seconds to get something clean to put on, then helped her to the bathroom down the hall. Maggie's legs were so weak that they felt like two shafts of cotton candy, but she gritted her teeth, determined to get behind a locked door, come hell or high water. Except the locked door didn't fly. A warning look in his eyes, Tony told her that if she locked it he was going to kick it down. Having more sense than to tempt fate, Maggie left it unlocked.

The hot steam was not a good idea. Her lungs decided it was definitely time to cough, and Maggie thought she was going to die for sure. By the time she got out and put on an old, worn-thin sweatsuit, she was so exhausted that she had to sit on the toilet to dry her hair, and even then her arms were so weak it took her fifteen minutes to do what she normally did in five. Using the wall as support, she crept back to her bedroom, stopping in the doorway to stare at her bed. It had been stripped down and remade, with the pile of used sheets and pillowcases wadded up in a corner. Moved to the verge of tears by his consideration, she crawled into bed on her stomach, burying her face in a pillow. Lord, she hadn't had anyone make a bed for her since she was really little.

Feeling ridiculously emotional, she concentrated on the scent of the clean bedding. She always hung her sheets and towels outside in the summer to dry because she loved the smell of sunshine and fresh air on her linen. For some reason it made her feel better.

"You were supposed to call me when you were done."

Wiping her face against the bedding, Maggie collected her strength and hoisted herself up against the stack of pillows. She managed a wan smile. "I'd hoped you'd taken Grandma's remedy and gone home."

He was carrying a cookie sheet with several items on it—a cereal bowl, a mug and a covered cooking pot, all emitting steam, and a glass of water with ice cubes in it. It struck Maggie that he was doing a darned good job of finding his way around her house—the fresh bedding, the cookie tray, ice cubes, the dishes. A nosy little trait he'd picked up as a detective, no doubt.

Giving her a reproving look, he set the tray on the foot of the bed. "Be nice, Burrows. I don't do this for just anyone." He picked up the bowl and stuck a spoon in it. "I made you a poached egg on toast, which," he said, giving her a stern look, "you are going to eat. And I made you some tea."

Maggie took the bowl, giving the tray a skeptical look. "That explains the bowl and mug," she said, her voice croaky after the coughing spell. "But it doesn't explain the pot, Parnelli."

"Ah," he said, his tone mysterious. "That's Grandmother's Special."

He handed her the glass of water. "All the water and every bite of food, Burrows."

She didn't have the energy to argue. She wasn't sure about the toast, but he had cut it up with the egg, pretty much turning it to mush, and it went down better than expected. She finished and handed him the bowl and empty glass, then tried to slip out of her end of the deal. "Lord, but I'm so tired," she whispered for effect. "I think I'll just go to sleep."

He shook his head and gave her an amused look. "Nice try, lady. But it isn't going to work. A deal's a deal."

He lifted the lid off the pot, and the unmistakable odor of garlic wafted up. He took out a steaming towel, and Maggie realized it was folded into a pad that was filled with some sort of concoction. The smell of garlic and something else hit her respiratory system, and Maggie nearly gagged to keep from coughing. She scuttled back in the bed, holding up both hands. "Forget it," she croaked. "You're not coming near me with that."

He stopped and looked at her, then cocked one eyebrow. "Either you do what I tell you," he said, giving her a smile that had I Dare You written all over it, "or I'll do it for you. It's entirely up to you."

She stared at him, not liking the determined glint in his eye. There was a brief, silent battle of wills; then she sighed and rolled her eyes. "Fine. What am I supposed to do? Make spaghetti sauce?"

He sat down on the edge of the bed facing her, his hip pressing against hers. The twinkle in his eyes got worse. "No, smart mouth. You're going to put this on your chest, and you're going to leave it there for twenty minutes." She folded her arms, an obstinate set to her chin. There was another brief staring match, and Maggie considered her options.

"You made a deal, Burrows," he reminded her.

Realizing he had her there, Maggie heaved a sigh and gave in. "Fine," she said flatly, taking the towel. "Go away and I'll do it."

With a knowing glint in his eyes, he folded his own arms and shook his head. "Uh-uh. I'm going to sit here and make sure you do it."

Giving him a defiant glance, she unzipped her sweatshirt to expose the top part of her breasts, flattening the hot, moist compress against her chest. "There. Happy?"

He reached out and zipped her up, then leaned down and pulled the sheet over her. "Not exactly," he said, grinning broadly. "But it'll do for now."

He set the cup of steaming tea on her bedside table and picked up the cookie sheet. "I'm going home to have a shower. I'll be back in fifteen minutes, and if that plaster isn't still there, we're going to start right from the top, Maggie. Just so you know."

"Thank you, Dr. Feel Good," she said, her tone as tart as she could make it under the circumstances.

He gave her an amused look, then went over and lowered the blind. "And no cheating."

Suddenly exhausted, Maggie rested her arm on her forehead and closed her eyes, the fumes from the garlic plaster oddly soothing. Here she was, sick in bed, smothered in garlic and being treated like a child. It just didn't seem fair.

She was vaguely aware of someone coming in later and removing a weight from her chest, then covering her up. Rolling onto her side, she stuck her hands under her cheek and sighed. Maybe if God was kind, he'd let her sleep for a week.

Tony wakened her again at ten to give her another dose of medicine and inflict another garlic plaster on her. She was so zonked out on medication that she was barely coherent, but she remembered giving him a very hard time, telling him in no uncertain terms to leave her alone.

She awoke again just before two in the afternoon, her head amazingly clear. The whole bedroom reeked of garlic, and the bedding smelled like the inside of a salami factory. She could even taste it in her mouth. But as dubious as she was about most home cures, her chest was so much better she couldn't believe it. She was still congested, but the congestion was loose and the searing pain was gone.

Pushing back the covers, Maggie hiked herself up against the pillows and stretched her arms over her head to ease the soreness in her back and shoulders. She felt as if every muscle in her body had been pummeled. Closing her eyes, she raked her fingers through her tangled hair, then sighed and swung her legs off the bed. God, she needed some fresh air.

Her legs still feeling a little wobbly, she went to the window and opened the blind, then the window. Folding her arms on the window frame, she rested her head on them and closed her eyes again, enjoying the feel of the warm breeze across her face. She smiled a little. Not a hint of garlic out there.

"What are you doing out of bed?"

Her heart gave a lurch at the sound of Tony's voice, but she didn't lift her head. "I'm breathing fresh air."

"Breathe it in bed."

"Go away," she said, her tone peevish. "I need to stand up for a while."

He grabbed her around the waist, and before she had a chance to react, he had her back on the bed and covered up. Jamming his hands on his hips, he glared at her. "You're pushing your luck, lady. I talked to your doctor, and he said this is nothing to mess around with."

Gripping the edge of the quilt, Maggie stared up at him with wide eyes. "How did you get the name of my doctor?"

He picked up the bottle of medication and held it two inches from her nose. "Where do you think?"

Annoyed by his attitude, Maggie pushed herself up against the pillows and glared back at him. "This isn't a big deal. I've had it before."

Bracing his arms on either side of her head, he leaned over her, a muscle twitching in his jaw. "I don't know what your problem is, but it's no crime to get a little help now and then. You scared the hell out of your daughter last night. I ran into her in the alley. She'd gone to get help from a neighbor, only she wasn't home. Maybe you need to think about that damned independent streak of yours. And how it makes other people feel. I'm here because I told Kelly I'd look out for you."

Experiencing an awful sinking feeling in her middle, Maggie stared up at him, wondering what had gotten into him. Then, in a flash of stomach-dropping clarity, she recalled what she'd said to him when he'd come at ten. She had been rude and obnoxious, and not at all nice. Realizing how ungrateful she must have sounded then, and just now when she'd told him to go away, she made a disconcerted gesture with her hand. "Tony, I—"

He shoved the medicine into her hand, picked up a covered cooking pot off the floor and slapped it on the bed beside her. "Here. You can do whatever you want with this."

Snatching up the jacket he had dropped on the foot of the bed, he turned and left the room. Maggie stared at the empty doorway, then closed her eyes. She had really done it this time. Flinging back the covers, she stumbled out of bed and started toward the hall, but the back door slammed before she got as far as her bedroom doorway. Closing her eyes, she rested her head on the door frame, so ashamed of herself that she felt like crying. He had every right to be ticked off. She had been downright rude, and the fact that she was sick wasn't a good excuse. Heaving a sigh, she straightened and raked both hands through her hair. Then she went over to the bed and dug through the jumble of covers for her prescription medicine, unscrewed the cap and drank a slug right from the bottle. She knew her prickliness was a defense mechanism. But it had backfired badly on her this time.

Putting the top back on the bottle, she set it on the bedside table, then stacked up the pillows and got back into bed. Her throat was unbearably tight, so she lifted the lid on the pot and took out the steaming compress, then very carefully applied it to her chest. Then she leaned her head back and closed her eyes, feeling totally wretched. Not once had she thanked him for what he had done.

Kelly arrived home at four and came straight to her mother's bedroom. She smiled when she saw that Maggie was awake, "Hi. You look like you're feeling better."

Maggie managed a faint smile. "I am. Much better." *Thanks to Tony,* her conscience whispered. She tried to put a little more energy into her smile. "How was your day?"

Kelly came over and sat down on the foot of her bed, crossing her legs Indian fashion. "Guess what?" she said, a sparkle of enthusiasm in her eyes.

Feeling nearly unbearable affection for this child of hers, Maggie had to wait for the contraction in her throat to ease before she responded. "What?"

Kelly gave a little shiver of pleasure. "Tony gave me a ride to school this morning, and we went in the Mustang. You should have seen the expression on the guys' faces when we pulled into the parking lot. Their eyes were bugging right out of their heads. A bunch of them came over and started asking questions, and Tony pointed at me and said, 'Ask the expert.' I thought I was going to die. But it was so neat."

Remembering what it was like to be a teenager and not part of the in-crowd, Maggie experienced a heavy burning sensation behind her eyes. Tony Parnelli had handed her daughter a whole load of self-esteem that morning, and Maggie was certain his actions were no accident. Tony Parnelli saw things most people didn't.

Folding her arms against a twinge in her chest, she gazed at her daughter. "Did anything else wild and wonderful happen?"

Kelly shrugged. "Not much. I got 98 percent on my math exam."

"Way to go, honey."

She made a sheepish little grimace. "I should have got a hundred. I made one stupid mistake." She shrugged, then looked at her mother. "Do you want me to get you anything?

I was going to go over to Stevie's gym and work out for an hour, if it's okay with you. She's got a new step machine that she wants me to try out.''

Maggie shook her head. "No. You go ahead. I'm fine."

"You're sure?"

"I'm sure."

Kelly bounced off the bed and headed toward the door, then stopped and turned. "Oh. I forgot to tell you. I stopped at the bakery on the way home and got Tony one of Mrs. G's rum-and-carrot cakes." She gave her mother a slightly embarrassed, slightly shy smile. "He wasn't there, so I put a note on it and left it in the shop, thanking him for being such a good neighbor. Was that okay?"

Feeling lower than low over her own behavior, Maggie made herself smile. "Very okay, honey. Thanks."

Kelly waggled her fingers. "See you later."

Maggie listened to her leave the house, then leaned back against the pillows and stared out the window. She had really made a mess of things. Her whole life was out of whack since Tony Parnelli had sauntered up her front walk. Now she was acting like a child, and it was her fifteen-year-old daughter who was acting like an adult. At least someone in the family had the decency and good manners to let him know his efforts were appreciated. And maybe it was better if she just left it at that. Especially after the way she had acted.

Feeling dangerously close to tears, Maggie shoved the pillows aside and stretched out on her stomach, burying her head in her arms. Damn it, she was not going to start crying again. It was better this way... except it didn't feel better at all.

It was going on eight o'clock when Maggie woke up again. She lay in bed, listening to the robins chirp in the backyard, trying to shake the dispirited feeling. Finally she sighed and crawled out of bed. She was going to have a shower, shampoo her hair and put on some real clothes, then make herself some tea.

Kelly was doing homework at the kitchen table, her math book propped up in front of her against an empty milk glass.

She looked up when Maggie entered. "Hi. How are you feeling?"

Maggie went over to the counter, got the teakettle out of the cupboard and filled it under the tap. "Better." She plugged in the kettle, then turned, bracing her weight against the counter as she considered her daughter. Kelly was sitting hunched over the table with the headphones to her Walkman clamped in her ears, her feet wound in the rungs of the chair. Her thick, glossy hair was pulled back in the usual French braid, a few wisps loose around her face with blond highlights from the sun beginning to show, and her clear, flawless complexion appeared almost translucent in the evening light. She had been such a little tomboy, and now she was almost grown-up. Maggie wondered if her daughter had any idea how pretty she was.

She moved her math textbook, and Maggie saw a partially eaten wedge of dark cake on a bread-and-butter plate. It looked suspiciously like Mrs. G.'s rum-and-carrot cake. Experiencing a funny flutter around her heart, she slid her hands into the front pockets of her slacks. Clearing her throat, she took a breath and spoke, her voice still hoarse. "Kelly?"

Pulling back the headphones, Kelly looked up at her. "What?"

Maggie indicated the cake. "Did you get another cake for us?"

Kelly shook her head. "No. Tony brought it over." She stuck her fingers in the crumbs, then licked them off her finger. "He's leaving first thing tomorrow morning. Didn't he tell you?"

At the mention of her nemesis's name, Maggie experienced an awful sinking sensation. She would give anything if she could just go back and retract all the thoughtless comments she'd made. On top of that, she hadn't even had the decency to thank him. And now he was leaving town, which made her feel even worse. Maggie released a heavy sigh and answered, "No."

Propping her chin in her hand, Kelly stared off into space, a dreamy, wistful look in her eyes. "They're taking six cars to a string of classic auto shows in the States. And in July, they're going to hit the stock-car circuit." She turned her head and looked at her mother. "Do you know how they move those cars, Mom? Mario and Tony's partners are old racing buddies, and they *bought* one of those big car-transport carriers to haul them to shows. They must be loaded!"

Trying to ignore the heavy feeling in her middle, Maggie unplugged the kettle, then opened the tea cannister. "All this to show some cars?"

There was a sigh of exasperation behind her. "No. Mom. It's not just to show them. They go to *sell* them. They buy a car, restore it, then sell it. Didn't you *ever* go to car shows with Grandpa?"

Recalling her experiences with her father, Maggie grinned and dunked a teabag in the cup of hot water. "No. Your grandfather taught me how to shoot pool and he took me to snooker tournaments. He took your aunt Katherine to car shows."

There was a giggle behind her. "Aunt Kate? At car shows? In her designer outfits?"

Maggie tossed the teabag in the container for the compost bin and turned, giving her daughter a pointed look. "That was before your aunt became a high-powered lawyer, my pet. But I'll have you know your aunt Katherine could rebuild a carburetor with the best of them."

"You're kidding, right?"

"No, I'm not. I didn't say she liked it, but she could do it."

Still sitting with her head propped on her hand, Kelly released an amused sigh. "Aunt Kate with dirt under her nails. I love it." Narrowing her eyes, she gave her mother an unwavering stare. "How come you never told me about this before?"

Cupping the hot mug in her hands, Maggie gave her daughter a wry look. "Because I didn't want to encourage you."

Kelly grinned and made a sassy face at her, then began doodling in her notebook. "Well, if Tony's Boss 429 is an example of the kind of work they do, they're going to make a killing. The least-expensive car on that load will likely go for around fifty thousand dollars."

Maggie nearly choked, sloshing her tea. "Pardon?"

Kelly looked up at her, a glint of satisfaction in her eyes. "These are *classics,* Mom. Collecting cars."

Her eyes watering from tea in her already congested lungs, Maggie wheezed, then finally gasped, "How do you *know* all this, Kelly Lynn?"

Kelly grinned. "I read, Mother. And I go to car shows."

Still trying to quell the need to cough, Maggie held her breath.

Kelly cocked one eyebrow, mimicking her Aunt Kate. "Nice show, Mary Margaret."

Finally suppressing the urge to cough, Maggie wiped her eyes and set down her mug. She reached for a paper towel in the dispenser under the cupboard, tore off a square, then crouched down and began wiping up the tea she'd spilled.

There was a peculiar offhand tone in Kelly's voice when she spoke again. "Did he stay all night?"

Not at all comfortable with the tangent this conversation was taking, Maggie wadded up the paper towel and tossed it in the garbage, then fixed her daughter with a reprimanding look. "Honestly, Kelly Lynn. What kind of question is that?"

Leaning back in the chair, Kelly began tapping her pencil on the table, studying her mother with far too much shrewdness in her eyes. She even had the nerve to smirk. "So did he?"

Feeling pretty much cornered, Maggie avoided her gaze by dumping her tea down the drain. Knowing she was probably stretching the truth, but not sure she was actually lying, she finally responded, her tone crisp with annoyance, "I have no idea."

"Hmm," said her daughter.

Maggie put the lid back on the tea canister and pushed it into place, then wiped off the counter. She could feel Kelly watching her, and she wished she'd stop. Her daughter was just a little too sharp for her liking.

The *tap tap tap* of Kelly's pencil finally stopped, and Maggie let her breath go. She finished wiping off the counter, then folded the dishcloth and hung it over the faucet. Her little burst of energy gone, she was considering whether she should just go back to bed or curl up with a pillow and blanket and watch some TV, when Kelly spoke again. "Too bad he's going to be gone for four weeks."

Maggie didn't like the too-casual tone in her voice. Nor did she like how her stomach did an unnerving nosedive. Irritated at herself, she picked up a box of tissues and headed toward the living room. He was leaving. Good. Maybe now she would be able to get her head back together. Her reaction to Tony Parnelli was nothing more than a case of middle-age crazies.

She was just going to stop thinking about him. And she was going to get everything back to normal. It was the only solution.

It was an excellent plan. Except it didn't work. Through bloody-minded determination and heartless lectures to herself, she managed to get her days back to the way they'd been before he'd turned up on her doorstep. Her nights, however, were a different ball of wax altogether. She bought herself some Spanish tapes and went to bed with Kelly's Walkman on so she wouldn't let herself slide into those dangerous nighttime fantasies. Which was fine. She could now count up to a hundred in Spanish and say "Hello, how are you?" and "What is your name?" three different ways. But it was after she fell asleep that her mind turned on her, and she started having these weird, disconnected dreams. She would have understood if they'd been hot and erotic, but they weren't. They were about guilt.

Every morning for two solid weeks she'd wake up unable to look herself in the eye because she felt so darned guilty. Finally she quit playing games with herself and confronted her feelings head-on. She felt like such a louse. Not only had she offended Tony by leaving his open house, she had been downright rude to him as well.

But what she was feeling truly awful about was that he had left without her saying one word about how much she appreciated what he'd done for her. Which was pretty unforgivable. No wonder she was having weird dreams, and no wonder she got this awful feeling in her stomach every time she remembered how ungrateful she'd been.

She felt just like she had when, at eight years old, she'd fallen off the garage roof and broken her sister's nose. She wasn't supposed to be up there in the first place, but she'd just gotten to the part in *Anne of Green Gables* where Anne walked the ridgepole, and Maggie just had to try it for herself. Kate had been watching from the ground, and when Maggie slipped and fell, she had tried to catch her. And Maggie had somehow managed to clip her older sister in the face with her knee. She had felt so terrible about smashing Kate's nose that for months after, Kate only had to touch her nose and complain of a headache, and Maggie would be absolutely stricken with remorse. Kate had gotten a lot of miles out of that broken nose.

Even now, her nose was still a tad off center, and Maggie still had the scar on her knee where she'd sliced herself open on Kate's teeth. Her sister still tried to use the broken nose to her advantage, and Maggie would show her the scar and they'd laugh.

But with Tony, she couldn't even go over and say she was sorry. He was gone. And he'd been so ticked off when he'd left, he probably wouldn't speak to her when he got back. Finally unable to stand it any longer and knowing she had to try to make amends, Maggie tried to write a thank-you note. But her half-dozen attempts all sounded stiff, formal and insincere.

Then, just by accident, she stumbled across the perfect card in the drugstore. One of those with bizarre, misshapen animals on it, it featured two Holstein cows standing on their back legs leaning against a fence, one chewing on a stalk of hay. And it went on and on about the milk of human kindness. Maggie laughed out loud in the store when she read it, and the woman beside her had looked at her as if she was completely nuts.

Feeling better than she had in days, she bought it, took it home and wrote a note in it, then slipped it through the mail slot at the shop. She knew he'd probably still avoid her like the plague when he got back, but after delivering the card, she at least started sleeping better. Dealing with guilt opened up a big hole in her defenses, however. Maggie tried to put Tony out of her mind, but there was no defense against loneliness. And at times it would sweep in—especially at night—and she'd feel absolutely bereft. She couldn't count the number of occasions that she'd find herself standing in front of the window, staring out at the falling twilight, loneliness weighing her down.

It probably wouldn't have been so bad if Kelly had been around more in the evenings, but she was training for a major swim meet and was hardly ever home. Maggie was sure all her daughter did was eat, sleep, go to school and swim.

Weekends weren't much different. Only this weekend it was Maggie's turn to drive the kids to swimming. She had to have them there by six-thirty, but she didn't really mind. She kind of liked early mornings. She hung around the pool for a while, watching them practice turns and starts, until the smell of chlorine stared to get to her. It was a little over three weeks since her bout with bronchitis, and although the cough was finally gone, there were some things that still set off a tickle in her chest. And the smell of chlorine was definitely one.

It was a beautiful, crystal-clear morning, with everything brushed with gold from the rising sun, the angle of the early morning rays making the dew on the grass sparkle like jewels. For one brief, insane moment, Maggie toyed with the idea of driving out to Banff, but she had no idea what she would do when she got there. She supposed she could sit and watch tourists ignore the Do Not Feed the Bears warning signs.

Instead, she went home and puttered in her garden under the watchful eye of Captain Hook, who was sunning himself on Stevie's garden shed. She tried to coax him down with a can of tuna, but he gave her a disdainful look and closed his eyes, as if above that kind of bribery. Maggie knew better. Wedging the can into a space in the fence, she turned her back on him and went back to staking up delphiniums. When she glanced up a little while later, he was gone and so was the can. She grinned to herself. Old Hook was no dummy.

Finishing with the delphiniums, Maggie decided to call it quits in the yard. She washed off her garden implements and put them away, then went into the house and made a fresh pot of coffee. She was going to have a long, hot shower, treat herself with some of her new gardenia-scented body lotion, then spend the rest of the morning lazing on the back deck with a good book. It was just too beautiful to stay indoors.

She'd had her shower and was just pouring herself a cup of coffee when there was a knock on the back door. Replacing the glass carafe on the element, she glanced at the clock on the stove. It was just a little after ten. Back door; Sunday…it had to be Stevie. Which meant La Goddess had set a new record. Maggie's across-the-alley neighbor had strong convictions that no living thing should be allowed outside on Sundays until afternoon, especially barking dogs, small children and people with loud lawnmowers. Smiling to herself, Maggie went to answer the door. Something earthshaking must have happened to get her out of bed this early.

Maggie opened the back door, prepared to give her neighbor a hard time, but her stomach immediately shot to her shoes and her heart skipped several beats.

It was a neighbor, all right. But the wrong one.

Tony Parnelli was standing there, looking across at his backyard, tapping a blue envelope against his thigh. A black leather jacket was slung over one shoulder. He had on black biker boots, blue jeans, a gray sweat top that had the sleeves hacked off at the shoulders, and a pair of aviator sunglasses hanging from the frayed neck. He looked more like some motorcycle desperado than an ex-cop. Her brain processed the fact that he wasn't due home for another week; her knees, on the other hand, wanted to cave in beneath her. With her heart racing a mile a minute, she pushed open the screen door.

He turned his head and looked at her with a steady, unsmiling expression, the angle of sunlight revealing gold flecks in his unreadable, dark brown eyes.

Resisting the urge to wipe her hands down her thighs, Maggie tried to get a breath past the crazy flutter in her throat. She gave him an uneven smile. "Well, hello. You're back early, aren't you?"

He didn't say anything. He just continued to watch her with that same unwavering gaze; then he raised his hand, showing her the envelope he had clamped between two fingers. She recognized her handwriting, and the nervous flutter slid to her chest. Running her palms down her slacks, she looked from him to the envelope, then back at him. He was still watching her, not a trace of expression on his face. A flush of discomfort crawled up her scalp, and she nervously cleared her throat, then forced herself to meet his gaze. It was not going to be easy, but she made herself say the words. "Thank you," she said, her voice catching on a lump of nerves, "for being there. I really did appreciate it."

He continued to watch her, as if processing information, then he narrowed his eyes just a little. "So it is from you."

Feeling as if her heart was warring with her lungs for space, she gave him a confused look, then nodded. "Yes. It's from me."

He held her gaze for a second; then, tucking the jacket under one arm, he folded the envelope in half. He slipped it into the back pocket of his jeans. "I wasn't sure," he said, his tone as unreadable as his face. "The handwriting was pretty similar to the note on the cake."

Experiencing a surge of remorse, Maggie cleared her throat again. "I was pretty rude, and it just seemed the right way to say I was sorry."

He held her gaze, a glint appearing in his eyes, and the laugh lines around his eyes crinkled just a little. "Yes, you were rude."

The knot of tension in her middle abruptly let go, and she gave him a rueful grin. "Well, at least we agree on something."

A smile lurked in his eyes. "So how have you been, Burrows?"

*Lonely.* Shaken by that random thought, she folded her arms. "Fine." She managed a small smile. "Although I smelled like a Polish sausage for a few days afterward."

The creases around his eyes deepened, but his gaze remained unwavering. "You don't smell like a Polish sausage now," he said, the glimmer in his eyes intensifying. "I'd say you smell just like gardenias."

Unnerved by his accuracy, Maggie resisted the urge to fidget under his unwavering scrutiny. "I doubt if you'd know the difference between gardenias and daisies, Parnelli."

"Ah," he said, his voice dropping a notch. "But I do. And you smell like gardenias."

Maggie couldn't think of a single thing to say. She just stood there staring at him, her insides suddenly tying themselves in knots. He held her gaze a moment, then his expression al-tered, almost as if he were pulling back. Propelled by feelings she didn't understand, she made a motion toward the kitchen. "I just made a fresh pot of coffee," she said, averting her gaze, unable to hold his an instant longer. "Would you like a cup?"

Catching her under the chin with one finger, he lifted her head, forcing her to look at him. Then he smiled a slow, breath-stopping smile. "Are you actually inviting me in?"

Her heart suddenly pounding and her chest too tight, Mag-gie stared back at him, as if his question was of a magnitude she just couldn't grasp. Fighting the urge to close her eyes and give herself over to his light, light touch, she wet her lips. "Yes," she said, her voice unnaturally weak.

His gaze still riveted on her, he rubbed his thumb slowly along her jaw; then he gave her another one of his heart-stopping smiles. "I would love a cup of your coffee, Maggie Burrows."

Feeling as if her legs wanted to cave in beneath her, she stepped back so he could enter. Instead of coming in, he caught her wrist, a twinkle in his eyes. "But I have a better idea. I was going to take my bike for a spin. How about you coming along for the ride?"

Maggie stared at him, not quite sure she'd heard him cor-rectly. "On your bike?" she asked, her voice rising a little.

His eyes glinting with pure, undiluted mischief, he grinned again. "Have you ever been on a Harley, Ms. Burrows?"

Not quite sure what to make of this, Maggie slowly shook her head.

"Well," he said, his eyes twinkling, "you're in for the ex-perience of your life."

The practical side of her brain knew she should say no. She'd been brought up when nice girls did not ride motorcycles. But there was another side, one that superseded her pragmatic na-ture, urging her to do something just a little bit reckless just this once.

Rubbing his thumb up the inside of her wrist, Tony watched her, the gleam in his eyes turning to a serious entreaty. "Come with me, Maggie," he said softly, his tone low and husky, his eyes urging her to say yes.

Feeling as if she were standing at the very edge of a high cliff, she stared at him, wanting to go in the worst way. She knew if she stepped off that cliff, she'd experience a rush like she'd never experienced before. But her sensible side urged her to keep her feet firmly planted on the ground.

His gaze turning intent, Tony watched her, something dark and compelling in his eyes. He stroked her wrist again, then spoke, his tone urging her on. "Come."

Something made her throw caution to the wind. Taking a deep, fortifying breath, she swallowed hard. "All right."

He didn't give her a chance to rethink her impulsive decision. Did she have boots?

Yes, she had boots.

Did she have blue jeans?

Yes, she had blue jeans.

What about a leather jacket?

It was so nice out she wouldn't need a jacket.

Tony was emphatic—yes, she needed a jacket. He explained that riding on a bike was not like riding in a car, and that a leather jacket was mostly for protection. When he started to graphically describe what the term *road rash* meant, she shuddered and hastily interrupted.

No, she didn't have a leather jacket of her own, but there was an old one of Haley's around somewhere.

By the time they got outside, Maggie felt as if she'd just been spit out by a tornado. Tony made sure she had her helmet fastened correctly, then he straddled the bike and flipped the switch to start it. He leaned forward so she could climb on behind him, then checked to make sure she had her feet where they were supposed to be.

Bracing his own feet on either side of the bike, he turned and looked at her, a glint in his eyes. "Four things, Tinker. Number one, don't let your legs touch those silver pipes. They're the exhausts and they get damned hot. Two, lean when I lean. Three—" he pulled her arms around his waist "—hang on and don't let go." He grinned and slipped on his sunglasses. "And four, trust me." He knocked away the kickstand and rolled open the throttle. "You're gonna love this."

The trip through town was downright scary, and the first few miles on the highway were terrifying. But then the terror gave way, pure, unadulterated exhilaration set in and Maggie felt as if she were flying. She hung on to Tony, grinning like an idiot, wanting to throw her arms in the air and yell into the wind. It was the most unbelievable sensation. And God, she loved it.

Tony took her to Banff, but he didn't take the four-lane highway. Instead he took the old route, and it was wonderful. No traffic. Fabulous scenery. And an unbelievable sense of freedom. Her legs were decidedly shaky when they finally stopped and she got off the bike, but it was the most fantastic experience she'd ever had. They gassed up in the resort town, had lunch and a bathroom break, and it was early afternoon by the time they headed back. Feeling a bit more experienced, Maggie reveled in the return ride, the smell of hot leather and sunshine mixing with the heavenly scent of the blossoming silver willow.

The road wind beat her to death, the warmth of the sun made her feel almost boneless and she felt as if she could sleep for a week. When they arrived at the city limits, Tony didn't take the ramp for Sarcee Trail. Instead he kept going, heading into the northwest part of the city. Maggie knew the area. Locals referred to it as "Little Italy," and it had some of the best restaurants in town. Feeling almost anesthetized from all the sunshine and fresh air, she didn't pay much attention, assuming he was stopping for a coffee.

But instead, he geared down and turned onto a shady street where huge elms nearly formed a canopy overhead. They were barely crawling along, and Maggie sat up and stretched her back, resting her hands on her thighs. The sounds of water sprinklers and children playing were distinguishable over the throaty rumble of the bike, and she inspected the yards as they passed by. The older homes were all set on big lots with beautiful big trees. This was clearly a comfortable kind of neighborhood where people put down roots.

Gearing down again, Tony pulled alongside the curb, then brought the bike to a halt. Bracing his legs on either side of the machine, he killed the ignition, then peeled off his helmet. Not sure why they were stopping, Maggie gratefully followed suit, glad to get the weight off her head. It felt like her hair was ground into her scalp.

Tony scrubbed his fingers through his own hair, then looked over his shoulder at her. "End of the road, Burrows. Time for a break."

Feeling as if she didn't have the strength to sit, let alone stand, Maggie braced her hands on his shoulders and stood up on the foot pegs, stiffly swinging off the bike. Her legs *really* feeling like jelly, she peeled off her jacket, dropped her helmet on the ground, then flopped down on the strip of grass between the sidewalk and the street. Flat on her back and feeling pretty much like mush, she drew up her knees, groaning as she forced the small of her back against the ground. "Lord, I think you killed me, Parnelli."

His eyes hidden by sunglasses, Tony grinned as he rocked the bike back on the kickstand. Removing the keys from the ignition, he dismounted, then stood staring down at her. "A little wobbly, are we?"

Feeling as she'd just delivered a full-sized elephant, she squinted up at him. "I don't know about you, but I feel like overcooked spaghetti."

He picked up her helmet, then glanced at her, amusement lurking around his mouth. "Speaking of spaghetti, how about dinner?"

Struggling to a sitting position, she looked up at him. "Right now I could eat dirt."

Grasping her jacket and the chin straps of both helmets in one hand, he reached down and caught her wrist, pulling her to her feet. He was grinning that devilish grin of his. "Then up and at 'em, Tink. I'm going to treat you to the best spaghetti in town."

Dusting off her bottom, Maggie groaned. "Are you going to make me get back on that thing?"

He chuckled and took her hand, pulling her onto the sidewalk. "Nah." With a lift of his chin he indicated a big old house. "Fifty feet and we're there."

Suddenly very suspicious, Maggie stopped. "That's somebody's house."

He turned and looked at her, grinning that bad-boy grin again. "God, but you're quick."

Stiffening her knees, Maggie tried to pull back, literally digging in her heels. "I don't like the look of this, Parnelli," she said, her tone wary.

"Sure you do," he said, giving her another tug, obviously amused by her mutinous behavior. "You just don't know it yet."

She tried to break his hold with her free hand, but he just kept walking, towing her along behind him on the lush grass as if she were on skis.

"Tony," she wailed, still trying to break his grasp, not knowing whether to laugh or cry.

"Don't be a big baby. We're just going to have dinner with my folks."

"They won't be expecting company." She nearly fell flat on her face when her skidding feet hit the sidewalk, and she grabbed on to his T-shirt to keep from falling.

Tony kept on walking, and she stumbled along behind him. "Yes, they are. I called them from Banff."

Planting her feet, she stopped dead in her tracks. "You did *what?*"

Still holding her wrist, he turned and looked at her, and she knew he was laughing at her behind those damned sunglasses. "I called them from Banff."

She didn't believe him for a minute. She lifted her chin. "When?"

He grinned. "When you went to the bathroom."

She stared at him, still not sure if she should believe him or not. "You did not."

"Yes, I did." He gave her another tug and started walking. "Come on, Burrows. Don't be such a chicken."

She was so stunned that she followed along behind him, at least until he stopped at the wide, wrought-iron trellis set in the neatly trimmed caragana hedge. Then she tried to resist again. Dropping back beside her, he hooked his arm around her neck, drawing her head against his shoulder. "Don't worry," he said, giving her a reassuring little squeeze. "It's not a big deal."

It was then that Maggie caught sight of the driveway on the other side of the hedge, and her stomach dropped to her shoes as she stumbled again. Cars. Lots of cars. She tried to correlate the number of vehicles to the number of people who must have arrived in them.

Putting two and two together, Maggie closed her eyes, an entire flock of butterflies taking off in her middle. It wasn't just Mom and Pop. It was the whole damned family.

Her stomach a mess of nerves, she tried to use some down-to-earth logic to put things in perspective. He'd taken her for a fabulous bike ride, and now he was inviting her to his parents' home for a spaghetti dinner. It wasn't a big deal. If it had been anyone else but Tony Parnelli, she wouldn't have thought anything of it. That's what her head said. Her insides were saying something else altogether.

The helmets and jacket still grasped in his hand, Tony lifted the latch on the gate just as a gust of wind caught in the bower of climbing honeysuckle overhead, sending a shower of delicate blossoms down on them.

The yard was a gardener's dream, filled with flowers and blossoming shrubs. A wide flagstone walk curved around a stand of clump birch and blue spruce, then made another curve around a bed of junipers. It was enough to take her breath away.

"This," she said, her voice soft with awe, "is absolutely beautiful."

His arm around her shoulders, Tony glanced down at her. "If you think this is something, wait until you see the back." He held up his hand to protect her from a low-hanging bough, then gave a soft, reminiscent laugh. "I'm afraid we didn't appreciate it much when we were kids. My mother used to put us to work out here every weekend in the summer, and we'd fight like hell over who had to do what." He grinned and gave her shoulders a reproving little squeeze. "But I can tell the difference between gladioli and gardenias, Burrows."

Restraining her amusement, Maggie narrowed her eyes at him in a quelling look, trying to ignore the flip-flopping sensation in her middle. Lord, but she wished she knew what was going on in his head.

They reached another wrought-iron trellis and gate, this one leading into the backyard. Tony withdrew his arm from around her shoulders and took her by the hand. He looked at her, his expression suddenly serious, then gave her hand a reassuring squeeze. "I'm glad you came," he said, his voice low and husky.

Suddenly feeling as if she had too much air trapped in her chest, Maggie gripped his hand back, unable to look away, her throat abruptly cramping with a rush of emotion. It was magic. The whole day was nothing but magic. But she had to keep reminding herself that magic was temporary.

As if reading her mind, he gave her a small smile, then squeezed her hand again. "Come on," he said, looking away. "I want you to meet my family."

Experiencing a rush of uncertainty, Maggie tightened her hold on his hand and took a deep breath. She felt as if she was fifteen and on her first date.

# Chapter 6

There had to be twenty people in the backyard. And they all started shouting catcalls when they saw Tony and Maggie.

"Eh, Antonio. What's the matter? Can't you tell time? Don't you know your way home yet?"

Tossing the helmets and jacket on the grass, Tony grinned and made an obscene gesture with his fist. "Hey, I told Ma we'd be here by three. It's three."

Someone said something in Italian, and everybody laughed. A petite, plump woman with silver streaks in her dark hair set down a pitcher she was carrying and came toward them. "Be nice. Don't pick on your brother." She smiled and stretched both arms, her gaze warm and welcoming. "We're so glad you could come," she said taking Maggie's face between her hands and kissing her on both cheeks. "Welcome, Maggie Burrows."

There was so much genuine warmth in her greeting that the wad of nerves in Maggie's stomach suddenly let go. She gave the older woman a small smile. "Thank you, Mrs. Parnelli. Especially after your son sprung me on you at the last minute."

Tony's mother patted her cheek. "Rosa, dear. Call me Rosa." She looked at Tony, her eyes twinkling, then patted his cheek, as well. "This son of mine. Never had any manners."

Tony gave her a level look. "Don't start with me, Ma. I'm not six years old anymore."

Her eyes still twinkling, Mrs. Parnelli pinched his cheek. "'Don't start with me, Ma,'" she mimicked, giving his head a little shake. "That's no way to talk to your mother, Antonio." She smiled up at Maggie, then touched her arm. "Come. You need to meet the rest of the family." She looked down to where Tony was holding Maggie's hand and disconnected his grip. "For heaven's sake, Antonio. We aren't going to eat her." She smiled at Maggie again. "Come and meet Tony's brothers and sisters."

Maggie's head was swimming by the time they had gone the rounds: three brothers, three sisters and an assortment of nieces, nephews and spouses, twenty-three in all. Sensing that Tony was watching her, she glanced back at him. He had taken off his own black leather jacket and was slouched down in a wooden lawn chair, his legs stretched out and his hands laced across his chest, an odd half smile on his face. That smile did weird things to her insides, and she looked away, suddenly feeling like a bug under a microscope. Lord, but she wished he would take those damned sunglasses off.

"Ah, there are the rest." Tony's mother took her by the arm and Maggie turned. A man was coming out of the house, guiding a tiny, withered woman who was leaning heavily on a cane. The man settled her carefully in a small wooden rocking chair in the shade, and Maggie heard him say something in Italian. The older woman shook her head and patted his hand, positioning a small string bag in her lap.

Tony's mother touched her arm again. "Come. These are the last."

The man turned and started toward them. His hair was totally white and he had a much stockier build, but he looked so much like Tony that Maggie wanted to laugh. Before Tony's mother had a chance to say anything, he smiled broadly and opened his arms wide. "Ah. This must be the Maggie who called the cops on my son."

Frantically wondering when Tony had told them about that, Maggie felt herself blush, at a total loss for words. The man didn't seem to notice. He gave her a big bear hug, then held her away from him and grinned. "But he had it coming, no?"

She started to laugh and covered her face with her free hand as Tony's mother scolded, "Marco, you big ox. Look, now you've embarrassed her."

He chuckled and ruffled Maggie's hair. "No, No, that pink is just from the sun. Come," he said, propelling her toward the old woman. "You must meet the guest of honor."

Maggie cast a helpless look over her shoulder at Tony. He was still slouched in the lawn chair, a bottle of beer held loosely in his hands, and still watching her, that same half smile on his face. It was as though he was waiting to see if she would sink or swim. Narrowing her eyes at him, she made the same rude gesture behind his father's back that he'd made earlier. He grinned at her, then lifted his bottle in a salute. She wanted to throttle him.

Drawing her arm through his, Marco Parnelli escorted Maggie over to where the other woman was seated in the shade of a huge May Day tree. She was very old, her face wrinkled with a thousands creases, her snow white hair looking as if it had just been styled. She had on a cornflower blue dress, the type Maggie's grandmother would have worn to church, and her black oxfords had been freshly polished. She was intent on the piece of handiwork she held in her stiff gnarled, fingers. But she looked up as they approached, and Maggie was struck by the astuteness in her intent brown eyes. This woman, she thought, was nobody's fool.

"This is my mother, *cara*," he said, his voice quiet with respect. "We are celebrating her eighty-fifth birthday today." He said something in Italian, which included Maggie's name, and the woman looked at her, watching her with a steady stare, as if evaluating the person standing before her.

Then her eyes started to twinkle and she smiled, her wrinkled face creasing into a hundred warm and wonderful lines. She reached up to Maggie, her hands gnarled with arthritis, the skin thin and blue veined. Sensing what the old woman wanted, Maggie leaned down, her throat suddenly tight. With the slowness of the aged, the old woman kissed her on one cheek, then the other. Still gripping Maggie's face, she leaned back and studied her again, slowly nodding her head, as if in approval. She said Tony's name, then spoke to him in Italian, and everyone started to laugh. Patting Maggie on the cheek, the old woman gave her a conspiratorial wink, the twinkle in her eyes even brighter. "It is about time," she whispered, her voice creaking with age, "my Antonio brings home to his family a good woman, *cara.*"

Maggie felt another flush creeping up her cheeks, but there was something about the twinkle in the old woman's eyes that invited collusion. She smiled at Tony's grandmother. "I think," she whispered back, "that your Antonio needs more than a good woman, Grandmother."

The old woman started to chuckle, and she grasped Maggie's hand. "Eh, he is a bad one, that Antonio," she said, wheezing a little from the effort. She gave Maggie's hand another conspiratorial squeeze. "But me, I like the bad ones best."

Maggie grinned. She knew exactly who had encouraged Tony Parnelli's bad-boy charm.

Aware that the whole family was blatantly eavesdropping and hanging on their every word, Maggie knew she was somehow going to have to get herself out of the tight spot the old woman had put her in. Hoping to distract her, she touched the handiwork laying in her lap. "This is lovely."

Grandma patted the side of her chair. "Here. You sit and I will show you."

So Maggie sat in the grass by the old woman's chair, watching her make the most exquisite lace Maggie had ever seen. She was fascinated by the speed at which the old woman's crippled fingers worked, but it was the work itself that truly impressed her. She had never seen anything so delicate. Realizing Maggie's interest was genuine, one of Tony's sisters went into the house and came out with several completed pieces. One was a huge tablecloth, easily the most beautiful thing Maggie had ever seen. She said as much and found out Tony's grandmother had a tiny streak of vanity in her. Looking quite smug, she told Maggie that she had been the best lace maker in her village when she was a girl. Tony's sister winked at Maggie, amusement in her eyes. It was obvious that the old lady's pride was a small foible the family was very well aware of.

Rosa Parnelli came over with a glass of wine for Tony's grandmother, setting it on a small table by the old lady's chair. Thinking of Kelly, Maggie rose, brushing off the back of her jeans. "Could I use your phone, Mrs. Parnelli? I should call home and check on my daughter."

The other woman raised her finger in a scolding gesture. "Rosa. Mrs. Parnelli is for the butcher and baker." She frowned suddenly. "You daughter is at home? I thought Tony said she was at swimming."

"She was, but she should be home by now. I just want to call and tell her where I am."

Rosa Parnelli looked scandalized. "Mother Mary, we can't leave her alone for Sunday dinner." She turned and yelled at Tony, who was stretched on his side on the grass, head propped on one hand, talking to a brother-in-law. "Antonio! Come here."

He got up and came toward them. He had taken off his hacked-up sweatshirt, and the claw marks from the Captain were still very evident. Maggie wanted to squirm when she saw them. That was a day she'd be a long time forgetting.

A chain around his neck glinted in the sun, and she studied it thoughtfully. She clearly—very clearly—remembered that his chest had been naked the day the cat attacked him, and she wondered what this was. Tony didn't seem to be the type who'd bother with jewelry. As he came closer, she experienced a funny rush in her middle when she recognized it as a small St. Christopher medal. It was the kind of thing a mother would give a son who did not always travel in safety. She wondered how many sleepless nights Rosa Parnelli had had when he was still on the force. For some reason, he was the type who invited trouble.

He looked dangerous and disreputable dressed in worn blue jeans and biker boots, with a five-o'clock shadow darkening his jaw and those damned sunglasses obscuring his eyes. And Maggie suddenly pictured him as an undercover cop, working the streets. *Lethal* was the first word that popped into her mind.

"What do you want, Ma?"

Rosa Parnelli brushed some grass off his chest, and Maggie's hands suddenly tingled. She quickly stuffed them in the pockets of her jeans.

"You go get Maggie's daughter and bring her back here for dinner."

Tony turned his head and looked at Maggie. He didn't say anything, but just stared at her, and Maggie realized he had been deliberately keeping his distance. He wasn't testing her, she thought with a start—he'd been letting her test herself. And right then, as if someone had just brought everything into sharp focus, she had another startling realization, one that really shook her. This was no friendly little game he was playing. He was deadly serious.

Feeling suddenly very nervous, she folded her arms and swallowed against the crazy flutter in her throat. He continued to watch her without a trace of expression on his face. The decision was hers. And it totally unnerved her that he understood her so well. She would never involve Kelly if this was just a one-time deal, and she knew if she said no, that would be it. But if she said yes . . . If she said yes . . .

Her heart started to pound and her mouth went dry, and common sense warred with a fierce longing. Yes. No. It was up to her.

Aware that Tony's mother was only a foot away, she took a deep, tremulous breath and finally spoke, her voice not quite steady. "Maybe I should call her first and make sure she's home."

A muscle in Tony's jaw twitched, then he released the air in his lungs. "Never mind," he said, reaching out and cupping his hand against her neck. "I want to take the bike back anyway." He gave a squeeze, drawing his thumb across the frantic pulse point there. The intimacy of that touch made her legs go weak, and it was all she could do to keep from tipping her head back and closing her eyes. His expression giving nothing away, he gave her neck another light squeeze, then let her go. "I'll be back in twenty minutes," he said, his tone abrupt.

With that, he went over to where his shirt was lying on the grass, swept it up and pulled it over his head. Maggie abruptly turned and followed Rosa Parnelli, so shaky inside she felt as if a riot was going on in there. Lord, but she had really jumped into the deep end this time.

Maggie almost—almost—had a grip on herself by the time Tony returned with Kelly. She was standing at the stove, one of the babies slung on her hip, stirring the spaghetti sauce and talking taxation law with Tony's sister who owned her own boutique. She had to smile when she saw her daughter. Kelly was looking pretty wary about this, but she had put on her good khaki walking shorts and a bright yellow blouse, and her trendy new hiking boots had obviously been cleaned. Her hair was freshly braided, and she had tied it with a bow that was the same color as her blouse. Maggie couldn't remember the last time she'd seen her daughter look so coordinated.

The baby grabbed a handful of Maggie's jersey and tried to stuff it in his mouth, then made a bid for her hair. Maggie turned her attention back to him, disengaging his chubby little fists. He was seven months old and belonged to one of Tony's brothers, and he was such a little Parnelli—big brown eyes, long, thick lashes and a grin that was enough to melt anyone's heart—that Maggie wanted to hug the stuffing out of him every time she looked at him.

She had no sooner disengaged his hands than he grabbed another handful of jersey and put his head to his fist, trying to get it into his mouth.

She laughed and loosened his fingers again. "You don't want to eat that, Slugger. It's going to taste pretty yucky."

Rosa appeared beside her and smoothed down the wrinkles in Maggie's top with maternal briskness. "Here, *cara*. Let me take the little one," she said, lifting the baby out of Maggie's arms. "His papa has his food ready."

It was almost like watching a bucket brigade, the way the baby was passed through the crowd in the kitchen from one set of hands to another until he was finally delivered into his father's arms. Maggie turned back to the spaghetti sauce, a funny feeling unfolding in her chest. She'd noticed right away how everything seemed to revolve around the kids. She was having an awful time sorting out which child belonged to who, because somebody was always holding someone else's baby or tying some other kid's shoes. Even the quiet reprimands were dealt out by whomever was closest, and Maggie had never seen better-behaved kids. Everyone was part of the family circle, and the most amazing thing was that they had automatically included her as one of their own. Their ready acceptance touched cords in her she didn't even know existed. It was the nicest thing that had happened to her in a long time.

Turning down the heat under the sauce, she glanced over to where Kelly was standing. She and Tony were off in a corner talking to the revered Mario, and Maggie could seen the flush of excitement on her daughter's face. Maggie smiled to herself. She wondered if that was the leverage Tony had used to get her daughter to come.

Tony glanced up and caught her watching them, and his expression went very still. He stood with his back braced against the window frame, his arms folded, one foot flat against the wall. There was something in his stillness, in the steadiness of his gaze, that made her heart skip a beat.

She inhaled and turned back to the stove. Lord, he was driving her to distraction.

It was a little after ten o'clock when they finally left. Kelly couldn't seem to wait to get into the car. She had a thousand questions to ask Tony, most of them about his brother and his career. But she also had quite a few about his family; who was married to the tall blonde, who did the twins belong to, who was the oldest, who was the youngest?

Her elbows hooked over the seat back and her chin resting on her hands, Kelly hung on every word, as if this whole thing was totally amazing. She was still asking questions when Tony pulled into the parking area behind his shop. Her chin still on her hand, she said, a hint of shyness in her tone, "You've got a really neat family, Tony."

Maggie saw the corner of his mouth lift before he switched off the lights and killed the engine. "We have our moments."

Taking the keys out of the ignition, he opened the door, and Kelly scrambled out. "Thanks, Tony. I had a great time."

In the faint glow from the light standard in the back alley, Maggie saw him tap the end of Kelly's nose. "That's what I was hoping for, Stretch."

Kelly shot her mother a quick glance over the roof of the car, then made a discomfited gesture with one hand. "Well, I've got school tomorrow, so I'd better head in." She jogged off toward the alley, calling over her shoulder, "Thanks again. It really was great."

Maggie's heart stammered and missed a couple of beats as she watched her daughter disappear around the corner of their garage, an acute case of jitters jamming up in her middle. Darn that kid. Maggie had been counting on Kelly to provide a comfortable escape route, and now she felt as if she'd just been stranded on a high wire without a clue how to get down.

Stuffing her hands in her pockets, she started walking toward the alley, trying to get rid of the nervous flutter in her throat. Tony fell into step beside her, his silence setting off a new wave of jitters. Lord, she wished he would say something. Anything. She could handle him when he was giving her a hard time and kidding around. This quiet side of him unnerved her no end and made her palms clammy. For some crazy reason the line from a commercial, about never letting them see you sweat, popped into her head. Right then, it seemed like good advice.

Taking a deep, not-quite-steady breath, she made herself speak. "You really do have a great family. Your mother is an absolute sweetheart. And I never had such fabulous food in my entire life."

More silence. Desperate to fill up the void, she babbled on. "And your grandmother is wonderful. That lace she makes is incredible. I don't know how she does it with her hands the way they are. She told me all about what it was like when she and your grandfather immigrated to Canada. It must have been so hard, coming to a strange country with two babies and not speaking the language. I can't imagine what it must have been like."

They'd reached her garage, and Tony stopped walking, resting his weight on one leg and folding his arms as he watched her with a tolerant half smile, letting her ramble on to the point of self-destruction.

She stopped for a breath, and he finally interceded. "Maggie," he said in a warning tone, as if trying to snap her out of it.

She shot him a wary look. "What?"

She experienced a wild churning sensation as he straightened and came toward her, backing her up against the double door of the garage. He braced his hands on either side of her head. "Just shut up, okay?"

From a dead start, her heart lurched into a breath-robbing frenzy, and she stared at him like a rabbit caught in a pair of headlights, the commotion in her chest immobilizing her. "You just don't know when to quit, do you?" he said, a tiny trace of humor in his voice. Before she had a chance to collect her senses, he lowered his head and brushed his mouth lazily back and forth against hers, stealing what little breath she had left. Closing her eyes, Maggie flattened her back against the solidness of the garage door and tried to hang on, every nerve in her body suddenly rioting. He was barely touching her, and she was practically incoherent.

Tony moistened her bottom lip with his tongue, then deepened the kiss with the same lazy thoroughness, the warmth of his mouth setting off frantic currents of sensation. Maggie fought to catch her breath, the sudden electrical charge paralyzing her lungs. He slowly licked her bottom lip again, and her legs went weak and she started to slide down the door, every bone in her body turning to jelly. Lord, she was going to turn into nothing but a puddle at his feet.

Laughing against her mouth, Tony caught her in midslide. Grasping the back of her head, he turned her face against his neck and straightened, his breathing rough and uneven against her ear. Maggie slid her arms around him and pressed her face tighter against his neck, her whole body quivering as she tried to haul air into her lungs. She felt as if he had blown every fuse in her body.

Tucking his head down against hers, he slid his hand deeper into her hair and pulled her hips flush against his, then tightened his arms around her. Releasing an uneven sigh, he spoke, his warm breath against her ear making her shiver. "So," he said, his voice husky and tinged with amusement, "what was this big deal with my grandparents?"

Still feeling as though her heart was stampeding around in her chest, Maggie managed a shaky laugh. "I don't remember."

He slid his hand up the back of her neck, his fingers tangling in her hair as he gave her head a little squeeze. Then he rubbed his stubbled cheek against her temple, cuddling her deeper into his embrace. He began massaging her scalp, his touch slow and mesmerizing. "This feels pretty damned good, Mag," he whispered huskily. "Even better than I imagined."

There was something in the gruff quality of his voice that got to her, and Maggie found herself suddenly struggling against a thick wad of emotion. She clenched her eyes shut and swallowed hard, nearly overcome with feelings for this man. Feelings that caused a painful ache deep in her chest. It had been a very long time since she'd been held like this, and it made her feel things she had no business feeling. She could so easily fall in love with him. So easily.

He rubbed his hand down her spine, hugging her closer, and she felt him smile. "I gotta tell you, though. You're harder to corner than that damned cat."

A rush of guilt nailed her squarely in the chest, and she flattened her hands against his back, wishing—oh, God— wishing this could be real. But common sense told her she was in way over her head. She gave herself a minute to fight back the awful sense of loss that was threatening to break loose, then swallowed hard and drew in an unsteady breath. Bracing herself for the bereft feeling, she started to pull away. "Tony, I—"

He pulled her back, tightening his arms around her. "Not a chance," he said, his tone gruff. Grasping her jaw, he lifted her face, covering her mouth with a soft, sweet kiss, one that made her pulse go berserk. Her heart was pounding so hard when he finally drew away that she felt the reverberation from her scalp to her toes. He combed her hair back from her face, then nestled her head firmly against his shoulder.

Tony gave her a tight hug, then began rubbing her back. "I'm not letting you off the hook this time," he said quietly.

Maggie pressed her face against the soft skin of his neck, her whole body trembling. She grasped the back of his head, holding on to him with what little strength she had. She took a deep, shaky breath, struggling to bring things back into focus.

He smoothed his hand up her back, his jaw pressed tightly against her temple. "Just so you know," he said, as if warning her, "I never throw in a poker hand, Burrows." He carefully tucked some hair behind her ear, his touch oddly comforting. When he spoke again, there was a touch of amusement in his voice. "And I sure as hell don't quit while I'm ahead."

That prompted a shaky laugh, and the tension abruptly drained out of her. "I didn't take you for a gambler, Parnelli."

He stroked her cheek with his thumb, then slid his fingers into her hair again. His voice was very soft when he responded, "I've been running a gamble ever since I saw you standing in the doorway, sweetheart." He held her for a moment, then withdrew his arms and took her face between his hands. Tony planted another firm kiss on her mouth, then tipped her head back so he could look at her. Finally he released an uneven sigh, his expression turning serious. "I'm leaving for Vancouver first thing tomorrow morning for a car auction. And I won't be back until sometime Friday." He inhaled deeply and tightened his hold, the soft glow from the alley light casting his face in strained lines. "I want to take you out Friday night, Maggie," he said, his voice very quiet.

Maggie stared up at him, her throat suddenly tight. She should say no. She knew she should say no. But a fierce longing overrode her common sense. She had to wait a moment for the contraction to ease, then managed an uneven smile. "You aren't taking me to a poker game, are you?"

He stared at her a second, then let his breath go in a rush and grinned at her. "Nah. I was thinking more along the lines of a blues bar." He rubbed his fingers up and down her nape, making her shiver; then he tightened his hold on her face and gave her another quick kiss. "I'll pick you up around nine."

Before she had a chance to agree or disagree, he covered her mouth with a final kiss. Only this one wasn't quick. It was devastatingly long and deep and very, very thorough. And Maggie's senses were whirling when he finally let her go. Shaken to the core, she stood there in some sort of sensory coma, her legs weak as water and her heart pounding. By the time she was able to swim through the overload of sensations and open her eyes, he was gone.

Still stunned by the effect of that last kiss, she dazedly turned and started toward the house, her knees threatening to buckle with every step. She felt as if she'd just been run over by a ten-ton truck.

It was not a good week for Maggie. One moment she'd be nearly giddy with expectation, the next so filled with apprehension that she'd be on the verge of a full-blown anxiety attack. It was during those times that their age difference seemed like a bad joke, and she'd ruthlessly remind herself that she was a middle-aged mother who had nine hard years on him. But her darned heart wouldn't always listen to her commonsense mind.

She was a mess. She really tried to put everything back into perspective, but would find herself reliving that last kiss, and more than once, she'd have to put her head down on the desk and wait for her heart to stop pounding and her body to stop pulsating. Then she'd get into another long talk with herself, trying to get a grip on the crazy emotions that kept surfacing, and a disconnecting thought would pop into her mind, like what did one wear to a blues bar. She'd never been to something like that in her whole life.

It was so bad that Frank started watching her with a perplexed look, and on Wednesday he demanded to know if she was getting sick again. And were their accounts receivable up-to-date? Feeling suddenly defensive, Maggie told him what he could do with his accounts receivable, then picked up her handbag and left. Frank looked like a confused little boy when she stomped out the door.

Maggie hoped that a long walk and a heavy dose of tough self-talk would straighten her out, but she somehow ended up at Stevie's fitness center.

The tall blonde took one look at her, fixed one of the club's for-whatever-ails-you tonics and made her down the whole drink.

Her head in her hands, Maggie stared blindly at the pink fizz remaining in the tall glass. She was going to ask her neighbor why life was so complicated, but that wasn't what came out of her mouth. "What do you wear to a blues bar?" she asked instead, a thread of panic in her voice.

Stevie, dressed in a mind-boggling dark purple-and-pink Lycra leotard, grinned and rested her arms on the table. Stevie was partial to pink.

Pure delight sparkled in the blonde's eyes. "Have you got a *date* to go to a blues bar, Maggie?"

Maggie shielded her eyes with her hands. "Don't give me a hard time, Stephanie. Or I'll saddle you with full custody of Hook."

The other woman laughed, pushed her chair back and stood up. "God, I love it when the mighty tumble." She shouted across the vast room to one of her employees. "Hans, keep an eye on things, will you? I'm going out for a bit."

She grabbed one of Maggie's arms and yanked it out from under her head, nearly giving her whiplash. "Come on, Mary Margaret. Most people would wear jeans and a T-shirt with a beer logo on it to a blues bar. But that won't do for you. So your Aunt Stevie is taking you shopping."

Maggie didn't really know why she let Stevie take over. No one in her right mind would ever give that woman full control, but she followed along like some lame duck. Fishing Maggie's credit card out of her wallet, La Goddess marched her into one of the trendy little boutiques along the main drag and slapped the card on the counter. Maggie's sense of humor surfaced. Only Stevie could get away with going shopping in an outfit that looked as if it had been painted on her very spectacular body. It was a wonder the blonde hadn't caused several major car wrecks on the short walk from her fitness center to the shop.

Stevie shopped with a vengeance, partly, Maggie thought with a small grin, when it was with someone else's credit card. She assembled an outfit in ten minutes flat. Dark brown slacks, a cream-colored silk blouse and a tapestry vest that had dark greens, browns and a background of ivory. Taking possession of the designer shopping bag, she marched Maggie out the door and into the hair salon next door. "Dot," she said in that same bossy manner, "will you please do something with this woman's hair?"

Dot, who had burgundy tresses, was wearing a flamboyant jumpsuit and dangling earrings the size of hubcaps. She came over and narrowed her eyes, scrutinizing Maggie with the intensity of a carpenter who had just been handed a major renovation job. She pulled at Maggie's hair. "Sure can. What do you want?"

Grinning broadly, Stevie pushed Maggie into a chair. "First of all, don't listen to anything she says."

Dot positioned herself behind the chair, meeting Maggie's gaze in the mirror, her eyes twinkling. "Buckle your seat belt, honey. This is going to be a blast."

Stevie came over to stand beside Dot, folding her arms and considering Maggie in the mirror. "She's got great eyes, Dot. And decent bone structure. Can you do something that will accentuate her eyes and jawline?"

Maggie gave Stevie a contrary stare. "Don't act like I'm not here, Stevie. It's *my* hair."

Stevie grinned at her again. "And it's nice hair, Mary Margaret. It's so thick, and that bit of natural curl is fabulous. But I gotta tell you, that style doesn't do a thing for you." She gave an excited little wiggle, positively radiating enthusiasm. "I can't believe I'm finally getting the chance to do this." She tipped her head, thoughtfully narrowing her eyes. "What do you think about adding some blond highlights, Dot? That light brown color is pretty, but it's kinda flat. You know what I mean?"

Maggie glared at her. "You're taking an awful lot for granted here, Stephanie."

Stevie just laughed at her. "Be quiet, Mary Margaret. There are two geniuses at work here."

Maggie wasn't sure about the genius part. Zealous? Yes, definitely. Eager and enthusiastic? Absolutely. Overbearing and pushy? Without question. They both totally ignored her as highlights went in and several inches of hair came off. Stevie had hung a towel over the mirror so Maggie couldn't see what Dot was concocting. Maggie finally gave up, folded her arms under the vivid drape and sat there like a lump. Whatever had possessed her to say what she had to Stevie? Of all people, she should have known better. She just knew she was going to end up with one of those severe bobs that all the smart young professionals wore.

Maggie expected one thing; what she got was something altogether different. It wasn't severe; it was soft and unbelievably feminine, expertly layered to make the most of what natural curl there was. And it definitely did something to her eyes.

She stared at herself in the mirror, not even sure it was her own hair.

Dot fluffed the back with her fingers. "This is absolutely a low-maintenance cut, sweetie, especially with that bit of curl. You shampoo it, then you do this—" she scrubbed her hands through her hair "—and you just let it dry naturally. And it's going to look like this every time. You could go out in a hurricane and it'll still look like this." She whipped the cape from around Maggie. "You'll need to come back every six to eight weeks," she said briskly. "And that's it."

Stevie looked so pleased with herself that she positively glowed. "Now isn't that better, M and M? You look ten years younger."

Maggie's insides rose, then dropped in a rush. Ten years. Okay, so it was really nine. God, was she out of her mind? He had been nine when she was eighteen. She could have baby-sat him. That realization made her want to put her head in a bag and never take it out. Who did she think she was kidding, anyway? This was never going to work. Never. She was just going to have to break the date. Did forty-plus women even refer to it as a date?

By Friday morning she had changed her mind so many times that she'd lost count. By seven o'clock that evening she had definitely decided that going out with Tony Parnelli was equivalent to throwing herself over the weir on the Bow River—suicidal. After pacing about the house for exactly forty minutes, she finally screwed up the courage to call. With her heart hammering at two hundred beats a minute, she phoned information and got the new listing, then dialed.

She let it ring twelve times. Panic assailed her as she hung up the phone. Then, without even realizing she'd changed, she found herself pacing around the house, this time with her hair freshly shampooed, her makeup and new clothes on. At that point she finally decided she was behaving like an idiot, and she made herself take ten deep breaths, then poured herself a large glass of wine. Thank God Kelly had gone to watch movies at Scott's and wasn't here to witness her mother having a nervous breakdown. This was not a big deal. It was an evening out, that was all. Only her stomach kept sending her an altogether different message.

It was one minute to nine when a knock sounded on her back door. Feeling as if she was fifteen and facing her first date, Maggie smoothed down the front of her slacks and went to answer it, her heart taking off in some sort of race. Pausing in the entryway, she took another deep breath, stuck a smile on her face and opened the door.

Tony had been standing with one arm braced against the door, his other hand resting on his hip, aimlessly whistling through his teeth. He glanced at her and his face grew very still. Then he slowly straightened, a glint of appreciation lighting up his eyes. Maggie closed her hands into fists. If he said something asinine, like "Gee, Maggie, you look terrific," she was going to slug him.

His gaze traveled from the top of her head to the tips of her new shoes, as if he was cataloging assets; then he looked into her eyes and a slow, off-center, totally engaging grin appeared. "I gotta tell you, Burrows, you clean up real well."

The knot of nerves in her middle abruptly let go, and she found herself smiling. She mimicked his perusal. He had on new jeans, some sneakers that looked very expensive and a yellow polo shirt that did not have the sleeves hacked to bits. He looked so sweet and adorable that she folded her arms to keep from hugging him. "You clean up pretty well yourself, Parnelli."

He grinned again, then made an impatient gesture with his head. "Come on, woman. Let's get this show on the road."

Maggie fortified herself with another deep breath and picked up her handbag, which was lying on the wicker stand.

She had just jumped into the deep end. She only hoped she remembered how to swim.

# Chapter 7

The Blue Hornet Bar was located in a seedy part of town, but Maggie knew from Frank, who was a big blues fan, that it had an international reputation and featured blues artists from all over North America.

Things were fine in the car—easy, comfortable, relaxed, as if they'd done this a hundred times before. Tony told her what he'd been doing in Vancouver; Maggie, on the other hand, did *not* elaborate on her week. Instead she told him about her kids.

By the time they arrived at the bar, she was feeling pretty stupid for making such a big deal out of this. It was a night out, that was all. And she was going to enjoy herself.

Tony warned her that the place would probably be jammed because a top-flight performer was in from the States. And he was right. The bar was dim, crowded and very noisy. Tony paid the cover charge, then touched the small of her back and pointed across the crowded room toward some tables along the wall. Following his direction, she wound her way through the maze of tables. She had never seen such a mix of people in her whole life—gray-haired businessmen, hard-core bikers, university students, punkers, office workers—all there because of their love of music. She smiled to herself. It was too bad they couldn't turn the whole world into one big blues bar.

Having navigated through most of the tables, Maggie glanced over her shoulder at Tony, not even trying to make herself heard over the noise. He lifted his chin toward a table halfway down the wall, and she followed his glance, her stomach immediately dropping to her shiny new shoes. There were four people already seated at the table—two men and two women—and Maggie suddenly felt fifteen all over again. Lord, she wasn't prepared for this. She wasn't. Tony gave her a nudge in the small of her back, and she took a deep, uneven breath and stuck a smile on her face.

As if sensing her sudden reluctance, Tony slid his hand down her arm, then laced his fingers through hers, giving her hand a firm squeeze. She looked at him, and he grinned and winked at her, as if to say "gotcha."

He led her over to the table, and without letting go of her, pulled out a chair. "Maggie, I'd like you to meet Spider Bronson and Jeanne Walker," he said, then indicated the two at the back of the table, "and that's Mark and Cathy Turner. This is Maggie Burrows."

Maggie recognized Spider and Jeanne from Tony's open house. She was a redhead who looked as if she might make her living as a mud wrestler, and he was a big, burly biker type with a beard and a tattoo the size of a dinner plate on his bicep. He looked as if he could rip apart a motorcycle with his bare hands. The other woman was pretty and petite, with a ready smile, and as soon as Maggie looked at her husband, she knew he was a cop. She wanted to pull a bag over her head. She just hoped to hell he hadn't heard about her calling the cops on Tony.

Spider hooked the legs of a chair with his boot and drew it farther away from the table, giving her a big grin. "I remember you from Tony's bash. You should have stuck around. You missed a helluvah party."

Maintaining a firm hold on her hand, Tony waited for Maggie to slide into her chair; then he pulled out his own and sat down. Resting their joined hands on his thigh, he glanced at her, a wicked glint in his eyes. "She misses out on a lot of things, Spider."

Spider chuckled, and Jeanne leaned her arms on the table. "Don't let them rag on you, honey. They can both be a royal pain in the ass." She leveled one finger at Tony, her very long, very scarlet nail looking lethal. "Now buy the lady a beer, Parnelli, and be nice."

Cathy Turner lifted her empty bottle and waggled it. "And you can buy me one, too, Anthony. You welshed last time."

Her husband leaned forward, digging his billfold out of his back pocket. Opening it, he drew out a twenty-dollar bill and tossed it on the table. He looked at Maggie, a twinkle in his eyes. "Nope, Maggie's beer is on me. I would have paid a month's wages to see Parnelli getting hauled out in cuffs."

Wanting to crawl under the table, she slapped her free hand over her face. She should have known she'd never be that lucky. His voice ripe with amusement, Mark Turner continued, "I also heard that you put Parker flat on his back and that Lipskow is now singing soprano."

Dropping her hand, Maggie turned her head and stared at Tony. He shot her a quick glance, then gave Mark a wry grin. "Lipskow is lucky he's singing at all. The son of a bitch tried to get me down in a headlock."

Cathy laughed and clapped her hands. "Oh, God. I love it! That must've wounded his ego." She looked at Maggie, laughter still dancing in her eyes. "Lipskow thinks he's God's gift to women, and he struts around like he's top cop." She looked at Tony, raising her empty bottle in salute. "Congratulations, Ex-detective Parnelli. The women of the world salute you."

Tony tipped his head in acknowledgment, a small, meaningful smile lifting one corner of his mouth. "It was definitely my pleasure."

The warm-up band started to play about twenty minutes later, and Spider looked at Tony and jerked his thumb over his shoulder, his eyebrows raised in an unspoken question. Tony nodded, then slid his chair back. He leaned over the table and spoke to Mark, nearly shouting to make himself heard. "We're going to check out the back room. Wanna come?"

Mark looked at Cathy. She shook her head, then spoke into his ear. He nodded and rose. "Cathy's going to stay here and hold the table for us."

Tony downed the rest of his beer, then gave Maggie a light jab in the shoulder. "Come on. It'll be quieter in there."

The "back room" made Maggie smile to herself. Six pool tables squatted in the large room, canopied lights suspended over them, the players intent on their games. Two tables at the far end were not in use, and she followed Mark down the side of the room. She assessed the tables as she passed. Standard billiards tables, but they were high quality and in fairly good shape. She smiled again.

For the first time all day, she felt on absolutely solid ground. She had started shooting billiards when she was six years old, when her father had sawed the end off a broken pool cue for her. Her father had been a top-seeded player, and she had played in competitions until she got married. And somewhere in the storage room there was a box of trophies. Aunt Kate might have been able to rebuild a carburetor, but Maggie could shoot pool. It had delighted her father no end when she'd beat him—and she'd beaten him regularly. She wondered what Tony would say if he knew.

Jeanne didn't want to play, so Maggie sat at the table with her, watching the men. Tony was good. Very good, as a matter of fact. Stretching out her legs and folding her arms, she maintained a conversation with Jeanne, but never took her eyes off the game. She wanted to pick up a cue so badly that her palms itched.

His cue in his hand, Tony came over to the table and took a swig from his fresh bottle of beer, then looked down at her, giving her a small smile. "Are you bored out of your mind?"

She shook her head. "Not at all. I like to watch."

Setting his beer down, Tony turned, then made a disgusted sound and swore. Maggie looked from him to the table. Three men were standing at the end talking to Mark, and there was something about all three that singled them out as cops. Mark said something, and they looked across at the table. The one who appeared to be about fifty came over to Tony. He grinned and reached out his hand. "Hey, Parnelli. I haven't seen you in a dog's age. How the hell are you?"

Resting the end of his cue on the floor, Tony grinned and took the other man's hand. "I'll be damned. I figured they would have pink-slipped you by now, Kennedy."

Kennedy chuckled and slapped him on the shoulder. "Naw. They got me flying a desk."

He jerked his thumb at one of the other two men, who'd come up behind him. "This is Dennis Larson—he's new since you left." He gave Tony a deliberately even-faced look. "And you know John Lipskow, don't you?"

"Yeah," said Tony, a nasty little smile appearing. "We've met."

Maggie had to bite down hard on her lip to keep from laughing. John Lipskow was probably in his late twenties, big and blond, with a body that had seen hundreds of hours pumping weights. And it only took one glance to see that Cathy's assessment was dead-on. This man definitely thought he was God's gift to women. Tony turned his back on the younger man, excluding him as he introduced Jeanne and Maggie.

It was a deliberate snub, and Maggie watched the little performance, biting down harder on her lip. She saw John Lipskow look from her to Tony, then back to her, and the big blonde telegraphed his intent the instant he tucked his T-shirt into his jeans, tightening the fabric down his chest. He stepped from behind Tony, reached out his hand toward Maggie and turned on the charm full blast. "Hi, there," he said, looking directly into her eyes and giving her a boyish grin. "It's a real pleasure to meet you, Maggie."

Somehow managing to keep her face straight, Maggie shook his hand, the urge to laugh compounding when he held her hand far longer than necessary. Withdrawing her hand, she looked up at Tony, expecting to see at least a glimmer of humor. There wasn't a trace. He was watching John, his eyes narrow and hard, his jaw rigid, and she saw John give him a challenging look. Maggie rolled her eyes heavenward. At least some things never changed. They looked like two bull moose ready to do battle.

Kennedy slapped Tony on the shoulder, breaking up the hostile staring match. "How about letting us in the game, Parnelli? I want a chance to clock your butt."

Tony gave him a wry grin. "You wish."

There was a debate about who was challenging whom, and Mark came over to where Maggie and Jeanne were sitting, an amused grin on his face. "I think I'll head back and keep Cath company. If something happens and all hell breaks loose, come get me." He glanced at John Lipskow, his grin deepening. "I think Johnny Boy is itching to start a fight." Setting his empty beer bottle on the table, he gave the two women a little salute. "Stay cool, ladies."

Spider and Tony paired off against Kennedy and Dennis Larson in a game of eight ball, and Maggie slouched down in her chair and watched, intent on the strategy. John Lipskow came over to the table, a beer in his hand. Leaning against the wall, he took a swig from the bottle, then shifted so the muscles in his chest flexed. He took another swig, then crouched down beside her, tipping his head close to hers. "Can I get you a drink, Maggie?" he asked, trying to sound sexy.

Maggie shifted away from him, giving him a level stare. "No, thank you."

He did the eye thing again, looking directly at her with a slow, sensual smile, and Maggie experienced a flicker of irritation. It was evident by his muscle flexing and his phony charm that she was supposed to be flattered that he was paying attention to her. She remembered the type—the big, muscled jock so stuck on himself that he figured every woman he met should fall at his feet. Maggie wondered how he ever managed to fit his massive ego into a patrol car.

She tried to give him a subtle brush-off by turning her attention back to the game, but Lipskow did not know the meaning of subtle. By the time the other men were down to the last few balls on the table, she wanted to smack him. She knew he was trying to rile Tony, and she resented the fact that he was using her to do it.

And she knew by the look on Tony's face that the patrolman was getting to him. He looked as if he'd like nothing better than to ram his pool cue down the cop's throat.

Tony sunk the last ball, his jaw as rigid as granite, and as he straightened and looked over at them, his eyes were brittle. A small smirk appeared on John's face, and he ran his knuckles down Maggie's arm. "So, Maggie," he said, his voice deliberately husky. "You ever played?"

She gave him a flat look. "Once or twice," she said, her tone short.

He rubbed his knuckles up her arm. "How would you like a lesson?"

She jerked her arm away and stared at him, about to say something cutting, but then saw him glance at Tony, as if checking his response. Her irritation turned to outright annoyance. If anyone needed a lesson, it was this ego-inflated Lothario.

She gave him a big, plastic smile. "I suppose I could give it a shot."

Dodging his closeness, she got up and went over to the pool table. She stopped in front of Tony, giving him a tight smile. "John's going to give me a lesson," she said.

Tony's eyes narrowed and he looked at John, the muscles in his jaw tensing; then he looked back at Maggie. There was something about the heated, protective glitter in his eyes that kick-started her sense of humor. She winked at him and grasped the pool cue he held in his hand. "Just hang on, and trust me, Parnelli."

Tony narrowed his eyes and considered her, a glint of speculation in his eyes. Then he released the cue. A funny flutter unfolded in her middle, and Maggie avoided looking at him. She rolled the cue on the table to check for straightness, then undid the cuffs on her blouse and folded them back. Picking up the cue, she smiled across the table at John Lipskow, who strutted over and expanded his chest. He dropped the coins in the slot, releasing the balls. "When you run into trouble, you just sing out and I'll show you what to do," he said smoothly.

Maggie gave him an innocent look. "I'm sure you will," she said. Not daring to look at Tony, she watched the cop rack up the balls, then gave him another saccharine smile. "You go ahead and break. I'll watch."

It was a sloppy break, scattering the colored balls across the table. The butt of her cue resting on the floor, Maggie wrapped both hands around the top, assessing the table. It was the kind of messy break that any good player prayed for. She looked at her opponent, resisting the urge to flutter her eyelashes at him. "It's my turn now, right?"

He came over and stood beside her. "That's right." He dropped his voice into a drawl. "How about if I help you line up your first shot?"

Up to that point, Maggie had been considering toying with him for a while, but the thought of him pressing up against her made her skin crawl, and she abruptly changed her mind. John Lipskow definitely needed to be taught a lesson.

"No," she said, leaning over the table and lining up the first shot. "I think I can do it all by myself." She sighted down the cue and called her shot. "Blue ball in the corner pocket."

And with that, she set out to annihilate him. Her concentration focused, she sunk one ball after another, deliberately choosing shots that were nearly impossible. She wasn't going to give him one single reason to think this was a case of beginner's luck.

That end of the room had gone suddenly very still, and Maggie was aware of the figures standing off to the side, watching the game. But she kept her attention focused; the last thing she wanted to see was the expression on Tony's face.

With the last of the solid colors gone, she sank the black eight ball, then straightened. Avoiding eye contact with everyone else, she met John Lipskow's gaze. His face was flushed and there was a furious glint in his eyes. She gave him a steady stare and shoved her cue into his hand. "Thanks for the game," she said flatly. Then she brushed past him and went over to the table, experiencing another rush of irritation. He was so thick that he probably hadn't even realized what had happened. She slung the strap of her handbag over her shoulder and turned, startled to find herself face-to-face with Tony. His arms folded and his head tipped to one side, he studied her, his gaze thoughtful. Then a small, amused smile appeared. "So what was that all about?"

She looked away and adjusted the position of the strap across her shoulder. "Sheer arrogance," she answered, her tone short.

She could tell Tony was grinning by the tone in his voice. "His or yours?"

She looked up at him, prepared to give him a sharp retort, but he reached out and placed his finger against her mouth, the twinkle in his eyes intensifying. "I'll be damned. I do believe you were showing off, Burrows."

She knew he was right and wished she hadn't been quite so obvious. Bracing one hand on the wall behind her, he looked directly into her eyes. Then he grinned again. "I don't know how he's feeling right now, but you shocked the hell out of me." Leaning down, he brushed a light kiss against the corner of her mouth. "What other surprises do you have tucked up your sleeve?"

The touch of his mouth against hers set off a flurry in her chest, and her eyes drifted shut. It took every ounce of will-power she had to make herself answer. "Just an arm," she answered unevenly.

He laughed against her mouth, then gave her a little squeeze. "You're pretty damned cute, do you know that?" He kissed her again, then straightened, sliding his arm around her shoulders. "Come on, hotshot," he said, hugging her against him, his tone suddenly husky. "Let's check out what's happening in the bar."

By the time they made their way back to the table, Spider was giving Mark and Cathy a play-by-play of the game. Kennedy and Dennis Larson had joined the others, and Dennis Larson stood up as they approached the table, giving Maggie his chair. Knowing she was in for a hard time, she sighed and sat down. Cathy had to have the whole story, and Maggie finally relented and told them about her father giving her her first cue.

Tony disappeared just as the lights dimmed and the MC introduced the main act. The band started to play, and the wail of a tenor sax filled the darkened room, the soulful sound moving through the semidarkness like a living thing. Maggie felt the loneliness of that solitary horn right down to her bones, the haunting sound touching her in the most elemental way. Glancing away, she spotted Tony along the back wall, standing off by himself, his arms folded. The light from the bar slanted across his face, and Maggie's heart went very still.

He stood apart, and even from that distance she sensed his solitude, as if he had deliberately isolated himself from the rest. There was something somber, something heavily introspective in his face, and it struck her that there was an intentness, a complexity, a depth of emotion in this man that few people realized. It was a side of him she had never seen before, and her throat contracted.

She abruptly looked away, a fierce ache expanding in her chest. The thought of him isolated and alone sent a huge wave of emotion washing through her, and she rested her head back against the wall and closed her eyes, locking her jaw against the awful knot in her throat. He made her feel things she shouldn't feel, and he made her want things that she had no business wanting. But the image of him standing there alone did something to her heart that she had no defense against.

She sat there until the ache eased a little, then slid the strap of her handbag over her shoulder, pushed her chair back and got up, slipping away from the table unnoticed.

For once not considering the right or wrong of it, she went over to where he was, knowing that no matter what, she could not leave him like that. He was so intent on the music that he didn't even realize she was there until she touched him. His gaze swiveled to meet hers, a flash of surprise registering in his eyes.

Maggie managed an uneven smile. "Do you mind if I join you?"

He stared at her a moment, his gaze almost guarded; then he exhaled sharply and straightened. "No," his said, his voice unnaturally gruff. "I don't mind at all."

He pulled her in front of him, then slid his arms around her waist, drawing her back flush against his chest. Maggie covered his hands with her own and tipped her head against his jaw, her throat suddenly so tight she couldn't swallow. God, he touched her in ways she'd never thought possible.

Taking a deep, unsteady breath, Tony tightened his arms around her, tucking his face against hers. It was almost as if he was trying to absorb her warmth.

Experiencing another rush of emotion, she closed her eyes, hugging his arms closer, the sound of the music suddenly not quite so lonely.

It was nearly one a.m. when Tony pulled into the parking area behind his shop. They sat in the car for a moment, neither one of them speaking, as if they were both reluctant to break the mood. The illumination from the light at the top of the steps slanted through the windshield, and Tony took her hand, his profile solemn and unreadable as he rubbed his thumb back and forth across her knuckles. He had been strangely quiet for the past several hours, ever since she'd gone over to stand with him. But it wasn't a withdrawn silence; it was as if there was no need to speak.

Finally he lifted his head and looked at her, his gaze dark and unsmiling. "I want to take you to my place, Maggie," he said, his voice steady.

The pulse in her neck suddenly beating in double time, Maggie stared at him, knowing what he was really asking. She thought of all the reasons she should say no. Her daughter, for one, who was at home asleep in her bed. Her own state of mind, for another.

But she simply could not bring herself to say it. And she couldn't even use raging desire as an excuse. He had not exerted an iota of pressure on her, not even in the subtlest way. He had simply held her; that was all. But he had touched something infinitely tender inside her in that darkened corner, and she couldn't bear to lose that now. The thought of never experiencing that kind of feeling again made her whole chest hurt. So it boiled down to one final conclusion, that one fear outweighing all the others.

The wild frenzy in her throat compounding, she drew in a deep, shaky breath and tightened her hand around his. Feeling almost paralyzed by the momentousness of what she was about to do, she gripped his hand harder. "I'd like that," she whispered, her voice wobbling.

He stared at her a moment, then gave her hand a firm squeeze. "Just stay there," he said, his tone gruff; then he opened his door and got out. The minute he shut his door, Maggie closed her eyes and tried to take a full breath, her hammering heart suddenly five times too large for her chest. Lord, she was so inept at this. And it had been so long. So long.

Tony opened her door and helped her out, maintaining a tight grip on her hand. He didn't say anything as he led her up the stairs, and he didn't say anything as he unlocked the dead bolt on his door. But he didn't let go of her once, not even for an instant.

Entering the apartment, he tossed his keys on a stand that Maggie could barely see in the faint glow from the streetlight outside. Releasing an uneven breath, he caught her by the back of the neck and pulled her into a fierce, enveloping embrace. Maggie slid her arms around him and turned her face against his neck, trembling from head to toe. Grasping her head, Tony tightened his arms around her. "Don't be scared, babe," he whispered unevenly. "We're going to take this slow and easy, and if you change your mind, that's okay. Okay?" When she didn't answer, he gave her a reassuring hug. "Okay?"

She drew a shaky breath and nodded her head against his neck, a panicky feeling unfolding in her, doubts about her own sexuality warring with a nearly unbearable longing. She wanted this more than she'd ever wanted anything, but the process scared her to death. She did not have a beautiful body, and her experience was limited, to say the least.

As if reading her mind, Tony rubbed his hand across her back, then spoke. "This isn't a contest, Maggie," he said, a soft reprimand in his tone. "Or an inventory of assets. So I don't want you worrying about that, okay?" He gave her another light squeeze. "Okay?"

Some of the awful tension let go, and she managed an uneven smile against his neck. "Okay," she whispered.

He continued to rub her back, his touch making her breathing uneven. He didn't say anything for the longest time, then he released a raspy breath and tucked his head against hers. "God, but this feels so damned good," he whispered, his voice rough with strain.

Closing her eyes tight, Maggie drew a deep, uneven breath, a frenzy of sensations making her pulse hammer. Swallowing hard, she cupped the back of his neck, her doubts giving way to an onslaught of emotions.

Tony exhaled sharply and pulled her hips hard against him, then roughly turned his face against the curve of her neck. He took a couple of deep breaths and smoothed his hand across her buttocks. "I need to hold you," he said, his voice strained, "but I don't think I can do it standing up."

The tiny trace of humor in his tone did something profound and overwhelming to Maggie's heart, and she clutched the back of his head and swallowed hard, so many feelings building in her that she couldn't distinguish one from the other. Waiting for the spasm to pass, she exhaled unevenly and relaxed her hold. His body tense, Tony hugged her once, then let her go and grasped her tightly by the hand. He led her through the darkened apartment and down a hallway.

By the time they reached the bedroom, Maggie was trembling again. Whispering her name, Tony caught her to him once more and weakly rested his head against hers, his breathing ragged. Her heart laboring painfully in her chest, she swallowed hard and placed her hand along his jaw, moved beyond reason when she felt how rigidly he had his teeth clenched. Tears burned her throat and she swallowed again, tightening her hold on his face. She could feel the awful struggle for control in him, and suddenly nothing mattered— not her own uncertainties about herself, not whether this was right or wrong. All she knew was that he was holding back because of her, and she didn't want that.

Managing to suck in a tight breath, she slid her hand into his hair and drew his head down, covering his mouth in a kiss that didn't have a shred of caution in it. Tony shuddered and made a low sound; then he wrapped his arms around her and responded, working his mouth hungrily against hers.

The desperation in that kiss set off shock waves of sensation in Maggie, and a weakening need coursed through her, making her whole body ache.

Sliding her arms around his neck, she pulled herself flush against him, and Tony emitted a low groan. She felt him try to gentle his touch, to slow things down, but there was no way she could let him go. Grasping his head between her hands, she caught a painful breath, then repositioned her mouth against his, urging him on.

It was as if she'd hit him in the solar plexus, and he shuddered and caved in around her. His face contorting at her touch, he grasped one of her legs and dragged it around his waist, then thrust against her. The feel of him, hard and heavy, set off a hot, throbbing need inside her, and Maggie sobbed against his mouth as she moved against him, sensation after sensation piling in on her.

As if realizing the conclusion was inevitable, Tony grasped her hair and tore his mouth away, pulling her arms down. His breathing harsh in the darkened room, he yanked his T-shirt off over his head, then caught her in a crushing hold, covering her mouth in a hot, wet kiss.

And Maggie lost all touch with reality. Somehow he managed to get their clothes off, his mouth moving with devastating urgency over her body, his touch driving her deeper and deeper into a fever of need. Clutching her against him, he carried her down onto the bed, breaking their fall with an outstretched arm. Holding her immobile, he wedged her legs apart with his knee; then he settled his weight between her thighs, making a low, guttural sound against her mouth as flesh came in contact with flesh.

It was as if that contact jarred him, and he tried to roll away. Through the fever in her mind, Maggie realized what he was after and why, and she locked her legs around his hips, clutching him. "It's okay," she gasped out. "Please. It's okay."

A violent tremor coursed through him, and he twisted his face against the curve of her neck, his heart hammering in unison with hers. Then he heaved in a deep breath and thrust one arm under her hips, covering her mouth in another scalding kiss. Making a ragged sound against her mouth, he lifted her hips and entered her in a long powerful thrust, and Maggie cried out and arched beneath him, an agony of need ripping through her.

Jamming his head against hers, he began to move, his breathing harsh and labored against her ear, and Maggie arched again, the heat building and building to an unbearable pitch. Then the tension gathered into one pulsating center, and with one final thrust, he pushed her over the edge, sending her soaring as spasm after spasm coursed through her. He gave two more hard, driving thrusts, then clutched her and ground his body against hers, a low, tortured groan wrenching loose. Overcome with emotion, Maggie pressed his head tightly against her neck, holding him with every ounce of strength she possessed as tears slipped down her temples. Nothing could ever compare to this. Nothing.

Locking her jaw against the unbearable ache in her throat, she turned her face to his and smoothed her hand up his naked back, the ache intensifying. More tears slipped down her temple and she swallowed hard, trying to will them away. She wished she could draw him inside her and keep him there forever.

Tony released an uneven sigh and stirred, cupping her face with his hand as he kissed the curve of her neck. He caressed her temple with his thumb, then went very still. Pulling out of her hold, he braced his weight on one elbow, then reached over and turned on the small lamp on his bedside table. His expression grave, he gazed down at her, drying the track of tears with one knuckle. "What's the matter?" he asked huskily.

Her chest full and her throat tight, she gazed up at him, her feelings nearly overwhelming her. She stroked his face with the back of her hand, knowing that above all else, she had to give him the truth. Swallowing hard, she tried to smile. "You are truly a miracle, Tony Parnelli," she whispered, her voice catching as a wad of emotion jammed her throat.

He stared at her, his gaze somber and intense, then leaned down and softly—so very softly, so very carefully—kissed away the new flood of tears. The care and gentleness undid her, and Maggie hugged him hard, pressing her face against his neck, afraid she was going to start crying in earnest. She had never felt so emotionally raw in her whole life.

Supporting her head with his hand, Tony rubbed his cheek against hers. He didn't say anything for the longest time, then she felt him swallow hard. Drawing a deep, uneven breath, he gave her a little squeeze. "The miracle is that we made it to the bed at all."

Realizing he was trying to lighten the mood and loving him for it, Maggie slipped her arms around his neck and gave him a hard hug, the wryness in his tone dragging a smile out of her. "Do you want a medal?"

"I wrecked the zipper in my new jeans," he said, his tone accusing.

Her arms still locked around his neck and her forehead pressed against the curve of his jaw, Maggie smiled again. "Too bad."

Grasping her head between his hands, he forced her back down onto the pillow, looking directly into her eyes, his gaze narrowing. "That's not all I just about wrecked." She was about to give him a flip retort, but he lowered his head and gave her a kiss that was long, sweet and unbearably gentle. Finally releasing a long, unsteady sigh, he hugged her to him. "I'm glad you're finally here," he whispered unevenly. The huskiness in his tone made her throat close up, and Maggie shut her eyes and tightened her arms around him, a funny catch in her heart. If she had one wish right then, it would be that she could take this night and make it last forever.

Finally Tony eased his hold on her, bracing his forearms on either side of her shoulders. He abruptly withdrew from her, sucking his breath through clenched teeth; then he rolled to his back, gathering her into a secure embrace. He rubbed his hand up and down her arm, then released a sigh. "I'm sorry this happened so fast," he said, his tone low and very gruff. "You deserved better than that, Maggie."

Smiling a little, she caressed the broad expanse of his chest. "If it got any better than that," she said, her tone laced with wry amusement, "I would have disintegrated."

He smoothed back her hair, then brushed a kiss against her forehead. "You're pretty damned forgiving," he said softly.

Tipping her head back, she looked at him. "I've nothing to forgive, Tony." She smiled and touched his bottom lip, slightly discomfited by the frankness of the conversation. "Let me put it this way. You definitely exceeded my expectations."

He returned her smile, but it didn't quite reach his eyes. He shifted his gaze and began fondling her hair. "I should have stopped and used something. I have it here."

The self-reproach in his tone made her heart skip a beat, and she shifted her head on his shoulder, running her hand down his arm. "I had a tubal ligation after Kelly was born," she whispered unevenly. "It's not a problem."

He outlined her ear with his thumb. "I've never been careless about sex, Maggie."

She ran her own thumb along his collarbone, a genuine smile surfacing. "Good. Now can we drop it?"

He gave her a quick squeeze, then continued fondling her hair. After a brief silence, he spoke again. "It's been awhile for you hasn't it?"

Maggie closed her eyes, suddenly feeling acutely unsure of herself. Tony withdrew his arm from around her, then braced his weight on one elbow. Grasping her jaw, he made her look at him. His eyes were dark and solemn, his gaze unwavering. "Hasn't it?"

Swallowing against the nervous flutter in her throat, she shifted her gaze and nodded.

"How long?" He applied pressure to her jaw.

Releasing an uneven sigh, she met his gaze. "Ten years."

He continued to watch, his expression unsmiling. "Your ex-husband?"

She shook her head and looked away. "No. An old boyfriend from high school." Guessing that he wasn't going to let it rest until she told him the whole story, she took a deep breath. "We'd gone together for about four months, then he moved away and we lost contact." She gave a humorless smile. "I thought he was the love of my life." Releasing a sigh, she continued, "Then I ran into him at a trade show. He was divorced and I was divorced. I thought for sure something fabulous was going to happen. But it didn't. In fact, it was pretty abysmal."

The heel of his palm resting against the curve of her jaw, Tony lowered his head and kissed her with infinite care. Then he slid his hand under her hair and kissed her on the forehead. "Thank God for that," he said, his tone blunt. Propping his head on his other hand, he caressed her throat with the back of his fingers, then tucked some hair behind her ear. "Ten years is a damned long time. That's something you can't just turn off." Maggie tried to look away, but he didn't let her. It wasn't a question; it was a statement of fact, and Maggie felt her face go hot. He gave her head a reprimanding little shake, his expression softening. "Hey," he whispered gruffly. "Don't be embarrassed about it. It's nothing to be ashamed of." He leaned over and gave her a light, reassuring kiss. "I just wanted to know."

Abruptly aware of just how different her life had been from his, Maggie closed her eyes, unable to meet his gaze. As if sensing the sudden uncertainty in her, he moved so he was above her, taking her face between his hands, covering her mouth in a kiss that made her pulse race. He trailed kisses across her face—her eyes, her cheek, the unbearably sensitive hollow below her ear. "This time," he whispered, moistening her bottom lip, "we're going to go so slow it'll seem like ten years."

Unable to hold on to a single coherent thought, Maggie clenched her jaw and arched her head back, the feel of his wet mouth moving down her body making her heart pound and her pulse stammer.

She would never survive this onslaught. Never. Because this time, it was going to be twice as devastating.

## Chapter 8

Maggie stared at the ceiling, trying to will away the threat of tears, feeling so much emotion in her chest she could barely hold it all in. Tony had made love to her for two solid hours, and he had brought her to so many climaxes that she had lost count. There wasn't an inch of her body he hadn't touched, and he had kissed her in the most intimate places, shredding whatever inhibitions she'd had. It had been an exercise in pure, raw sensation, and her body still throbbed from the earth-shaking releases. And he had touched her so deeply, so profoundly that she knew she would never be the same again. She also knew this was a mistake she was going to pay for for a very long time.

A muscle-car sped past, the howl of the engine shattering the silence, and Tony stirred, shifting the leg he had draped across hers. Tightening her arm in a protective gesture, she smoothed down his tousled hair, letting her hand rest over his ear. Her throat aching, she softly kissed his hair, holding him with heart-wrenching tenderness. He sighed and nuzzled his face deeper into the curve of her neck, then slid his arm around her midriff. Resting her cheek against the top of his head, she swallowed hard and began slowly running her fingers through the long hair at the nape of his neck, a wrenching sense of loss filling her chest.

She should never have let this happen. But she had, and now hard, cold reality was staring her in the face. She was nine years older than him, and that bothered her. A lot. Maybe it wouldn't be such a gap if she didn't feel this way, but she did— she felt every single year. It made her feel almost guilty, but there was more to it than that. This was an illusion, and Tony Parnelli saw her as something she wasn't. And maybe that's what scared her more than anything.

But if she had it to do all over again, would she change anything? Closing her eyes, she lightly tightened her hold on his head, hugging him to her. No. She wouldn't. She wouldn't give up this night with him for anything. It was something she would treasure for the rest of her life.

Swallowing with great difficulty, she turned her head and looked at the clock radio on the table beside his bed. Four forty-seven. She should have left hours ago.

Encircling his head with her arm, she pressed another kiss against it, holding on to him one moment longer. She wanted everything about this moment to be etched permanently in her mind, so she would never forget the feel of him asleep in her arms. One more minute. Then she would slip out of his bed and out the door. And if she was strong enough, she'd slip out of his life. There was just too much wrong to make it right. She had let herself be mesmerized by the feelings he aroused in her; now she would have to deal with the empty, hollow feeling eating a hole in her gut.

The minute passed far too quickly. Struggling with the nearly suffocating sense of loss, she kissed him again, then gently—very gently—eased his head onto the pillow. Bracing herself for the final separation, she closed her eyes and clenched her jaw, then with careful deliberation tried to ease her arm out from under him.

"No," he mumbled, tightening his grasp around her middle. The ornery tone in his voice almost made her smile, and she caressed the back of his neck, pressing her mouth against his head.

"Shh," she whispered. Giving him a moment to settle, she continued to stroke his neck, a faint trace of humor surfacing. And she'd thought this part was going to be simple.

After a few moments, his arm went slack. She gave him a couple of seconds longer, then very carefully tried to ease away again.

He shifted his leg, effectively trapping her. "You aren't going anywhere," he mumbled, pulling her back.

Maggie wasn't sure if she wanted to laugh or cry. But she knew she was going to unravel if she didn't get out of there soon. She gave his head a little shake. "Tony?"

He didn't move a muscle. Hoping that her explanation would register enough so he would let her go, she shifted his arm. "I have to go," she said, her voice wavering a little. "Kelly will be getting up soon to go swimming."

He didn't move for a minute; then he withdrew his arm from around her and released a long sigh. "What time is it?"

Unable to stop herself, she ran her hand down his stubbled jaw. "It's nearly five. And I don't know when she swims today."

He rolled onto his back and dragged his hand down his face; then he turned his head and looked at her. And Maggie, who had struggled to a sitting position with the sheet clutched around her, made an unnerving discovery. If she thought Tony Parnelli was dangerous to her mental health when he was up and moving, he was twice as dangerous all sleepy-eyed and sexy after a night of heavy lovemaking.

Rising up on one elbow, he caught her by the shoulder and pulled her down for a slow, sensual kiss that nearly destroyed her resolve. Sliding his hand down to her arm, he gave her a quick squeeze. "Just give me a minute," he said, his voice still thick with sleep, "and I'll walk you home." He gave her arm one last caress, then rolled away, getting to his feet. Still shaken by the kiss, Maggie closed her eyes and rested her forehead against her upraised knees, a stark feeling washing through her. She wasn't sure she could face him.

She stayed like that until she heard the bathroom door close; then she slid off the bed and started collecting her scattered clothes. Somehow she had to get through this. Somehow.

She was completely dressed except for her vest when Tony came back into the room, wearing a rumpled white T-shirt and a faded pair of jeans. Still looking half-asleep, he sat down on the edge of the bed with his back to her, fishing a pair of old leather dock shoes from the jumble of clothing on the floor. Dropping them in front of him, he scrubbed his face with one hand, as though trying to rid himself of leftover sleep.

Maggie watched him, her heart feeling as if it was about to break into a thousand pieces. Realizing that she was storing up one last image of him, she dragged her eyes away and slipped into her vest. "There's no need for you to walk me home," she said, struggling against the awful clogging in her chest.

He jammed his foot into one shoe, then fumbled with the other one. "I'm going to walk you home," he said, that same intractable tone in his voice.

Maggie stared at him, dread making her lungs tight. She had wanted to sneak away in the night, to disappear out of his life just like that. Around three in the morning, she had made a decision that a letter would be the easiest way to explain why she had left and why she wouldn't see him again. But she should have learned that nothing was ever simple with him. Feeling as if she didn't have an ounce of color left in her face, she said quietly, "I don't think that would be such a good idea."

He rose and turned to face her, the heavy stubble along his jaw giving him a hardened look. Shifting his weight onto one leg and resting his hands on his hips, he stared at her across the room. All traces of sleep gone, he continued to watch her, his gaze sharply alert. Then he narrowed his eyes and spoke, his tone soft and ominous. "Just what in hell does that mean?"

Steeling herself to say to his face what she had intended to put in a letter, Maggie clenched her hands and eased in a tight, painful breath, meeting his gaze head-on. "This shouldn't have happened, Tony," she said, her voice not quite even.

He glared at her, shifting his weight to the other leg. "Why the hell not?"

She flattened her hands against the sides of her legs to still their trembling as she groped for the right words. "You're young and attractive, and I was lonely—"

He cut her off in midsentence, a dangerous glint in his eyes. "Are you insinuating that you were *using* me?"

Grasping at an easy out, she abruptly shoved her hands in her pockets and lifted her chin. "Maybe I was."

He gave her a tight smile, shaking his head. "Nice try, Burrows. But it won't fly." He paused, his eyes drilling into her, the tightness in his face easing just a little. "So why don't you spit out what's really on your mind?"

Determined to keep the sudden threat of tears at bay, she looked away, waiting for the nearly crippling contraction in her throat to ease. A charged silence stretched between them, and Maggie tried to assemble all the reasons in her mind. Finally she met his gaze, her expression controlled. "Do you have any idea how old I am?"

He stared at her a moment, then made a derisive sound and looked away, shaking his head in disgust. Maggie's insides felt like an overextended bow by the time he fixed his attention on her again. "Assuming you weren't five years old when you had your son," he said, his tone cutting, "I think I've pretty much figured that out."

Suddenly cold from the inside out, she wrapped her arms around herself, afraid that if she started to shiver she would never stop. Hating what she was doing to him, she tried to reason with him. "I'm forty-three years old, Tony—nine years older than you are." She made a helpless gesture with her hand. "And that's a big difference for you right now."

He tipped his head to one side, a hard glitter in his eyes. "You mean it would be fine if you were eighty-nine and I was eighty. But it's not all right because you're forty-three. Is that what you're saying?"

The look in his eyes made her falter, and she lifted her hands in another helpless gesture. "Yes." She took a deep breath. "No. That's not the point."

"What is the point, Maggie?"

She swallowed hard and folded her arms. "I feel as if I'm robbing you, Tony. And to be honest, I'd feel guilty every time we got a funny look. We're at different phases in our lives. You'll probably want kids someday."

With his gaze riveted on her, he came toward her in a loose-hipped saunter, an unnerving expression in his eyes. "I might. I might not." He folded his arms and tipped his head to one side, narrowing his eyes in contemplation. "Although I must admit, this is a damned interesting topic, seeing as we've known each other less than a month and been out on one date."

Feeling outmaneuvered and trapped by his comment, as well as totally exposed, Maggie turned away and tried to reorganize her thoughts. Drawing up her shoulders, she turned to face him, not quite able to meet his gaze. "I'm sorry," she said, her voice subdued. "That was pretty presumptuous of me. But I was trying to make a—"

He cut her off. "I never said it was presumptuous, Maggie," he corrected. "I said it was interesting."

Thrown off balance by the look in his eyes, she folded her arms and looked away. Finally she spoke. "What I'm trying to do," she said, her tone even, "is to stop this before someone gets hurt."

"I see. And what does that mean, exactly?"

She turned her head and looked at him. She hesitated for a moment, then answered, "Our life-styles are continents apart, Tony. Surely you can see that."

He braced his arm on the closet door and rested his hand on his hip, scrutinizing her with unnerving steadiness. "No," he said flatly. "I can't. Why don't you draw me a picture?"

A tight lump formed in her throat, and Maggie looked up at the ceiling, waiting for the burning sensation behind her eyes to pass. Exhaling unevenly, she rubbed the aching spot between her eyes. There was a long pause, then she lifted her head and looked at him. "Your life is exciting," she said, her voice barely above a whisper. "*You're* exciting. You take life by the throat and live it, Tony. I don't. In fact, my life is pretty dull. *I'm* pretty dull."

Still standing with his arm braced against the closet door and his hand jammed on his hip, he studied her for a long while, as if contemplating her very existence. "So?"

A funny flutter unfolded in Maggie's midriff, and she turned and stared out the window, nervously rubbing the side of her finger with her thumb.

"Come on, Maggie," he said, his tone unrelenting. "Don't leave me hanging. Let's get right down to the bottom line. Why are you so ready to bail out before we've really got started?"

Rubbing her palms together, she swallowed hard, the flutter in her middle moving up to her throat. Sensing his gaze on her hands, she shoved them into the pockets of her slacks.

"I'm not letting you out of here until you level with me."

Withdrawing her hands from her pockets, she folded her arms, her heart suddenly pounding.

"Maggie?" he prompted.

Feeling as if the room was closing in around her, she stared out the window once more, unable to come up with a sound answer. She took a deep, uneven breath and finally replied, not sure if it was the truth or not, "I think I'm just a passing fancy."

There was a brief silence, then he asked, his voice oddly quiet, "So you think I'm using *you?*"

Badly shaken by his question, she whirled and stared at him, every bit of warmth draining from her face. "God, no," she whispered, horrified that he might think that. "No."

He straightened and rested his hands on his hips, watching her with a considering gaze. He studied her a moment, then spoke again, his unshaven face giving nothing away. "What do you think I see in you?"

She made a helpless gesture with her hands. "I don't know."

He continued to stare at her, his eyes unreadable in the soft light coming from the bedside lamp; then he shifted his weight and spoke again. "Okay. Then what do you want from me?"

Feeling suddenly very close to tears, Maggie rubbed her upper arms. It took her a minute before she could get the words out. "I want us to be friends."

The muscles in his jaw twitched and a hard glitter appeared in his eyes. He came toward her, like a big cat stalking its prey. "I don't want to be your friend," he said, his voice dangerously soft. "And I'm sure as hell not looking for another mother or sister. So that doesn't leave us much, does it?" He stopped a foot from her, his eyes glinting with anger. "But I gotta tell you, Burrows. You are, without a doubt, the most thickheaded woman I've had the misfortune to meet. And I've met a few." He stared at her, his voice growing even softer. "Last night wasn't about friendship, babe. Don't think for a minute that it was."

Upset because she had angered him, and doubly upset because she was afraid she was going to cry, Maggie folded her hands into fists to keep from touching him. "This isn't really about me, Tony," she pleaded, trying to make him understand what she was trying to say. "It's about you. Can't you see this is all wrong?"

"I'll tell you what I think," he said with ominous quiet. "I think you have a pretty damned shallow perception of me. I do not go to bed with every woman I meet, and I'm not some high-flying swinger."

Realizing she had made it worse instead of better, Maggie turned away. Without meaning to, she had somehow managed to destroy the very thing she had wanted to protect. Knowing she was on the verge of coming apart, she picked up her handbag from the footlocker at the end of the bed. "I have to go," she whispered unevenly.

"So you're going to walk. Just like that."

Her back to him, she nodded once, her throat so tight she couldn't even swallow.

"Fine. If you think what happened between us is so damned insignificant that you can walk out of here without a second glance, then I'm sure as hell not wasting my breath." He crossed to the bedroom door and rested his shoulder against the frame, partially blocking her escape route. Then he folded his arms, his face cold with anger. "Just remember, Mags. This decision is yours, not mine. I was willing to give this thing between us a shot, but you won't even give it a chance. I thought you had more balls than that." He paused, then spoke again, his tone cutting. "So go home, Maggie. And hide in your house. And watch life pass you by. Just remember that sometimes there aren't any second chances."

Feeling as if he had just cut the ground out from under her, Maggie brushed passed him, her vision blurring and a cold, sick feeling radiating through her. There was nothing left for her to say. He had said it all.

Maggie sat at her desk, a computer printout spread before her, but the glare from the desk lamp made her eyes burn, and she reached over and shut it off. She had turned off the overhead lights for the same reason, but nothing helped. Propping her elbow on the printout, she covered her eyes with her hand, trying to get rid of the ache in her throat. Lord, but she was a mess. She couldn't eat. She couldn't sleep. She was miserable all the time, and she had a big, aching, empty hole inside her that just would not go away. It was more than a week since she'd walked out on Tony, and it wasn't getting any better. In fact, it was getting worse. Nothing made sense—not her life, not her job. And definitely not the account she was working on.

Resisting the urge to rip the printout into tiny pieces, she snatched a tissue out of the nearly empty box wedged beside her computer and angrily wiped her eyes and blew her nose. Then she tossed it in her wastebasket, which was damned near full of wadded-up tissues.

That made her eyes fill up again, and she braced her elbow on the desk and covered her eyes. This was ridiculous. She hadn't fallen apart this badly when Bruce had walked out on her. Or when the kids had left home. Or when she'd had to have the dog put down. She could stack all those losses together and they still wouldn't add up to what she was feeling now.

It was so stupid. This was what she'd wanted. Well, maybe not exactly. She hadn't wanted to make him angry. And she hadn't wanted him to see any of her shortcomings. But she had. And he did. And now she was a mess.

She should have known better. She'd sensed he was a load of dynamite the minute he'd come up her walk. But had she used her head? No, of course not.

"What are you doing?"

Wishing her boss would just leave her alone, and irritated by his abrupt tone, she snapped back, "I'm having a stroke. Is that okay with you?"

Frank chuckled, and she felt him rest his considerable weight on the corner of her desk. "You know what I think?" he asked, as if she actually cared. "I think you're coming down with that flu again, Burrows. You look like something the dog dragged in. Your eyes are red and puffy all the time, and you sound like you've got horseradish stuffed up your nose."

The horseradish thing almost made her smile. "You're such a comfort, Frank," she retorted, her voice laced with sarcasm.

He patted her awkwardly on the shoulder. "Go home, Mary Margaret. Have three hot toddies and go to bed. You gotta start taking care of yourself."

Feeling mean about snapping at him, Maggie heaved a sigh and dropped her arm. Avoiding his gaze, she turned and pressed a key on the computer, deactivating the screen saver. "I'm fine," she lied. "It must be allergies or something."

He patted her shoulder again and stood up. "Hey, just don't think you have to stick around here. Hell, I'd leave if I had a good enough excuse. Except I've got some work I gotta do."

He lumbered back into his office, and Maggie almost smiled when she heard a distinctive bomb blast a few seconds later. Frank had a lot to do all right. He was in there playing computer games.

Swiveling her chair around so she could look out the window, Maggie propped her chin in her hand, watching the traffic go by. It was rainy and heavily overcast and just plain dismal, the steady drizzle turning everything gray. She'd always liked days like today. For some reason she found them oddly comforting. She stared out the window a moment longer, then heaved another sigh and turned back to her computer. With all the lights out and the grayness from outside infiltrating the room, maybe she'd be able to get through this account after all.

It rained all the next week, which suited Maggie just fine. She had started taking another route from work, which took her a block out of her way, but was better than walking past Tony's shop every night.

On Friday they found out one of their clients was being audited by Revenue Canada, which made Frank rub his hands in glee. The news made Maggie's head ache, but it gave her an excuse to go to work on the weekend. There was a swim meet in town, and the thought of sitting in a crowd of clapping, cheering people was more than she could handle. Except the thought of rattling around in an empty house was even worse.

By Monday, a kind of numbness had settled in, and she was able to more or less operate on remote control during the day. She went to work, came home and tried to find something to do to keep herself busy.

Nights were the worst. She'd fall into bed around ten o'clock, absolutely exhausted. But sleep never came easily. The awful sense of loss would rise up in her, and she would hurt so badly she could barely stand it. Then she'd get up and wander around the house, going over things again and again in her mind, and sometimes terrible doubts would seep in and her heart would start to pound. And then she'd try to convince herself it was for the best. But one thing remained constant: she had never missed anyone the way she missed Tony.

Wednesday night was particularly bad. The loneliness was so intense that she couldn't stand it, and it was just going on four-thirty in the morning when she finally gave up on sleep and went out to the kitchen. Night was starting to fade, and in spite of the fine mist falling and the overcast sky, early morning gloom had seeped into the house. Without turning on the light she filled the teakettle and plugged it in, then got the hot chocolate mix and a mug out of the cupboard.

She opened the window above the sink to let in some fresh air and the clean scent of rain. It was so still outside that the fine drizzle was coming straight down, pricking the surface of the puddle behind Tony's shop. Leaning against the counter, she folded her arms and stared out, an awful heaviness settling in her chest. It was not good for her mental health to be standing where she was. Not only did the window overlook the back of Tony's shop, from where she was standing she could see the stairs leading up to his apartment. And sometimes, when the loneliness was really bad, she'd stand there in the middle of the night, hoping to catch a glimpse of him.

The kettle started to boil, and she reached over and un-plugged it, then pried the lid off the chocolate mix with the end of her spoon. She smiled a little. Her morning bouts with hot chocolate were turning into some kind of addiction.

She heard the approach of a fast-moving car, the dawn stillness carrying the sound. There was a squeal of tires on wet pavement in front of her house, then the solid clunk of a vehicle jouncing over a curb, and a police cruiser, red and blue lights flashing, careened through the space between her fence and Tony's shop. The car had barely rocked to a stop when the apartment door slammed, and Tony came sprinting down the stairs two at a time, his shirt unbuttoned, his jogging shoes in his hand. He yanked open the passenger door, dived inside, and before he even had the door closed, the car shot out of the parking area and into the back alley.

A cold, sinking sensation filled her stomach as Maggie stared after it. It had to be an accident. She closed her eyes, her legs suddenly shaky. She prayed to God it wasn't someone in his family.

The awful anxiety stayed with her, and she spent the next hour going from the kitchen window to the one in the front room, then back again. She hated this helpless feeling. There was nobody she could call, nothing she could do but pace and chew her nails.

She watched Tony's place until six-thirty, then made herself get dressed for work. Maybe it wasn't an accident at all. Maybe it had something to do with an old case Tony had worked on. Maybe he had to go identify somebody.

Dumping her cold chocolate down the sink, she made a pot of coffee, trying to talk herself out of feeling the way she did. She was probably making mountains out of molehills.

Switching on the radio to catch the seven o'clock news, she opened the door of the fridge to get a basket of strawberries.

The announcer's voice echoed in the silence. "...And a Calgary undercover police officer was shot early this morning. The downed officer was discovered at approximately 4:00 a.m. when he failed to report in. Sergeant Peter James Layden received a bullet in the chest in what a police spokesperson described as a single shooting. Sergeant Layden, a fifteen-year veteran on the force, was rushed to Calgary General Hospital, where he is reported to be in critical condition. KS 87 will issue news bulletins as more details become available. Also on the news this morning..."

The broadcaster's voice droned on, and Maggie straightened, feeling the color drain from her face. It all fit together. She'd be willing to bet her life that they had come to get Tony because of the shooting.

Her stomach churning, she set the berries back in the fridge and closed the door, then went to stand in front of the window overlooking her backyard. Folding her arms, she stared out. She remembered what it had been like when her father had been admitted to the hospital in critical condition. Only this was a gunshot wound, and that would probably mean surgery, which meant Tony could be waiting for hours before there was any word.

Releasing a heavy sigh, she turned from the window. Lord, she wished it would stop raining.

The report of the shooting was the feature story on every news broadcast that day. Maggie finally had to shut off the radio at work because every time they mentioned it, her insides would ball up. She would start wondering how Tony was coping, and then she'd feel even worse.

It wasn't until nine that night that news of the officer's death was finally released. The brief update on TV also reported that he was survived by his wife and two small children. Experiencing a rush of nausea in the pit of her stomach, Maggie shut off the TV and went to stand in front of the living room window, thinking about the young wife and family he'd left behind. She could only imagine what the woman was feeling right now—the shock, the horror, the numb feeling of disbelief. And how scared she must be.

A fine drizzle again spattered against the window, sending thin rivulets of water down the pane, and Maggie watched, her expression somber. The cloud cover had settled even lower, casting the street in a premature dusk that neutralized all color.

"Mom?"

Maggie turned from the window. "In here."

Kelly appeared in the archway, dressed in an old pair of her grandfather's flannel pajamas. "Do we have any more double-A batteries? I need 'em for my Walkman."

Maggie nodded. "In the second drawer of my desk." She leaned back against the window frame. "Are you going to bed already?"

"Yeah. Some of us are going to try and get some lap time before school tomorrow, so I have to be up by six."

Kelly started down the hallway. "Kelly?"

She turned and looked back. Maggie tried to keep her voice even. "I think I might go for a walk. Being cooped up all week is beginning to get to me."

Kelly nodded. "Just make sure you've got your key. I can't hear the doorbell from down there."

Maggie nodded. She watched Kelly disappear from view, then straightened. Feeling totally drained, she went over to the front closet and got out her raincoat. She felt as much like going for a walk as she felt like flying, but she just had to get out of the house.

Heavy dusk had settled in by the time she'd walked all the way down to Fourteenth Street and back, but she didn't feel any better. All she could think about was the shooting and what an awful tragedy it was. And the young widow left to raise two small children without a father.

Stuffing her hands in the pockets of her raincoat, she turned down the final block, her mood as heavy as the weather. It was ironic how life could blow up in your face. Her grandmother had always told her to live each day as if it was her last. Maggie had always thought Gran had used that philosophy as an excuse to be slightly frivolous, but she was beginning to realize she had missed the fundamental message her grandmother had been trying to pass on. Maggie fingered her grandmother's wedding ring. Too bad she hadn't understood that message sooner.

Bruce had spent their whole married life worrying about their old age and hoarding for the future. He was so focused on that that he had never really taken a deep breath and made the most out of the present. And, she realized, neither had she. She had never thought about what her regrets would be if she were to find out she had only one more day to live. There would be several—but one that stood out above all the rest.

Skirting a huge puddle by the curb, she crossed the street, a funny feeling unfolding in her when she saw that one of the big bay doors of the Parnelli shop was open.

The faint sound of music was coming from the battered radio on the workbench, and it wasn't until Maggie was just outside that she realized it was Debussy. The music was unexpected, but the sight of Spider under the hood of a car was doubly so. One corner of her mouth lifted. Spider listening to "Clair de Lune"—who would have thought it.

She hesitated a moment, then walked up the cement parking area and entered the brightly lit garage, the smell of very old coffee overriding the smell of motor oil.

He glanced up from under the hood when he heard her approach, then straightened, a wrench in his hand and a twinkle in his eye. "Well, if it ain't the red-hot mama with the big pool cue."

She gave him a wry smile. "Watch it, Spider, or I'm going to blab it around that you listen to Debussy and your tattoo is a phony."

He chuckled and pulled a rag out of his back pocket, wiping a spot of grease off one of the chromed engine parts before crawling back under the hood. Maggie watched him work, knowing enough about engines to recognize this was a piece of art. He tightened a bolt, then turned his head and glanced at her. "You here to check out my tattoo or you got somethin' on your mind?"

She held his gaze for a moment, then looked down and shifted a bolt with her foot, feeling as if she were trespassing. Finally she lifted her head and looked at him. "I saw a police cruiser at Tony's this morning, and I wondered if it had something to do with that shooting."

Spider made a disgusted sound and tossed the wrench into a big red tool chest. "It had something to do, all right. Him and Tony worked the strip together for two or three years. Hell, when I broke parole, them two kept my ass out of a sling. Got me work with Mario, made sure I kept my nose clean, told the parole officer there was extenuatin' circumstances. Helluvah good guy. I tell you this—I'd like to get my hands on the bastard that shot him."

The fact that Spider had been on parole really didn't come as a surprise, but the fact that two cops had bailed him out certainly did. Huddling her shoulders against the damp chill, she studied him. There was hard, cold anger in his expression, but the tight lines around his mouth said something else altogether. A feeling of recognition closed around her chest, and she looked away. She knew that expression. She'd seen it on her own face when her father died. Staring across the street, Maggie stuffed her hands deeper into her pockets, experiencing a rush of remembered grief. She wondered how Tony was coping with the loss of someone he'd been so close to.

As if reading Maggie's mind, Spider said, "The boss got home a couple of hours ago. Looks like hell, but he ain't talkin'. Don't expect he'll surface for a day or two."

Maggie gazed at the mechanic, not quite sure how to respond, but Spider was intent on reconnecting a hose. She looked away, feeling hollowed out inside. She was probably the last person Tony would want to see right now, and that was hard enough. But knowing he was upstairs alone was even worse.

Spider tossed a clamp into the tool caddie, the loud clatter jarring the silence, and Maggie shifted her gaze. He selected another wrench and braced one hand on the engine, reaching down into the maze of hoses and belts. "Yep," he said, as if talking to himself, "he ain't in good shape at all."

Locking her jaws against the ache forming in her throat, Maggie lifted her head and stared across the street, the fine drizzle glimmering like threads of silver in the light spilling out from the open bay door. She couldn't bear to think of him alone. She just couldn't.

Without giving herself a chance to reconsider, she turned and walked out of the garage, the rain cold against her face as she turned toward the back of the building. Her stomach churning, she climbed the stairs, the beads of moisture on the handrail dampening her hand. Reaching the top landing, she faced the door. Then, steeling herself, she raised her hand to knock on the wooden panel. Reconsidering, she hesitated, then tried the knob, her insides giving a lurch when the latch gave beneath her hand. Taking a deep breath, she closed her eyes for a second, then pushed open the door.

The apartment was dark except for a faint blue glow in the living room and the illumination coming from a light in the hallway. As she closed the door soundlessly behind her, she heard the distinctive shuffle of a CD cartridge, and an old Otis Redding song started up. Wiping her damp hands down the front of her jeans, she swallowed hard, then moved toward the sound.

The blue light was coming from the muted TV, the screen silently displaying the printed text of the information channel. Tony was sitting on the sofa, his feet propped on the coffee table, a bottle of rye wedged between his thighs. He looked dangerously grim, his unshaven jaw rigid with tension, his mouth compressed into a hard, unyielding line.

Reaching the archway, Maggie paused, her stomach turning into a mass of knots. Trying to compress the awful flutter in her middle, she drew in a deep breath, then spoke. "Tony?"

Without so much as a glance in her direction, he closed his eyes and took a swig from the bottle, his rebuff as pointed as it was silent.

Maggie experienced a heavy, sinking sensation in her middle, and her first impulse was to turn and leave. But something kept her rooted there. And it was then—when she saw the hard lines of control in his face—that she realized just how much she had hurt him. He took another drink, and the deliberateness of what he was doing cut through her. She crossed the room, her throat so tight her jaws ached.

Kneeling beside him, she tried to pry his fingers off the bottle. "Let me have it, Tony," she whispered unevenly.

He jerked the bottle out of her grasp, his tone rough with anger. "Get out. I don't want you here."

Feeling as if she had somehow betrayed him, she again tried to disengage his hand from the bottle. "If you want me out," she whispered, her voice uneven, "you're going to have to throw me out."

He abruptly let go, and she rested her forehead against the neck of the bottle, relief making her pulse hammer. Composing her expression, she set the bottle on the coffee table and turned back, her heart contracting painfully when she saw the stark lines etched in his face. Sucking in a raspy breath, she gave his hand a reassuring squeeze, and Tony abruptly bent his head, gouging at his eyes with his thumb and forefinger. Unable to stand it any longer, she moved onto the sofa, then slipped her arm around him. Whispering his name, she tried to draw him against her. For an instant he resisted, then he let his breath go in a shaky rush and turned his face against her neck.

Her chest full and tears burning her eyes, Maggie tightened her hold, trying to offer what comfort she could.

It was a long time later when Tony released an unsteady sigh, then slid his hand under her raincoat. "You're wet," he whispered gruffly.

She swallowed hard and stroked his hair, her voice wobbling a little when she answered, "I was out walking in the rain." He inhaled unevenly, then relaxed his hold. Without meeting her gaze, he eased her away from him, then slid his hand in the front opening of her raincoat, as if he were cold.

Untangling herself Maggie stood up and stripped off the damp garment. She tossed it on the coffee table, then reached down and grasped his hand. "Come on," she whispered unevenly. "You're going to bed."

He stared at her for a split second, then looked away, the muscles in his jaw bunching. Without meeting her gaze again, he slowly got to his feet, as if the effort was more than he could handle. Her own emotions far too close to the surface, Maggie turned and started toward the hall, her chin set with resolve. She was going to take care of him, whether he wanted her to or not.

Once she got him to the bedroom, she let go of his hand and started straightening the tangle of bedding. A fresh frenzy of nerves unfolded in her belly, and the flutter climbed higher as she smoothed out the sheets. He never spoke, and neither did she; it was almost as if they were two strangers, neither one sure of the other.

Her whole body stiff with tension, she tossed the comforter onto the bed, then tugged it straight. She heard the rasp of a zipper, then heard him shucking off his jeans as she turned her back to the bed and began picking up some clothes she had swept onto the floor. The bed shifted, and her heart gave a lurch. Closing her eyes, she forced in a deep, steadying breath—one wrong move, and she knew she was going to fall apart.

Maggie finished folding a T-shirt and placed it on the dresser. Resisting the urge to wipe her hands down the front of her jeans, she turned back toward the bed. Tony was stretched out on his back with one arm draped across his eyes, the sheet covering the lower half of his body. He looked as tense as she felt.

She hesitated, self-doubt churning through her. Then, drawing up her courage, she went around the end of the bed.

Her legs feeling like jelly, she sat down beside him, then very carefully combed back his hair. Trying to will away the wild flutter in her throat, she said, her voice catching a little, "Can I get you anything?"

Without moving his arm, he shook his head, the muscles along his jaw tight. Worried, Maggie went to smooth her fingers along his temple, but Tony caught her wrist, trapping her hand. He didn't say anything for a moment, then he spoke, his voice low. "Don't."

Maggie stared down at him, a surge of regret making her heart contract. She had never meant to hurt him. But she had been so caught up in her own self-doubts that she had never really looked at things from his point of view. He was right: she hadn't given them a chance. In all her agonizing over the right or wrong of Tony Parnelli, she had missed one critical fact: nothing was for certain. Nothing. One dead police officer was testament to that. She had been wrestling with all the reasons why she should back away. She had never looked at all the reasons why she should take whatever time she had with him and hold on to it for however long it lasted.

A nearly unbearable swell of emotion rising in her, she closed her eyes and touched his face with her free hand, trying to communicate by touch alone what she was feeling.

The muscles in his jaw flexed and he tightened his grip on her hand, as if he was trying to ward off some deep, painful emotion. And Maggie knew it was because of her.

Braced by that realization, she twisted her wrist out of his grasp and stood up, her motions jerky as she kicked off her shoes, then stripped off her wet slacks, angry tears burning her eyes. God, she had been so stupid.

Tossing her slacks on top of his jeans, she slipped into bed beside him, then slid her arm under his neck. "Come here, love," she whispered, her voice catching. "Let me hold you."

He remained stiff and unmoving for an instant, then he let his breath go and turned into her arms, a tremor coursing through him. Swallowing hard against the lump in her throat, she drew his head onto her breast and cradled him against her, tightening her arms around him. She had not worn a bra under her thin cotton sweater, and the rough stubble on his jaw prickled her skin, but she didn't care. Nothing mattered except that he was letting her hold him.

Clenching her jaw against the awful ache in her throat, she drew him tighter into her embrace and pressed her cheek against the top of his head, cherishing the hard warmth of his body against hers. She would be content to hold him like this all night long, if he'd let her.

A cool, damp breeze wafted in through the open window. Maggie drew the sheet up over his shoulders and nestled closer, trying to ward off the chill. Tony stirred and released a heavy sigh, pulling away from her as he rolled onto his back. He rested his arm across his eyes again, and Maggie glanced at him, apprehension warring with concern. She didn't know if he was withdrawing from her specifically or if he had just retreated deep within himself. Uncertainty made her waver, and she sat up, debating whether she should stay or go. But before she had a chance to make up her mind, he moved his arm and looked at her.

Even in the half light spilling in from the hallway, Maggie could see the taut set of his jaw and the hard, unwavering expression in his eyes. He stared at her a moment, then spoke, a demanding edge in his tone. "Do you mind telling me what you're doing here?"

Feeling every inch of the distance between them, Maggie looked down, a terrible sense of loss radiating through her. She had really messed things up. Maybe to the point where she couldn't put them right. The ache in her chest expanded, and she fingered a loose thread in the hem of the sheet, trying to will away the threat of tears.

With that same insistent tone in his voice, he prompted "Maggie?"

She tried to clear away the cramp in her throat, but a renewed sense of loss welled up in her and her vision blurred. How could she explain that this wasn't about sympathy, it was about regret?

The bed dipped as he shifted his weight, then he grasped her face and pulled her head around, forcing her to look at him. He was propped up on one elbow, watching her with an unwavering stare, the dark stubble accentuating the stern set of his jaw. Compelled by the pressure of his hand, she held his gaze, desolation nearly overwhelming her. Trying to clear her throat, she took a deep, unsteady breath, then forced herself to speak. "I've made such a mess of things," she whispered, her tears finally spilling over. "And I needed to tell you that I'm sorry."

He studied her, as if weighing her response, then closed his eyes and released his breath in a rush. Grasping the back of her neck, he dragged her down into a crushing hold, his hand tangling in her damp hair. "God, Maggie," he whispered hoarsely. "I'd just about given up on you."

A sob of relief escaped her, and Maggie slid her arms around him and hung on, not wanting to cry, afraid she was going to. But Tony never gave her the chance. Dragging her beneath him, he spanned her jaw with his hand and tipped her head back, a heated message in his dark, intent gaze. Then, leaving his hand as a barrier against his beard, he closed his eyes and covered her mouth in a kiss that decimated her. Another sob escaped her, and Maggie tightened her hold and opened her mouth beneath his, tears slipping down her temple.

This was more than she had hoped for. And all that she wanted.

# Chapter 9

Maggie lay with her head on Tony's shoulder, snuggled deep in his embrace, drifting in a haze of lassitude as she listened to the sound of the rain on the roof. Her whole body sated, she drowsily watched the blind wavering in the breeze that was coming in through the open window, feeling cocooned in the warmth of their shared body heat. Their lovemaking had been fast and wild, her climax shattering, and she'd felt as if her body had exploded into a million little pieces. But now boneless lethargy had set in, and she wasn't sure she could have moved even if she'd wanted to.

His jaw resting against the top of her head, Tony slowly stroked her arm, as if he was there but his mind was somewhere else. Reminded of the tragedy that had brought her to him, and feeling guilty because she had temporarily forgotten his loss, she smoothed her hand up his rib cage. "Spider told me what happened," she whispered softly. "I'm really sorry, Tony."

He released a heavy sigh and gave her shoulder an acknowledging squeeze. There was a brief pause, then he spoke, his tone resigned. "Yeah. Unfortunately, it happens."

She raised up on one elbow and looked at him, her expression solemn. "Do you want to talk about it?" she asked, her tone soft.

He caught a piece of her hair and rubbed his thumb against it, the light from the hallway casting shadows across his unshaven face. Finally he looked at her, his gaze flat and unreadable. "So is that what this is about? You delivering condolences?"

Realizing how ready he was to mistrust her motives, Maggie experienced a hollow rush of remorse. She had done that to him. A sick feeling radiating through her, she swallowed against the sudden cramp in her throat. Covering his hand with her own, she shook her head, unable to speak.

He stared at her for an instant, his expression unsmiling, then he exhaled heavily and caught her arm, pulling her down against him. Brushing her hair back, he pressed a kiss against her forehead, then nestled her head on his shoulder. He continued to rub his fingers up and down her spine, and Maggie knew from the stillness in him that he was staring off into space. Finally he gave her a light squeeze and spoke. "I don't want you here for the wrong reasons, Maggie," he said firmly.

She turned her face against him, then exhaled unevenly. She knew she owed him her honesty, for what it was worth. She took a deep breath, then closed her eyes tight. "I don't know what I'm doing," she whispered, her voice breaking a little. "I'm just a damned mess."

She felt him smile against her forehead. She hadn't been sure how he would respond to her confession, but she definitely had not expected a smile. He gave her neck another reassuring squeeze, then answered, a tinge of amusement in his voice, "Confusion I can handle, Burrows. As long as you don't keep slamming doors in my face."

Experiencing a nearly unbearable swell of emotion, Maggie slipped her arms around him and hugged him hard, trying to control the mounting pressure in her chest. Just like that, he had forgiven her. She had never experienced that kind of generosity in her whole life.

Pressing her face against his neck, she held him with every ounce of strength she had, trying to tell him by touch alone how grateful she was.

Tony released a long, uneven sigh, then dragged her up on top of him, enveloping her in a tight embrace. He turned his head and kissed the curve of her neck, clamping her hips flush against his. Then he separated her legs with his knee and settled her more intimately against him, his mouth hot, wet and arousing against the unbearably sensitive hollow of her throat. Maggie clenched her eyes shut, her breathing suddenly ragged, her heart suddenly too big for her chest. Tony caught her knee and drew it up alongside his hip, opening her to him, and she clutched at him as he slowly, so slowly, rubbed himself against her. With one touch, her senses swam out of focus and she was lost in the sensations he aroused in her. Every time was like the first time with him.

It was slower, sweeter, softer that time around, but for Maggie, twice as devastating. With every touch, every slow stroke of flesh against flesh, it was as if Tony was memorizing every sight, every taste, every sound—every single sensation. The level of intimacy was like nothing she'd ever known before, and by the time they were finished, she didn't know where his body left off and hers began.

Now, twenty minutes later, she felt totally cleansed—and closer to him than she'd ever thought possible.

She was still lying on top of him, and Tony slowly stroked his hand down her head, pulling her hair back behind her ear. Thrusting his fingers along her jaw, he lifted his head and softly kissed her forehead. "Are you okay?" he whispered huskily.

Without opening her eyes, she nodded and smiled. "Perfect." He stroked her hair again, and Maggie arched under his touch. She'd had no idea how wonderful it felt just to be petted.

Finally forcing herself to move, she propped her head on her hand and gazed down at him. Earlier Tony had turned on the small bedside lamp so he could watch her as they made love, and now she studied his face. When she'd moved, he had let his hand drift down to the base of her spine, and he was lying with his eyes closed, slowly caressing a vertebra with his thumb.

His mouth tempted her, and she ran her finger along his bottom lip. "How about you?"

His eyes still closed, he responded with a wry smile. "I think I blew a valve."

There was something about his smile that struck her as forced, and Maggie considered him, her expression sober. Knowing she was going to have to be the one to broach the tragedy that had happened early that morning, she began fondling his tousled hair. Keeping her expression neutral, she asked, "Just how bad was it at the hospital?"

His whole body stiffened and he tried to push her away, but Maggie had her arms around him before he could roll free. Grasping the back of his head, she held him to her. "Just talk to me, Tony," she whispered against his hair. "Tell me about him. You can't shut everything up as if nothing happened."

He remained stiff and unyielding for several seconds, then released his pent-up breath in a rush. Turning his face against her neck, he held on to her, as if trying to absorb something from her. Finally he eased his hold and pulled away. "I need a cigarette," he said, his voice taut.

Not sure what was going on, Maggie let him go. His back to her, he got out of bed and pulled on his jeans. Not bothering to do up the zipper, he left the bedroom. Tucking the sheet around her, Maggie sat up and locked her arms around her upraised knees. Her expression stark, she stared at the empty doorway, debating whether she should go after him or not. She was running on gut reaction as far as he was concerned. And maybe that was absolutely the worst thing for him right now.

She was still sitting there, trying to figure out what she should do, when Tony came back into the room with a lighted cigarette, a pack of cigarettes and an ashtray grasped in one hand. His face devoid of expression, he picked up a chair and swung it around to face the bed. Still without looking at her, he sat down and propped his feet on the mattress, taking a deep drag on his cigarette. Balancing the ashtray on one thigh, he knocked off the ash, his face etched with strain.

Maggie watched, hurting down to her soul for him. Trying to ease the tense silence, she said, "So when did you start smoking?"

He finally looked at her, a small smile lifting one corner of his mouth. "When I was about twelve."

She gave him a stare that she'd often used on her kids. "Don't play games with me, Antonio."

A glimmer of real amusement appeared in his eyes. Finally he answered, "All right, Warden. I quit about eight years ago. This is the first time I fell off the wagon since, okay?"

She raised her hand in an arresting gesture. "Hey. You don't have to make excuses to me. They're your lungs."

He continued to stare at her, the glint intensifying. "Fine. Now do you want to tell me about the cigarette burn I saw on the dresser in your bedroom?"

"No," she answered, staring back at him. "I don't."

Amusement still hovered around his mouth as he gave his head a little shake. "I didn't think so." He took another drag on the cigarette, and Maggie watched him, her arms still locked around her sheet-draped knees.

The smile fading, Tony looked down and rolled the lighted end of his cigarette along the lip of the ashtray, his expression shuttered. A frown appeared, and Maggie knew he was wrestling with some very deep feelings. Then without lifting his head, he started to talk.

He told her about the first case he and Pete Layden were assigned to, how they both eventually worked undercover, how the stress finally got to Pete and how he had started drinking. He told her about how he'd finally talked his partner into getting some help, and why he had decided to leave the force.

It was a long story, and Maggie didn't ask any questions. She didn't offer any comments; she just listened, knowing that's what he needed from her right then. After crushing out his second cigarette, he told her how Pete had finally realized that the undercover work and the whole dirty drug scene were screwing with his mind, and he had finally asked to be taken off the drug squad.

It was at this point that Tony stopped talking, and Maggie watched him, wishing with all her heart that there was some way she could make it easier for him. He was slouched in the chair, one leg cocked across the other knee, and there was so much strain in his face that it made her heart ache just to look at him. A cool breeze wafted in through the window, and she tucked the sheet tighter around herself, then rested her arm on her upraised knee as she solemnly assessed him. Somehow they had to get through the rest of it. Somehow.

She hesitated for a moment, then asked, "So how come he was out there alone last night?"

Tony broke apart the filter of a burned-out cigarette, his expression impassive. "They suspected that an old drug operation was gearing up again, and Pete knew all the players. He offered to go back in with the unit. I guess he figured he could finger the kingpins."

"But something went wrong."

Tony wiped his fingers on his jeans, then began folding the foil from the cigarette package. "Yeah. This slimeball met Pete at a bar. He was a small-time dealer when Pete and I were working together. We'd leaned on him pretty hard a couple of times, and he'd coughed up some key names that led to a major bust. The narcs didn't know that he'd moved into the big leagues, and no one had tied him to this new operation. I guess when he saw Pete in the bar, negotiating a buy, he went a little nuts. Some of the players in this operation were the same guys that he'd fingered when Pete and I had leaned on him. There's a big Colombian connection with this new operation, and he knew he'd turn up dead if anyone ever put two and two together."

His face like granite, Tony picked some fibers from the shredded filter off his jeans, then rolled them into a ball between his fingers. A muscle in his jaw jerked, and he tossed the bits of rolled-up fiber into the ashtray. There was a flat, bitter edge to his voice when he continued, "So he waited for Pete to leave the bar, then followed him. He cornered him in a back alley and screamed at him for mucking up his life. Then he shot him."

The horror made her stomach turn, and Maggie looked away, waiting for the awful feeling to settle in her middle. So violent. So senseless. She could only imagine what this must have done to Tony.

Knowing they couldn't stop now, she asked, her voice quiet, "Then what happened?"

Tony gave another lifeless shrug. "When Pete didn't check in, they sent a squad car out looking for him. As close as they can figure, he was in that alley for over two hours before they found him."

The lack of emotion in his voice wrenched at her, and it was all Maggie could do to keep from going to him. Trying to retain some emotional distance, she looked down and began pleating the fabric lying across her knees. She gave herself a few seconds, then she spoke again. "I take it they notified you right away."

Tony shifted in his chair, then exhaled heavily. "Yeah. Pete regained consciousness after the paramedics got him in the ambulance, and he kept asking for me. He knew I'd be able to ID the guy because of the other case." There was a brief silence, then he added, "Pete died on the operating table. The doctor said with the amount of blood he'd lost, he didn't know how he'd hung on that long."

Feeling the emotional weight of that admission, Maggie looked at him, trying to think of something that could ease his burden just a little.

Still sitting with one leg cocked across the other, Tony pulled at a loose thread in the stitching around the cuff of his jeans, his expression fixed. "I joined the force because I thought law enforcement could make a difference." He yanked the thread loose and tossed it into the ashtray, his jaw rigid with anger. "But our system is so screwed up that the victims get nothing, and the civil libertarians go to all lengths to make sure the perps have their rights protected. There's no damned justice anymore."

Maggie looked at him, her expression somber. She understood his anger. She felt pretty much the same way herself. But she sensed the anger was only a cover-up for something that went much deeper. A nervous sensation unfolded in her belly, and she looked down, her expression even more somber as she smoothed out the wrinkles in the sheet. There was a line she wasn't sure if she should cross or not. Making her decision, she lifted her head and looked at him. "Don't start blaming yourself because you weren't there to cover his back, Tony," she chided softy. "You came through for him in the end, and that's what's important."

The muscles in his jaw bunched as he abruptly looked away, and Maggie caught the sheen of moisture in his eyes. Her own chest tight, she reached over and removed the ashtray from his knee, set it on the floor, then grasped his hand. "Come on," she whispered softly. "Come to bed." He didn't respond, and Maggie gave his hand another tug. "I want to hold you."

His face haggard with strain, he finally relented, expelling a shaky breath as he came into her arms. Cradling his head on her shoulder, Maggie flipped the comforter over them both, then tightened her arms around him, offering him what solace she could. Tony slid his arms around her and roughly turned his face against her neck, and she closed her eyes against the sudden contraction in her throat. God, he was so cold.

Pressing her face against his, she began rubbing his back, trying to warm him. If she kept it up long enough, maybe he would drift off to sleep. She released a soft sigh and settled deeper into the warm comfort of the bed. She could spend forever like this. Absolutely forever....

A low grumble of thunder brought her awake. It took a minute for consciousness to kick in; then she wet her lips, stirring a little against Tony's weight. Somewhere along the line, they had changed positions as they slept. She was now lying on her side with his body curved around her back, his one arm shoved under the pillow, the other locked around her middle. Feeling coddled, content and drowsy, she let her eyes drift shut as she smoothed her hand down his arm.

Maggie smiled to herself. She might have known that Tony Parnelli was a cuddler. What she hadn't known was how unbelievably good it would feel to wake up snuggled in somebody's arms. She lay there for another moment, savoring the feeling; then she sighed and opened her eyes. Raising her head, she looked at the clock radio on the bedside table. It was 2:17 a.m.

Maggie dropped her head back to the pillow, staring at the ceiling. As much as she wanted to remain right where she was, she knew in good conscience that she couldn't. She had a fifteen-year-old daughter she was supposed to be setting a good example for. Bracing herself for separation, she released another sigh, then carefully lifted Tony's arm away and pushed back the comforter. Now if she could only leave without waking him . . .

She turned off the lamp, hoping she wouldn't disturb him, then used the light from the hallway to collect her clothes. Slipping soundlessly out of the room, she went into the bathroom across the hall to get dressed, wishing with all her heart she didn't have to go. The last thing she wanted to do was leave him, but she really had no choice. There was Kelly to think about. Reluctance dragging at her, she pulled her cotton sweater down over the waistband of her slacks, then ran her fingers through her hair. Maybe she could find some paper and leave him a note; maybe then she wouldn't feel like such a traitor. She looked around the bathroom, then realized she had forgotten her shoes.

Trying to be absolutely silent, she entered the bedroom, then tiptoed around the end of the bed. It blocked the faint light coming from the hallway, and she crouched down, feeling around on the floor for her shoes. She had just located one when Tony spoke, an embittered edge in his voice. "Bailing out again, Burrows?"

Bracing her hand on the mattress, Maggie swiveled to look at him, his tone stopping her cold. She stared at him, her insides dropping away to nothing. After what she had done to him, she really couldn't expect him to think anything else. Letting go of her shoe, she sat on the edge of the bed, her touch deliberately soft as she caressed his face. "I'm not bailing out," she whispered unevenly. But she might as well have been touching a block of wood.

Feeling very small for hurting him the way she had, she ran her thumb along his jaw, then took a deep, shaky breath, knowing it was up to her to make things right. Gazing down at him, she said, her voice husky with sincerity, "I'd give my right arm to stay here tonight, Tony." She ran her fingertip across his brow, trying to will away the sting of tears. "But I have to think of Kelly. She's only fifteen, and I don't want to set a bad example."

Tony stared up at her, the muscles in his jaw set, and for one awful instant, he didn't say anything. Then he removed her hand and looked away. "Fine," he said, his tone as flat as the expression in his eyes.

Alarmed by his mistrust and knowing she deserved every bit of it, Maggie felt the color drain from her face. Realizing she was going to have to set her own self-doubts aside, she tried to bridge the gap between them. "Of course, you *could* come home with me. I can't offer you shared accommodations, but I have a great sofa in the living room."

He glanced back at her, his gaze intense and unwavering as he considered her.

Feeling desperately uncertain, she forced a small, wobbly smile and added, "And you'll have to behave yourself. I don't want to put any ideas into her head."

He considered her words for a moment, then shifted his gaze as he reached up and tucked her hair back. "No," he said, his voice suddenly gruff. "I'd better not. I don't want to put any ideas into her head, either."

Encouraged by his answer and unwilling to leave him when he was unsure of her, she softly caressed his ear. "Come home with me, Tony," she pleaded softly. "I don't want to leave you here alone."

He looked back at her, his expression less guarded. She smiled again. "I'll make you breakfast."

He stared at her a moment, then gave her a lopsided smile. "You will, huh?"

She leaned down and kissed him. "Yes, I will," she whispered against his mouth. Grabbing her by the back of the head, he opened his mouth and kissed her back, the moist caress of his tongue making her heart hammer. Clenching her hand into a fist, she tried to catch her breath, a heady weakness coursing through her. As if realizing where they were headed, Tony dragged his mouth away, forcing her head down against his. He held her immobile for a moment, then drew a deep breath. "I think we'd better get the hell off this bed," he whispered roughly. "Or we're going to be in big trouble here."

Maggie waited until the hot wash of desire dissipated a little, then she eased away, feeling definitely shaky. Tony swept her hair back with both hands and gave her neck a little squeeze. "Can you give me ten minutes?" he said, his voice still a little husky. "I'd like to grab a quick shower first."

Relief making her shaky inside, she forced herself to pull away. She managed another wobbly smile. "It's going to take me ten minutes to get my breath back."

He gave a husky laugh and sat up, planting a quick kiss on her nose. "I do like your style, Burrows." He threw back the blankets and got up, and Maggie closed her eyes, her heart still skittering around in her chest. Tony Parnelli was simply more than she could handle.

She had the bed made, the ashtray emptied and the living room straightened by the time Tony reappeared. He had on a clean pair of navy blue sweats and a white T-shirt, and he had shaved. His face was still etched with exhaustion, but he had some life back in his eyes.

Maggie gave him a smile. "Ready to go?"

He nodded and picked up her coat from the coffee table. He helped her put it on, then ran his hand up the back of her neck, pulling her hair free. "Are you dead sure about this?" he asked, his voice very quiet.

Adjusting the coat on her shoulders, she turned and faced him. "Yes," she said, meeting his solemn gaze. "Very sure."

He watched her a moment, then turned and picked up a navy windbreaker lying on the end of the sofa. The jacket had a police-department insignia on the shoulder, and Maggie experienced a rush in her middle. Not wanting him to see her reaction, she turned and pushed a cushion back into place on the sofa with her knee. Making sure her face gave nothing away, she turned and watched him shove his arms into the sleeves. He pulled up the collar and did up the bottom snap, then looked at her, his gaze dark and unreadable.

Needing to touch him, she ran the back of her fingers down his cleanly shaven cheek. "Nice," she said, smiling into his eyes.

He closed his eyes and grasped her shoulders, resting his forehead against hers. Finally he inhaled unevenly and released her. "We'd better go."

He waited for her to precede him, then shut off the lamp with the switch by the archway.

Maggie shoved her hands in her pockets and closed them into fists. She had a feeling it was going to be a long walk home.

And it was. By the time they reached her front door, she was so wound up inside that she was having trouble breathing. As if sensing the tension in her, Tony took the key from her hand and unlocked the inside door, pushing it open so she could enter. Kelly had left a light on in the front entrance, and Maggie felt as if the brightness was stripping her skin off. Certain she would unravel completely if she so much as looked at him, she kicked off her damp shoes. She heard the click as he closed the door and set the dead bolt; then she heard him toss the keys onto the entranceway table.

Maggie stripped off her coat and hung it in the closet, then closed her eyes and tried to force a deep breath into her lungs. She wanted to feel him against her so badly she could hardly stand it. Tony hung his jacket alongside hers, then caught her arm. Turning her to face him, he pulled her close, then enfolded her in a tight, protective embrace. "I know, babe," he whispered roughly. "I know."

He kissed her ear, then forced her head against his neck. Slipping her arms around him, Maggie expelled a shaky breath and flattened her hands against his back. Never in her life had she experienced such an overwhelming need to be held. Clutching him tighter, she turned her face into the curve of his neck, absorbing the clean, rain-damp scent of him, trying to regulate her breathing. Tucking his face against hers, Tony massaged the small of her back, holding her even tighter, his own breathing uneven. He smoothed his hands across her hips, then spoke, his voice low and strained. "Maybe it'd be a good idea if I cleared outta here."

Tightening her hold, she shook her head.

He wrapped both his arms around her, hugging her hard. "I won't let anything happen here, Mag," he said, his voice husky with assurance.

Maggie closed her eyes, trying to regain her equilibrium. She didn't want anything to happen here. Well, that wasn't quite true, but it would be enough if she could just hold him. One thing was for sure—she couldn't bear to let him go.

Tony turned his head and pressed his mouth against her neck, giving her another tight, oddly communicative squeeze. He held her like that until the surge of need eased, until she could relax her hold just a little. Then he smoothed his hand down the full length of her spine, his firm touch sending a fuzzy weakness through the lower half of her body. Looping his arms around her hips, he rubbed his jaw against her temple, then said, a touch of amusement in his tone, "I gotta tell you, you cook up one hell of a breakfast, Burrows."

Maggie let out her breath with a shaky laugh and hugged him back. "Maybe we'd better move to the kitchen."

Rubbing both hands down her buttocks, he kissed the sensitive spot below her ear, then released a heavy sigh. Sliding one hand down her arm, he laced his fingers through hers, then turned toward the front room. "Later," was all he said, his voice gruff.

Skirting the large coffee table, he led her over to the sofa, then tossed all the loose cushions except one onto the floor; that one he propped against the arm. Then he stretched out, pulling her down with him. Snuggling into a comfortable position, he drew her head onto his shoulder and wedged one knee between her legs. Nestling her deeper into his embrace, he cupped her face, his fingers tangling in her hair as he pressed a soft kiss against her forehead. "I don't want breakfast," he said gruffly. "I just want to hold you."

Closing her eyes on a swell of emotion, Maggie tucked her face under his jaw and slid her arm under the small of his back, turning deeper into his embrace. She wished she could climb right inside his body.

Tony brushed back her hair and sighed. "God, this feels good," he whispered unevenly.

Unable to answer him because of the sudden aching tenderness in her heart, Maggie tightened her arm around him, holding him closer. Dear Lord, this wasn't good. This was heaven.

The sound of a distant alarm clock brought Maggie out of a deep sleep, but it was the feel of a hard male body against her, of strong arms wrapped snugly around her that brought her fully awake. And it was the sound of the alarm being shut off that made her eyes snap open. Kelly. Six-o'clock swim. Mother all tangled up on the sofa with a man. Great! *Great way to set an example, Mary Margaret!* She closed her eyes, silently chastising herself. What would Kelly have thought if she'd walked in here and seen them?

*That her mother had finally got a life,* a tiny voice rebutted.

Maggie smiled. Kelly was nobody's fool.

Shifting her head on Tony's shoulder, she stared into space, unwilling to leave the secure warmth of his arms. This was the nicest of all possible ways to wake up. Warm. Surrounded by another person's heat. Feeling physically connected to another human being. There was only one flaw: the arm she was lying on was numb from her shoulder to her fingertips.

She heard the shower come on downstairs, but stayed right where she was. Ten more minutes. As soon as she heard the shower shut off, she'd get up. She wanted just a few more moments to savor waking up like this.

Tony sighed and stirred, slowly shifting one leg. Then he tightened his arm around her back, smoothing his hand—which she finally realized was *underneath* her sweater—up her rib cage to cup her naked breast. Maggie went dead still, her breath jamming up in her chest. It struck her that Tony Parnelli was just as dangerous asleep as he was fully awake. Closing her eyes and forcing herself to take deep breaths, she gave herself a moment to settle down, then started to ease away. He stirred again and tightened his hold.

Using the back of the sofa as a brace, she looked down at him, a small smile on her face. He did look adorable first thing in the morning. She watched him sleep for a minute, then tried again to extricate herself, but his only response was to turn his head and settle into a deeper sleep.

She gave his shoulder a little shake. "Tony?"

He rubbed his thumb along the swell of her breast, that one light touch nearly sending her through the roof. She gave his shoulder another little push and he turned his face toward her, but his eyelids remained closed. "Hmm?"

Feeling as if she was connected to a live current, she reached down to disengage his hand. "I have to get up," she said, her voice quivering a little. "Kelly will be up in a minute."

He slid his other hand under the waistband of her slacks. "No."

Maggie didn't know whether to laugh or to throttle him. "Tony," she said, striving for firmness, "I have to get up. Kelly will be coming upstairs any minute."

He finally opened his eyes, but then closed them again. "Hell," he muttered, his tone disgruntled. But he relaxed his hold.

His irritability made her smile, and she leaned down and gave him a light kiss. "Just go back to sleep, Parnelli." He didn't make it easy for her when she tried to disengage herself, but the minute she was free of him, he rolled onto his side, one arm hanging over the edge of the sofa. The early morning coolness made her shiver, and she picked up the antique afghan of her great-grandmother's that was draped over the sofa—the one she had forbidden anyone to touch—and covered him with it. Unable to just leave him like that, she brushed back his hair, then leaned down and kissed him again. He didn't move a muscle.

Hearing the shower shut off downstairs, Maggie resolutely turned toward the hallway, trying to rub some circulation back into her numb arm and feeling as if she was on some kind of high.

She washed her face, combed her hair and changed into an old sweatsuit in two minutes flat. She was in the kitchen putting on a pot of coffee when Kelly came up the back stairs. Dropping her canvas backpack on the chair at the end of the table, she shot her mother a curious glance as she went to the fridge. "How come you're up so early?"

Not quite able to meet her daughter's gaze, Maggie closed the lid on the tank of the coffeemaker, then slid the carafe onto the element. "I heard your alarm," she responded, keeping her tone perfectly casual. "And I wanted to warn you that Tony's asleep on the sofa."

Her hand on a pitcher of orange juice, Kelly went dead still. "Pardon?"

Maggie wiped some dribbles of water off the counter. "Tony's asleep in the front room." She tossed the cloth in the sink, then turned, bracing herself to face her daughter. Leaning back against the counter, she folded her arms, wishing she could spare her the brutal truth, finally she met her gaze. "The police officer that was killed yesterday was Tony's ex-partner," she said quietly. "They sent for Tony early yesterday morning, and he was at the hospital all day. I went over to see him last night. He was there by himself, so I brought him home."

A stricken expression on her face, Kelly set the pitcher down on the counter with a thud. "Oh God, Mom, how awful."

"Yes, it was," she answered softly.

A worried look appeared in Kelly's eyes. "How is he?"

Maggie gave her a reassuring smile. "It's hit him pretty hard, but he's okay." She looked down and straightened the fringe on the mat with her toe, then met Kelly's gaze dead on. "He doesn't need our sympathy, honey," she said quietly. "He just needs us to be here, okay?"

Kelly nodded and shoved her hands in the pockets of her shorts, her expression stark. "I feel so bad for him."

"I know you do." Straightening, Maggie went to her daughter, giving her shoulder a reassuring pat. "So do I." The teenager stared at her for a moment, then sighed and opened the cupboard to get a glass. "Are you going to stay home with him today?"

Maggie gave a warped smile. "You mean play hooky, Kelly Lynn?"

Kelly shot her a glance over her shoulder, a look of wide-eyed innocence on her face. "Gee, Mom. What's that?"

"Yeah, right," she answered wryly.

Kelly grinned. "You should try it, Mom. A little larceny is good for the soul." She got down two glasses, then gave her mother a bright, mischievous look and went to the archway. "Hey, Parnelli," she yelled. "Do you want some orange juice?"

There was a loud thump in the living room.

Maggie shot her a reproving look. "Kelly! He was sleeping, for heaven's sake. What possessed you to do that?"

Kelly grinned and fluttered her eyelashes. "Gee, Mom. I don't know. Maybe because I didn't want him to think he had to hide out in there."

Tony appeared at the doorway, his eyes bleary with sleep, looking as if he just climbed out of somebody's ragbag. He also looked just a little bit cranky. "Damn it. You scared the hell out of me."

Kelly grinned and poured two glasses of orange juice. "I take it that's a yes."

He raked his fingers through his tousled hair, then scrubbed his face. Resting his hands on his hips, he gave Kelly a baleful look. Her eyes dancing, she handed him a glass of orange juice. "What was that big crash? Did you fall off the couch?"

He narrowed his eyes at her, a glint of humor appearing. "What are you doing? Pushing your luck?"

She held up both hands in a conceding gesture. "Hey. I know better than to poke a bear." She nudged the bottom of his glass. "Have a slug, slugger. I think your blood sugar is a little low."

He gave her a long, cautioning look, then lifted the glass and downed half of the contents. Folding his arms, he leaned back against the counter and fixed his attention on Kelly. "Are you always this loud in the morning?"

Finishing her juice, Kelly opened the fridge and reached in for a bagged lunch. Pushing the door shut with her elbow, she looked at him, clearly enjoying herself. "Are you always this sweet and adorable?"

Staring at her, Tony shook his head, a glint appearing in his eyes. "You're just full of sass and vinegar, aren't you?"

She grinned at him. "Yep." The teenager picked up a banana from the basket of fruit on the table and stuffed it in the pocket of her jacket. She gave her mother a mischievous look.

"Have fun playing hooky, Ma. And stay outta trouble, okay?"

She raised her hand in a farewell salute to Tony. "See you later."

Kelly left, letting the back door slam behind her, and Maggie glanced at Tony, amused by the look on his face. "Considering it was your first skirmish of the day, you held up relatively well."

Bracing his hand on the corner of the fridge, Tony stared at her. "You could have warned me about her."

Maggie smiled as she reached into the cupboard and got out two mugs. "I take it you're not exactly a morning person."

"Not exactly."

Maggie filled the mugs with coffee, then handed him one, trying not to laugh. "Here. Maybe this will get your engine started."

He took it, then looked at her, a glimmer of amusement appearing in his eyes. "You think it's funny, don't you?"

She grinned at him. "Yes, I do."

He stared at her, the glint fading, changing to something dark and intense, something that made her pulse falter. Without taking his eyes off her, he set his cup on the counter, then took the steaming mug from her hand, setting it beside his. The steady, somber look in his eyes set off a wild flutter in her chest, and she stared up at him, unable to move. He caught her wrists, placing her arms around his neck; then he drew her flush against him, his gaze locked on hers. "So..." he said, his voice very soft, very husky. "Are you going to work or are you going to stick around?"

Maggie gazed up at him, knowing the question had nothing to do with her going to work or not; this was about them. She experienced a rush of fear. He was so much younger, and their life-styles were so very different. She was terrified of the day when he would realize it was all a big mistake, that she couldn't give him what he wanted.

But she would worry about that later. Now all she had to do was for once in her life throw caution to the wind. Take a chance. Let go. Step onto the high wire.

Her heart hammering like a wild thing, she drew a deep, shaky breath and took the biggest step of her life. "I'll stick around."

Letting his breath go, Tony closed his eyes and rested his forehead against hers. "You sure as hell took your sweet time making up your mind."

Cupping the back of his head, Maggie closed her eyes and swallowed hard, loving him so much her chest hurt. It wasn't quite so scary on the high wire when he was holding her like this.

Taking her face between his hands, he tipped her head back, covering her mouth with a sweet, searching kiss that robbed her of breath and made her legs want to buckle. And by the time he finally pulled away, she was breathing like a long-distance runner. Rubbing his thumb along her bottom lip, he smiled down at her, a twinkle in his eyes. "You ever played hooky, Burrows?"

Mesmerized by the gleam in his eyes, she shook her head.

"Well," he said, giving her a grin that had trouble written all over it, "we have to start by taking our clothes off."

Her uncertainties fading away to nothing, she gave him a steady look, somehow managing not to laugh. "Really?"

He slid his hands down her back and under the elasticized waistband of her sweatpants, the gleam in his eyes intensifying. "Yep." Then he cupped her buttocks, pressing her flush against him. "You can even play it on the kitchen table if you want."

She gave a little huff of laughter, resisting the pressure of his hands. "I think I need to buy you a dictionary, Parnelli."

He gave her another grin that came straight out of the bedroom, then lowered his head, lightly brushing his mouth against hers. "Nah. I'll show you instead."

Suddenly out of breath and tingling all over, Maggie tightened her arms around him, then grasped a handful of his hair. "Then you'd better show me fast," she demanded, putting pressure on his head.

He laughed against her mouth, tightening his arms around her hips. "You gonna participate?"

She gave his hair a firm jerk. "I'll show you participation, Parnelli."

He laughed again and backed her hard against the fridge, thrusting his knee between her legs. Then he pulled her up against him and kissed her in earnest, turning her whole body into one big erogenous zone.

Maggie opened her mouth beneath his, her senses slipping out of orbit. To hell with tomorrow. She was going to live today.

## Chapter 10

Maggie stared at the printout spread on her desk as if it were written in some foreign language, her mind refusing to compute the data. It was a company's year end, and the deadline for filing was four days away. And right now she felt like pulling all her hair out. Trying to release the tension in her shoulders, she closed her eyes and tipped her head back, willing up some calm. Okay. She was going to get focused. She was going to quit letting her mind wander and she was going to get down to business.

Dropping her hands, she stared blindly at the flashing cursor on her computer screen, the little blinking block taunting her. It was Friday afternoon, the last week of July, and she wasn't due to take the rest of her vacation for another two weeks. Which was not good, seeing that she had developed the attention span of a two-year-old. If she were Frank, she would have fired herself. She was about as productive as a slug, and her damned mind kept taking long-distance trips. And it was all Tony Parnelli's fault.

Realizing the absolute irrationality of that thought, Maggie dropped her head to her desk, letting her arms hang and wishing with all her heart that she could unplug what was left of her mind.

She didn't know what she was doing—maybe she was just manic-depressive. One minute she would be so high she felt as if she were flying, and the next so low she couldn't have dug herself any deeper with a steam shovel. Up and down, up and down—it was as if she was trapped on some crazy emotional roller coaster and there was no way off.

She wiped away a tear that had mysteriously leaked out. Without lifting her head, she pulled a tissue from the box on her desk and listlessly blew her nose, not caring one iota that she was lying all over someone's business receipts.

God, but she was a mess. She was so much in love with Tony, she couldn't even think straight. And everything was wonderful, wonderful, wonderful when she was with him. He dragged her to the races, he'd managed to talk her into learning to drive his bike and he did the most adorable things—like when he climbed into her bedroom in the middle of the night to bring her some roses, which he had swiped out of her own garden. And on top of all that, he was an honorable man. Even that night he sneaked in with the roses he wouldn't stay because of Kelly.

Maggie blindly reached for another tissue, wiping ineffectually at her nose. And all those times when they had some privacy together—those times in his apartment, in his car or in a field somewhere—she couldn't even bear to think about because they were so unbearably beautiful, so damned electric that her insides would turn to jelly just remembering them.

Managing to expel most of the pressure built up in her chest, she took a deep breath, aware that there was a paper clip pressing into her face. Okay, okay. She was just going to lie here for a moment and get herself together. She wasn't going to let that awful sinking feeling take root in her belly—that feeling that would rise up to haunt her in the middle of the night. That one that she couldn't quite control. Resting her forehead on the stack of receipts, Maggie closed her eyes, gathering her determination. She was going to brace herself, then she was going to finish this damned account and then go home and make dinner for Kelly and Tony. Once she was with him, everything would be okay.

"Are you in a coma or are you just in the middle of a heart attack?"

Maggie resisted the urge to bang her head against the desk. Heaving a sigh, she sat up, trying to look halfway competent. She picked up a pencil. "Go away, Frank. I don't want to talk to you."

Her boss chuckled, then reached over and picked the paper clip off her cheek. "Maybe we should just get your nose pierced." He tossed the bright green paper clip onto the printout. "Then you could have a whole string of paper clips hanging from your left nostril."

Maggie experienced a tiny flicker of amusement. "Hang them on your own left nostril and leave mine out of it."

He leaned over her shoulder and looked at the printout. "Having trouble?"

She placed her arm across the paper, as if they were in elementary school and he was trying to cheat. "No."

Before she had a chance to stop him, he snatched the statement from under her arm. "Hmm," he said, scanning the columns.

Maggie snatched the printout back and slapped it on her desk. "Don't mess with me, Frank."

Folding his arms, Frank hitched his hip on the corner of her desk. "Now, Mary Margaret," he said, adopting a patronizing tone, "you would be doing me a big favor if you'd just have a fit and dump that on my desk. My wife says we gotta go looking at wallpaper tonight, and I ask you, why me?" He gave her a hangdog smile. "But if *you* didn't get your work done, then I'd have to work late, wouldn't I?"

Maggie propped her chin on her hand, enjoying his performance. Frank could look like the most pathetic person alive when he put a little effort into it.

"So you gotta give me that file, Maggie," he said, looking woeful. "I'd rather deal with head lice than shopping. What in hell do I know about wallpaper, for Pete's sake?"

"You're so cute when you fib, Lucciano. You know that?"

"I am not fibbing." He actually started to sweat. "She's decided to redecorate the whole damn house. It's a fifteen-room house—do you know how many rolls of wallpaper that's going to take?"

Maggie gave him a long, scrutinizing look. "You aren't just trying to be nice because you caught me with my face planted in my desk?"

"Hell, no!" He tried to pull the printout from under her elbow. "Give it to me, Burrows. Pink pansies on blue flocking—" he shuddered "—are enough to give me cold sweats."

Maggie studied him for a moment, then lifted her elbow, letting him pull the file free. He was such a sneaky devil that she wasn't entirely sure she bought the blue-flocking business.

He headed toward his office, pausing at the door to yell, "Go home! I don't want you hanging around, screwing up my alibi."

Her head still propped in her hand, Maggie considered him as he closed his door. She would swear she could hear him whistling. A touch of humor surfaced. Blue-flocking, indeed. In a pig's eye. He was so sweet.

A heat wave had hit the city the week before, and it was sweltering. There wasn't a whiff of breeze, and heat radiated off the sidewalk like a blast furnace. By the time Maggie walked home, she was so hot she hardly had the energy to put one foot in front of the other. She had stopped off at the store, and the bag of groceries she was lugging felt like it weighed a ton. She smiled a little when she saw the Keep Off sign on her freshly painted front step. Tony had run compressor hoses from the shop to her house the night before, and he and Spider had sanded the step, then used a spray gun to paint it. It took them less than an hour to do what it would have taken her a week to accomplish.

Skirting the wet paint, she followed the sidewalk around to the back of the house and opened the old-fashioned-wrought iron gate, relieved to get in the shade. If she'd known it was so hot out, she would never have left the air-conditioned comfort of the office.

She rounded the corner of the house and stopped in her tracks. Tony was stretched out on one of the chaise longues, his T-shirt draped over the back of the chair, his arms folded across his naked, tanned chest. He had on a pair of faded cut-offs, with a baseball cap pulled down over his eyes, and he looked as if he didn't have a care in the world. There was a large, frosty pitcher of lemonade sitting on the table beside him, along with two ice-filled glasses.

Her day suddenly lightened, and she found herself smiling. "Hi. You expecting somebody?"

It wasn't until he lifted his hat and pulled off a headset that she realized he'd been listening to a Walkman. Tossing his hat on the deck, he used the two collapsible arms to hoist himself out of the chair; then he crossed the deck and met her at the top of the steps. He shot her an amused look as he took the bag of groceries from her. "I called the office, and your boss said he'd sent you home. He gave me some big story about finding you with paper clips stuck to your face." The gleam in his eyes intensified. "So I figured you must have flipped out on poor old Frank." Resting the bag of groceries on the railing, he leaned over and gave her a light kiss. Then he straightened and grinned at her, the devil dancing in his eyes. "So what happened, cookie? Did you loose a dime?"

Slipping out of her shoes, she pulled the bag out of his grasp. Not wanting to discuss what had happened at her desk, she narrowed her eyes at him. "I did not flip out. And if I were you, I'd be careful what you say, Parnelli. There are three New York steaks in that bag, perfect for barbecuing. If you aren't nice, I'll feed yours to Captain Hook."

He tried to reclaim the bag, finally yanking it out of her grip, and tearing it down one side in the process. "Forget it, Burrows. You're going to sit down in that chair, put your feet up and have a long, cold drink. Then—" he touched the end of her nose "—we'll worry about steaks."

She had on a loose-fitting, dark green cotton dress with buttons up the front, the long skirt gathered onto a simple bodice just below her bust. The dress itself was cool, but she was going to die of heatstroke if she didn't get out of her panty hose and half-slip. Tony had set the groceries on the table and was filling both glasses. Pulling her hair back off her hot face, she said as much to him. And that she needed to change.

His back to her, Tony paused, then set down the pitcher. Turning on his heel, he came toward her with a loose-hipped saunter, a glint of mischief in his eyes. He stopped inches from her, the heat of his body reflecting off her, making her own body temperature climb several degrees. Watching her with a steady stare, he slowly—so slowly—ran his hands up the back of her legs, dragging up the fabric of her dress. "Really?" he said. "You have to change?"

The feel of his hands moving over her flesh made her heart falter, and she had trouble catching her breath. Transfixed by his gaze, she nodded, and he moved his hands higher and kissed her again. Before she grasped his intent, he'd hooked his thumbs in the waistbands of her panty hose and slip, and quicker than lightning yanked them down. Maggie was so stunned by what he'd done and the speed with which he'd accomplished it that she stood staring at him, her mouth hanging open. Lifting one of her feet, then the other, he stripped away the garments and rose, tossing them on the table by the grocery bag. He turned back, clearly laughing at her. "So now you don't."

She waved her hands and started to sputter something, but he caught her face, tipped her head back and covered her mouth in a kiss that sizzled all the way down to the tips of her toes. When he finally drew away, she was gripping his wrists and breathing as if she'd just run five miles, and her heart was pounding like a crazy thing in her chest. Shutting her eyes, she hung onto him, her senses totally off balance, the heat from their bodies making it nearly impossible to breathe.

Still holding her face, Tony brushed a kiss on one corner of her mouth, then the other. Easing away, he stroked her cheeks with his thumbs. "Open your eyes, Maggie," he demanded softly. "Or things are really going to get out of hand."

Finally able to drag some air into her lungs, she looked up at him, staggered by the erotic kick of one very long, very thorough kiss. He drew one finger along her bottom lip, then gazed at her, his eyes dark and intent. Finally he managed a small, warped smile. "I think," he said, pausing for emphasis, "that wasn't a very good idea."

Still gripping his wrists, Maggie swallowed hard and closed her eyes again, weakly resting her head against his. Lord, he could rattle her senses.

Sliding one hand to the back of her neck, Tony squeezed lightly. "Come on," he said, his voice still husky. "Sit down and I'll put the groceries in the house."

Maggie was so shaky she wasn't quite sure how she made it into the lounger, but the minute she had the solid frame beneath her, she tipped back her head and closed her eyes, feeling as if she'd got nailed with a high-voltage wire.

She heard the screen door close when Tony came out; then there was the scrape of another chair on the deck. Turning her head, she opened her eyes.

He had moved the chair right beside hers, but he had turned it around so he was facing her. It took him a couple of adjustments to get it exactly right, but when he sat down, his shoulder was aligned with her torso, his body nearly upright. Her chair was positioned in a semireclining position, and he reached over and tucked her hair back, then rubbed his knuckles along her collarbone. His gaze was dark and intimate. "How are you doing?" he asked softly.

Maggie's heart gave a crazy little flutter, and she eased in a deep, careful breath. "I'm doing okay." She waited for the flutter to settle, then smoothed her hand across the back of his and gave him a small, off-center smile. "So how come you're here? Did you run away from home?"

He grinned at her, turning his hand to lace his fingers through hers. "After I talked to Frank, I figured you might need a little R and R."

Maggie experienced a swell of emotion deep in her chest, and she tightened her fingers around his, not daring to speak. Somehow he was always able to create a wonderful safety zone for her, where nothing could touch them. It was as if they were living in some sort of glass bubble that kept them separate from the real world. And maybe that's why she had this recurring feeling of dread. All it would take was one misstep, and the bubble could shatter. But she didn't want to think about that now; it scared her to death when she did.

"What's the matter, Mag?" Tony asked, his tone quiet.

Not wanting him to know, she met his gaze, forcing a small smile. "I'm just hot and tired. And I'm glad it's Friday." She gave his hand a little squeeze, real amusement surfacing. "Although I'm not nearly as hot as I was."

He laughed and let go of her, then leaned back and ran his hand up under her dress, caressing her bare leg. "Glad to hear it." Leaving his hand on her thigh, he turned, picked up one of the glasses of lemonade and handed it to her.

The cold glass was wet with condensation, and Maggie closed her eyes and pressed it against her flushed face. It felt wonderful. She opened her eyes and gave him a grateful smile. "You're a good man, Charlie Brown."

Leaning back in his chair, Tony took a drink from his own glass, then glanced at her, his eyes twinkling as he moved his hand higher. "Wanna go look at my etchings?"

She trapped his hand between her legs to stop the upward assent, choking on laughter and lemonade. Her eyes watering, she shot him a look of rebuke. "You don't have any etchings, and if you move your hand another inch higher, you're going to be in big trouble, bucko."

His eyes half-closed, he grinned at her and moved his hand downward. Gently he manipulated her kneecap, sending a fizzle of sensation along her leg. "So how was your day?"

She gave him a long, level look. "Rotten. How was yours?"

"All aces. I got a line on a Shelby Cobra in Kansas that's up for sale. Mario is leaving early next week to hit a bunch of shows—he's probably going to be gone six or eight weeks—so he's going to pick it up on the way home." Resting his glass on the wide arm of the chair, he tipped his head back, his other hand still caressing her knee. "I ran into Big Bertha today. I guess some of the businesses are putting together a big block party and street fair for the Labor Day weekend. Wanted to know if we were interested." He gave a small shrug. "I think it sounds like a hell of an idea."

They talked about that for a while, then fell into a comfortable silence, then talked some more, the heat of the day settling on them. And it was nice. It was better than nice. For Maggie, it was sheer heaven. It would never have entered Bruce's head to take an afternoon off and spend it with her because she'd had a rotten day at work.

But it wasn't just that that filled her with warm fuzzies; it was how Tony made her feel. And the bottom line was that he made her feel like a woman—not just a person or a mother or a wife, but a woman.

A very aroused woman.

A different kind of heat radiated through her, and Maggie closed her eyes and clenched her jaw against the rush in her middle. If he didn't quit stroking her leg, she was going to go through the deck. Or melt. Or both.

There was the sound of a car door slamming in the back alley, and Tony slid his hand to the inside of her thigh. "I think we've got company."

Drugged senseless by his slow, arousing touch, Maggie forced her eyes open. "Pardon?" she said, her mouth very dry.

He grinned at her. "I think I hear your daughter coming, cookie," he said, giving her leg a firm squeeze.

He might as well have dumped the pitcher of ice-cold lemonade in her lap. Bolting upright, she thrust his hand away and shoved down her dress, totally flustered.

Laughter dancing in his eyes, Tony folded his arms across his tanned chest and watched her, clearly amused. "Shame on you, Mary Margaret. You're such a hussy."

She shot him a disparaging look, then straightened the fabric across her knees. Tony laughed at her, and she wasn't sure if she should laugh back or smack him.

Kelly came up the walk, the straps of her backpack slung over one shoulder. She grinned at her mother. "Are you guys playing hooky *again?*"

His back to Kelly, Tony cocked one eyebrow at Maggie, the devil in his eyes. "Later," he mouthed, and Maggie felt herself blush to the roots of her hair.

"Frank let me off early," she answered, her voice cracking a little. Clearing her throat, she tried to act halfway normal. "How was your day?"

Kelly had a summer job teaching handicapped kids to swim, and she loved every minute of it. The teenager dropped her backpack on the deck, then poured some lemonade into Tony's empty glass. "Great. Michael—he's one of our Down's syndrome kids—actually got his face in the water today." She drank the lemonade and set the glass back on the table. Locking her hands together, she stretched her arms over her head. "So it was a really good day. So what are you guys up to?"

Maggie glanced at Tony, narrowing her eyes at him. "Nothing," she said pointedly. "Not one thing."

He gave her a grin loaded with innuendo. "Later," he said, clearly enjoying himself. "We'll do something later. After it cools off."

Oblivious to what was really going on, Kelly fished a piece of ice out of the glass and popped it in her mouth. "You guys should take the Harley out for a spin later. Drive out to Banff."

Tony answered, "Maybe tomorrow. The traffic will be nuts tonight, and I don't want to take your mom out there when everybody'll be driving like idiots."

Kelly grimaced in acknowledgment. "Never thought of that." She picked up her backpack and slung it over her shoulder. "So what's for supper, Ma?"

Tony flicked a mosquito off his bare thigh, then looked up at Kelly. "How about you and I handling supper tonight? Your mom's had a long week, and I think she needs to veg out for a while."

Kelly shrugged. "Sure." Then she shot Tony a glance over her shoulder. "So what are we going to make? Spaghetti and meatballs?"

"In your dreams, kiddo." He shoved himself from the chair and pushed it out of the way, then leaned over and kissed Maggie's eyes closed. "And keep 'em shut," he commanded. She felt him smile against her skin. "You're going to need all your energy for later."

"Later" turned out to be much later. Scott came around eight with two movies he'd rented. But then he and Kelly got into an argument about applying the laws of physics to billiards. It ended with Scott and Tony challenging Kelly and

Maggie to a game of eight ball. Only they made Maggie play left-handed. One game stretched to three; then the teenagers insisted that Maggie and Tony watch the movies with them.

They made it through the first one, but Maggie started yawning twenty minutes into the second, which was amazing, considering that the movie was one of those awful, grisly things. After watching her trying to smother another yawn, Tony got up, then hauled her to her feet.

Tucking his T-shirt into his cutoffs, he spoke to the two teenagers stretched out on the family-room floor. "We're calling it quits, guys." He didn't get so much as a flicker of response, and he gave Maggie a nudge in the small of her back. "Do you get the feeling they don't really give a damn?"

She stifled another yawn, then shivered. "Do you really care?"

He grinned and looped his arm around her neck, putting her in a playful headlock. "You're mocking me, Maggie."

"You have to be conscious to mock, Parnelli."

He followed her up the steps to the back landing, then paused in the darkened entryway. Resting his hand on the latch of the screen door, he leaned over and gave her a quick kiss. "I'll call you in the morning."

Maggie shivered again, but for different reasons. "I'll walk you out."

Even though it was nearly midnight, it was still warm, the usual cool night air from the mountains held back by the heat. A soft breeze caught at the skirt of Maggie's dress, and she turned her face into the breeze, inhaling the scent of flowers. God, she loved nights like this, when the air was laden with a mix of floral fragrances.

They reached the side door of the garage, and Tony stopped. Turning to face her, he slid his hand under her hair and caressed the back of her neck. "This is as far as you're going," he said. Then he leaned down and brushed her lips with a soft, undemanding kiss. Maggie closed her eyes and opened her mouth beneath his, not wanting him to leave, knowing she couldn't ask him to stay. Tony held her head still as he deepened the kiss, his mouth moist and warm as he leisurely worked it back and forth against hers. Her lungs malfunctioned, and she grasped his arm to steady herself, a tingling weakness traveling from the top of her head to the tips of her toes. Sliding his fingers into her hair, he increased the pressure, and the kiss turned deep and carnal. The tingling weakness turned into a rush, and Maggie tightened her grip on his arm, her senses swimming out of focus.

Releasing a shaky sigh, Tony eased away, then swore softly and gathered her up in a snug, comforting embrace. Rubbing his jaw along the top of her head, he locked his arms around her hips. "You could tempt a saint," he whispered roughly. He held her like that for several moments, then he caught her under the chin, lifting her face for one last, soft kiss.

Maggie slid her arms around his neck, and what started out as a final farewell suddenly escalated into something more. Tony abruptly widened his stance, pulling her up tighter against him, and Maggie clutched at him, hot, urgent desire pouring through her. Dragging up her skirt, Tony flattened his hand against her buttocks, pressing her hard against him; then he tore his mouth away, his breathing labored. "Maggie— honey," he whispered raggedly.

Feeling almost desperate, she tightened her arms around his neck. "Oh, Tony..."

Abruptly shifting his hold, he reached behind her and shoved open the garage door. With his arm locked around her rib cage, he got her inside. Then he closed the door and backed her against it, their breathing harsh and labored in the dark. Shoving her skirt out of the way, Tony pressed her to him, and Maggie dropped her head back and clenched her jaw as she wrapped her legs around him. With one hand braced beside her head, he used his weight to hold her as he grasped the side seam of her panties, ripping them in two and pushing them out of the way. He fumbled with his fly, then with a repressed groan, thrust into her. A surge of raw pleasure seared through her, and she sobbed out his name as her whole body turned to liquid heat. He moved in her hard and fast, lifting her up and up, until the blackness finally exploded into a million shards of light, her release coming with a blinding force. He gave one final thrust and went rigid, and a tremor shuddered through him. Roughly turning his face into the cleavage between her breasts, he hauled in a jagged breath, his arms trembling.

Her face wet with tears, she cradled his head with both arms, unbearable tenderness filling her to the very brim. God, but she loved him. Right down to her soul.

Tony didn't move for the longest time, then he exhaled with a shudder and shifted his hold. "I'm going to have to sit down," he whispered unevenly. "Just don't let go."

Maggie couldn't have let go if her life depended on it, and she nodded and stroked the back of his head. Tightening his grip around her hips, he turned, using the metal-clad door as a back brace as he lowered them both to the ground.

The garage floor was concrete, and cold on Maggie's legs as she tucked them back, straddling his hips. Still cradling his head against her breast, she pressed a soft kiss against his hair, the pitch blackness inside the garage making her even more acutely aware of him.

Running his hands up her arms, he turned his head and kissed her just under her ear, then spoke, a faint trace of amusement in his voice. "For someone who was half-asleep, you sure went from zero to sixty pretty damned fast."

Smiling in the dark, Maggie bracketed his face with her hands, resting her forehead against his. "You just know how to rev my engines, Antonio."

He chuckled and gave her a quick hug. "I think you have a fuel-injected ignition there, cookie. And I also think I slipped my clutch."

Laughing, Maggie slid her arms around his neck and hugged him back. "You're an opportunist, Parnelli. And don't tell me you're not."

She felt him smile, and he tightened his hold and gave her a firm hug, his hand warm against the back of her neck. He held her like that for several moments, then eased his hold and expelled his breath. "We'd better go, babe," he whispered, his voice soft with regret. "With our luck, Scott'll come out here looking for a bicycle pump or something." Hooking his thumb under her chin, he angled her head, giving her a soft, sweet kiss; then he released another sigh. Grasping her by the waist, he supported her as she eased off him, swearing softly as she completely withdrew. The total darkness affected her sense of balance, and Tony held her arm until she steadied herself; then he got up, brushing against her.

Groping for her ruined underwear, Maggie stuffed them into the pocket of her dress, the utter blackness leaving her disoriented. She heard Tony do up the zipper on his cutoffs, then he reached for her, sliding his palm down her arm to grasp her hand. "You ready, Freddie?"

She smiled, tightening her fingers around his. She felt like a teenager, sneaking around in the dark. "Sure am, Sam."

He gave her hand a shake. "You think you're cute, don't you?" Then he fumbled for the door and pulled it open.

Maggie's eyes were so dilated from the blackness that it took her a minute to adapt, and she gripped his hand even tighter. Once outside, Tony pulled the door closed and draped his arm around her shoulder. "This time," he said, humor in his tone, "I'm going to walk *you* home."

They were just about to go up the steps to the deck when Maggie stopped dead, horror washing through her. "Oh, my God," she whispered. "They're in the kitchen making popcorn."

Tony grasped the top of her head, shoving her down; then he grabbed her hand, dragging her behind him in a commando crouch until they were out of the rectangle of light spilling from the kitchen window. It was so ridiculous, two adults sneaking around in the dark, that Maggie wanted to laugh.

Reaching the side of the house, he flattened his back against the wall, and Maggie knew he was definitely up to no good; she thought he was insane. She opened her mouth to tell him so, but he caught her around the neck, clamping his hand across her mouth, and she probably would have laughed out loud if she'd been able to.

"Geez, woman," he whispered in her ear, his voice quivering with his own suppressed laughter. "Be quiet. I don't know about you, but *I* don't want to try explaining what we've been doing in the garage for the past half hour."

Fighting to contain herself, she nodded, her shoulders starting to shake. Tony let go and warned her to silence; then he turned, his hands on his hips as he studied her bedroom window—the very bedroom he'd climbed into less than a week ago. The sill was a good seven feet off the ground, and as far as Maggie was concerned, it might as well be seven miles. He looked back at her, his eyes glinting in the faint light coming from the alley. Reading his intent, Maggie shook her head, held her hands up and backed away, nearly overcome by a fit of silent giggles. If he thought she was going to climb in her bedroom window—in a dress, with no underwear on—he was out of his mind.

Shaking off her resistance, he gestured that it would be a piece of cake. She shook her head again, but he totally ignored her. Grasping the wooden ledge, he hoisted himself up and popped out the screen, then jumped down, dusting his hands off on the seat of his jeans. Turning to her, he grinned and locked his hands together, indicating that he was going to boost her up. Drawing a deep, quavering breath to control the laughter that kept bubbling up, she held out her skirt in a fake curtsy, silently indicating that she was hardly dressed to scale a wall.

He looked from her to the window, then, before she realized what he was thinking, he grasped the sill again. Without making a single sound, he pulled himself up, the muscles across his shoulders straining. Hooking one arm over the sill, he hauled himself into the aperture, then disappeared from sight.

Tony reappeared at the window. Bracing his weight against the wall, he leaned out and motioned for her to raise her arms. Feeling like Rapunzel in reverse, she took a deep, tremulous breath, giddily wondering if he had hernia insurance.

She really wasn't much help. With a lot of grunting and straining, he finally pulled her up. Once she got her knee on the sill, he grabbed her around the waist and lifted her in. She very nearly knocked him over, and he grabbed the window frame, his arm going around her to steady her. He was breathing heavily, partly from exertion, partly from laughing, and he weakly rested his forehead against hers, his chest heaving. "That's the last time I rescue you," he whispered, pulling her against him. "You're no bloody help at all."

Stifling another fit of laughter, she slid her arms around him and turned her face against his damp neck. "We could have just used the ladder, you know."

She felt him smile. "Now she tells me." He brushed her hair back with both hands, then, tightening his hold on her face, leaned down and kissed her, his mouth warm and moist and unbearably tender. Maggie experienced a rush of emotion so intense that it made her lungs clog up. Suddenly the laughter was gone, replaced by something very painful. She wondered how long it would be before the bubble would burst and reality would sweep in, and all this magic would disappear from her life forever.

Tightening his hold on her face, Tony released his breath and drew away. His expression sober, he stared down at her, the faint light from the alley casting shadows on his face. His eyes fixed on hers, he said quietly, "What's up, Maggie?"

Trying to smile, she shook her head. "Nothing. I'm just—"

He pressed his thumb against her mouth, his gaze unwavering, as if he was assessing her. There wasn't a trace of amusement in his voice when he spoke again. "I only want to know one thing. Are you planning on bailing out again?"

There was something in his tone that made her heart roll over, and for a minute, she was afraid her eyes were going to fill up. She shook her head. "No," she whispered.

His expression very somber, he drew his thumb across her bottom lip; then he met her gaze again. "This isn't some game I'm playing, Maggie."

"I know," she whispered.

He continued to watch her, his expression still thoughtful; then he spoke, an angry edge in his voice. "You really have a problem with who you are, don't you?"

Feeling as if he'd pulled the ground out from under her, she stared at him. It was as if he'd peeled away some protective layer, leaving her without any defenses, and blood rushed to her ears.

He stared a second longer, then gave her a small, twisted smile and let her go. "I'll see you in the morning," he said. He gave her one last, soft kiss, and before she could collect her fragmented thoughts, climbed back out the window, lowering himself to ground with barely a sound. Her expression frozen from the emotional jolt he had given her, Maggie watched until he disappeared around the corner of the garage. Then she closed her eyes and rested her head against the window frame, suddenly very shaky inside. She didn't like the feeling in the pit of her belly. She didn't like it at all.

# Chapter 11

It was not a good night. Tony's comment about her having a problem with who she was had scored a direct hit on a big, exposed nerve. And Maggie spent most of the night huddled in the corner of her bed, feeling like she had when she was four years old and afraid of the dark. Like something unknown and indistinct was hovering out there in the darkness, and she was afraid to reach out and touch it for fear of what she'd find. With all that racing around in her mind, there was no way she could fall asleep.

Of course, the damned mosquitoes didn't help. With the screen off the window, they invaded her bedroom like squadrons of miniature attack bombers, circling around her head, their annoying buzz worse than Chinese water torture. Around four, Maggie finally got up, went outside in her nightshirt and retrieved the screen, then stomped back into the house, muttering threats to the entire mosquito population. Once back in her room, she fitted the screen into place, then fumigated her bedroom with enough insect spray to kill every bug within a hundred-mile radius. Holding her breath against the dense fog of insecticide, she snatched a pillow and a light throw from her bed, then left, slamming the door behind her. They could all rot for all she cared; she was going to sleep on the sofa.

But Maggie couldn't get comfortable on the sofa, or at least that's what she thought. One minute she was wrestling with the blanket; the next, bright sunlight was streaming through the window and someone was shaking her awake. She buried her head under the pillow, trying to block out the voice.

"Come on, Ma. Time to get up."

Maggie clasped the pillow over her ears and considered suffocating herself.

Kelly gave her a solid nudge. "Nice try, Mary Margaret, but I know you're faking it," she said, yanking the pillow away. "Now up and at 'em."

Her defense gone, Maggie groaned and rolled over onto her back, squinting at her daughter. "You're as irritating as the mosquitoes."

Kelly grinned down at her. "I just love it when you don't make any sense, Mother." She caught Maggie's arm and gave it a solid tug. "Come *on*. There's a crazy Italian loose in our kitchen, and he's scrambling eggs in the wok."

The mention of a crazy Italian brought Maggie sharply awake, and her stomach gave a little lurch. She draped her free arm over her eyes. Tony. Breakfast. Oh, God. After spending most of the night feeling like a four-year-old, she wasn't sure she could face him. Or look him square in the eye.

Ignoring her lack of enthusiasm, Kelly braced her foot on the edge of the sofa and dragged Maggie off. "Not a chance, Mother. You're getting up, whether you want to or not."

Dumped onto the floor, Maggie gave her daughter a baleful look, resigned to the fact that she didn't have much choice. Kelly made a happy face at her. "See, that wasn't so bad."

Maggie was considering the pros and cons of debate, but Kelly never gave her a chance. She waggled her fingers, then headed toward the kitchen. Maggie watched her go, feeling as if she had an overinflated tire in her head. This was not going to be a good morning. She could feel it in her bones.

Her bedroom smelled only faintly of insecticide when she went to get clothes, and by the time she'd brushed her teeth and had a shower, she felt considerably better. She still had the jitters about facing Tony, however, and what made it worse, she wasn't even sure why. Maybe it was because she felt as if she'd done something wrong. That she had upset him. But that didn't make much sense. He was here making breakfast, wasn't he?

Bracing herself with a deep breath, she ran her hands down the front of her light cotton slacks, then plucked up her courage. She couldn't stay in the bathroom forever.

The tantalizing smell of food greeted her the minute she opened the bathroom door, and her stomach responded. Maggie wasn't entirely sure if it was from the mouth-watering aroma or from the butterflies struggling to get out, but by the time she reached the kitchen her insides were in full revolt.

Tony was standing in front of the stove, a spatula in his hand, his attention focused on something he was cooking in the skillet. He was wearing another pair of cutoffs and a faded yellow tank top, the pale color accentuating his dark tan, the cut of the garment revealing the heavy muscle development across his chest and shoulders. There was something about the sight of him standing there watching breakfast cook that struck her. And Maggie knew that, no matter what happened, this image of him would be forever imprinted on her mind.

Trying to will away the butterflies, she spoke, her voice not quite steady. "Good morning."

He turned and looked at her, his face unsmiling, a thoughtful expression in his eyes that set off another war of nerves in her stomach.

Rubbing her hands down her slacks once more, she tried to dredge up a smile, feeling closer to tears. "You're here awfully early."

Tony stared at her as if he was taking her apart piece by piece; then he set down the spatula and came toward her. His gaze still solemn, he hooked his knuckles under her chin and lifted her face and studied her. Not even sure why she felt like crying, Maggie gazed up at him, a terrible weight forming in her chest.

"Hey," he said softly, "it's okay." Catching her by the back of the head, he drew her against him and wrapped her in a big, comforting embrace.

Closing her eyes against the sting of tears, Maggie slid her arms around him and turned her face against his neck, finally letting her breath go in a shaky rush. God, but she loved him. And she wasn't quite sure what she would have done if he hadn't shown up this morning.

Tucking his head against hers, Tony rubbed his hand up and down her back. She tightened her hold and pressed her face deeper into the curve of his neck, grateful for him. So grateful.

Tony continued to massage her back, and Maggie was finally able to release the terrible pressure in her chest. Taking a shaky breath, she ran her hand across his shoulders, the tension seeping out of her body.

He smoothed his hand up her neck and nestled her closer, his jaw resting against her temple. He didn't say anything, but continued to hold her until she was able to let go and totally relax in his arms. Then he tipped his head lower and gave her a little, attention-getting squeeze. "Don't you want to know what I'm cooking up, Burrows?"

Five minutes earlier, Maggie would never have thought it possible, but he actually made her smile. "You're always cooking up something, Parnelli. And not necessarily on the stove."

He chuckled and gave her another squeeze. "You've got a dirty mind, you know that?" Letting his arms settle around her hips, he gave her a little shake. "So ask me. Come on, ask me."

She smiled to herself, then decided to humor him. Using the same tone she used on the kids when they exasperated her, she asked, "What are you cooking up, Tony?"

She felt him grin as he pinched her bottom. "I'm cooking up scrambled eggs and bacon. I'm cooking up hash browns and sourdough toast." He slid his hand down her bottom in a very explicit, intimate caress. "And I think I'm cooking my own goose."

With laughter bubbling up in her, she lifted her head and looked at him. "Then maybe you better turn down the heat, Parnelli."

He stroked her bottom again, giving her that slow, lazy smile that always made her pulse flutter. "So," he said, his tone low and suggestive, "do you want to check out the garage?"

She held his gaze, watching for his reaction. "Yes," she answered evenly. "I do."

It was as if she'd touched him with a hot iron. He went stock-still, then let out his breath in a rush. "Geez, woman," he said, sounding annoyed. "Don't do that to me first thing in the morning." Then he grasped her face in his hands and gave her a kiss that could have fried eggs at twenty paces. When he finally broke it off, he was breathing heavily and so was she, and Maggie felt as if every nerve in her body had been incinerated. Tony let go of her and abruptly turned away, raking his hand through his hair. "Big mistake. Really big mistake."

Closing her eyes against the squall of sensation, Maggie put her hand against the fridge to steady herself, certain that if she moved a muscle, she'd turn into a big puddle on the floor.

She heard Tony give a low, unsteady chuckle. "Good," he said with pure male satisfaction. "I don't see why I should be the only one around here ready to jump out of my skin." There was a slight pause, then he expelled a heavy breath and took her by the arm. "Come on," he said softly. "You need to sit down."

Feeling more than a little inebriated, Maggie let him lead her over to the table and shove her into a chair. Grasping her jaw, he leaned down and gave her another kiss, only this one was unbearably sweet and tender. Tightening his hold, he drew away and looked down at her steadily. "If you had any idea," he said, his tone gruff, "how much I want to take you to bed right now, you'd go into the bathroom and lock the door."

Maggie shivered and tried to make her lungs work. "I couldn't make it to the bathroom if I tried."

A glimmer of amusement appeared in his eyes, and he gave her hand a reprimanding squeeze. "You're doing it again, Maggie," he warned.

The back door slammed, and Kelly came bouncing into the kitchen. "Hey, you guys. Quit goofing off. I've watered the flower garden and set the table outside, and exactly what have *you* done, Mother?"

"I think," Maggie said, looking directly at Tony, "that I've just had a stroke."

Kelly grinned. "Nice try. But you still have to help." The teenager went to the stove and leaned over the skillet, inhaling the mouth-watering aroma. "Mmm. Smells terrific."

Resting his free hand on his hip, Tony tightened his hold on Maggie's fingers and watched Kelly, a wry expression tugging at his mouth. Maggie wondered if he felt like stuffing her daughter down a hole right then; she knew she did. He absently stroked her palm with his thumb, then looked down at her and gave her hand one final squeeze, a silent message in his eyes. *Later,* he was saying. *Later.*

Maggie swallowed hard and squeezed his hand back. She felt as though she had a million buzz bombs zipping around in her bloodstream. As if tuned in to her thoughts, Tony suddenly grinned and let go of her, then waved his fingers back and forth as if he'd just got burned. Maggie braced her elbow on the table and covered her face with her hand, trying not to laugh. He could say more things without saying anything at all.

They had breakfast out on the deck, and afterward, Maggie stretched out in one of the loungers and soaked up the sun, watching Tony and Kelly at the picnic table. He had given her daughter an old carburetor to disassemble, and Kelly had been thrilled to bits. They were sitting across from each other, various tools scattered on the table between them, and as Kelly took the thing apart, he explained how everything worked. Maggie smiled to herself. A match made in heaven.

She caught a flash of black out of the corner of her eye and lazily turned her head, watching as Captain Hook sprang from the fence to the roof of the garage. Maggie smiled again. Good old Hook. Out doing the rounds.

She watched the cat groom himself, then shifted her gaze, noticing the Harley parked by the back fence and two helmets lying on the grass just inside the gate. She looked back at Tony. "Don't tell me you *rode* over here this morning, Parnelli."

He glanced up, giving her a long, level look. "No, I did not ride over here this morning. I had to go to the store to pick up some stuff for breakfast."

She stared back at him, keeping her face straight. "Of course you did."

He narrowed his eyes at her. "Don't push your luck, lady."

Feeling as lethargic as Hook, she responded by smiling sweetly, then sticking her tongue out at him. Which was the wrong thing to do. He got up, stepped over the bench attached to the picnic table, then came toward her, a dangerous glint in his eyes. "Ah, Maggie," he said. "You shouldn't have done that." Before she had a chance to react, he grabbed the chair, collapsed the brace and folded her up in the heavy tubular frame. With her knees wedged under her chin, she was truly trapped, and she started to laugh. Darn it, she couldn't get away with one thing with him. Pleased with himself, he left her to struggle for a minute, then got down so he was eye-to-eye with her. "Take it back, Burrows."

Her lungs compressed from laughing and the position she was in, she gasped for breath. "I take it back."

He considered her a moment, as if deciding whether to believe her or not, then grinned. "I won."

"Let me out, Parnelli!"

Still grinning, he unfolded her, using his foot to secure the support. Bracing his hand on the arm of the lounge, he leaned down and gave her a kiss that knocked the wind right out of her. "Now behave yourself," he said against her mouth.

Maggie was about to respond when Kelly's voice intruded. "Dad! What are you doing here?"

It was a shot of cold water, and Maggie froze. Bruce? Here? She grasped Tony's wrist and sat bolt upright, swiveling her head. Yes, it was definitely Bruce standing by the garage, dressed in an immaculate gray business suit and crisp white shirt. And he looked about as stunned as she felt. She glanced up at Tony, who had straightened and was staring at the newcomer, a hard glitter in his eyes. The sudden silence was deafening.

Feeling at a disadvantage sitting down, she got out of the chair, brushing against Tony as she turned to face her ex-husband. She folded her arms and spoke. "This is unexpected."

Bruce looked from Tony to Maggie, then back, his expression rigid. "I would like you to leave. I want to talk to my wife."

Kelly rose off the picnic bench like she'd been shot out of a rocket, and Maggie felt Tony stiffen behind her. She saw red. "If you want to talk to your wife, I suggest you call her in Vancouver. And you don't have the right to tell anyone to leave *my* house."

Bruce's face turned livid, and he looked at his daughter. "Kelly! Go in the house. I want to talk to your mother."

Kelly moved over to stand beside Tony. She looked her father square in the eye. No," she said, deliberately provoking him, "I won't."

He opened his mouth again, but Maggie cut him off. "Just what are you doing here, Bruce?"

He looked at Tony and back to her, anger mottling his face. "I want to know what's going on here," he demanded.

It was a struggle, but Maggie kept her voice perfectly even. "Actually, it's none of your business."

"When my daughter's involved, it is my business," Bruce snapped. "Now I want to know what's going on here. And whose motorcycle is that?"

Maggie counted to ten under her breath, then answered in the same even tone, "I don't have to make any explanations to you."

Bruce took a couple of steps toward her. "Well, I just happen to disagree. You'd better grow up, Margaret, and start acting your age."

Tony started to brush past Maggie, and she caught his arm, holding him back. Her heart took a little nosedive when she saw the look on his face. He was furious, and he was staring at Bruce as if he wanted to tear him apart with his bare hands. Turning her back on her ex-husband, she squeezed his hand. "Tony?" she said softly. He acted as if he didn't hear her, the muscles in his jaw flexing as he glared at Bruce. She gave his hand a little shake. "Please."

He finally met her gaze, his face set, white lines of anger carved around his mouth. She could barely believe it—two men ready to bash each other over her. A sliver of humor surfaced, and she couldn't help but smile. The smile was something Tony obviously wasn't expecting, and he narrowed his eyes, as if not entirely sure it was real or not. She'd never wanted to hug anybody so badly in her whole life. "Maybe I should call 911 again," she said, just loud enough for him to hear.

He stared at her, then one corner of his mouth lifted a little. She smoothed her hand up his arm, trying to calm him. "I'm going to have to talk to him," she said very softly.

The muscles in his jaw contracted, and he glanced at Bruce, his face hardening dangerously. Maggie ran her hand up and down his arm, hoping to distract him. "Please, Tony," she pleaded. "Just give us an hour."

He turned his gaze back to her, his eyes like ice. "If he so much as lays a hand on you, I'll break his damned neck."

Maggie tried to produce another smile. "He won't. He just wants to give me a big lecture."

Continuing to stare at her, Tony didn't say anything for a moment, his expression flat and unreadable. Then he expelled his breath. "Okay. An hour." Gripping her shoulder, he very deliberately kissed her. With one final warning glance at Bruce, he started toward the steps, fishing his bike keys out of his pocket. Sticking her chin out in defiance, Kelly followed him.

The veins in Bruce's temples looked as if they were ready to rupture when he stepped in front of his daughter. "Kelly Lynn! You aren't going anywhere."

Kelly gave him a murderous look and stepped off the sidewalk to avoid him. "Just watch me," she retorted. Then she ran and caught up to Tony. She said something to him, and he put his arm around her shoulder, then bent down and swept up both helmets. They reached the bike, and Maggie saw Tony hand one helmet to her daughter. Her own anger making her stomach roil, she turned and started for the back door.

"Are you actually allowing her to go with *him* on *that?*" Bruce demanded.

Maggie whirled and glared at him. "She can go with him if she wants to. But if you want to talk to me, then you'd better talk to me now. Because you aren't going to get another chance." With that, she turned and yanked open the door, letting it slam behind her. She stomped into the kitchen, so furious with him she couldn't keep still, and she had paced back and forth across the kitchen three times by the time Bruce followed her in.

The instant he entered the kitchen, she rounded on him, so infuriated that she was shaking. "You'd better have a damned good explanation for the way you acted out there," she snapped. "I am not your wife. I haven't been for a very long time, and I resent the hell out of you acting like I am. I don't have to make any explanations to you—not a single damned one."

Bruce stripped off his suit jacket and hung it on the back of the chair; then he looked at her, his face stiff with anger. "You don't need to sink to the same kind of language as your...companion, Margaret. You didn't used to be that crass."

Maggie took two deep breaths, determined to get her own anger under control. When she spoke, her voice was shaking. "Who I spend time with and my use of language are none of your business, either, and I'll be crass if I feel like it. Now what are you doing here?"

"I had to fly into town on business this morning, so of course I wanted to see Kelly Lynn. I was very disappointed that she wouldn't come to the coast for spring break." He gave Maggie a bitter smile. "Which, I'm sure, you encouraged."

Maggie stared at him, unable to believe her ears. He knew darned well why Kelly had refused to go, and it had nothing to do with her. She gritted her teeth, waiting for the new burst of anger to ease, then laid it on the line. "The problem between you and Kelly isn't *my* problem, it's yours, Bruce. You make it pretty obvious that you disapprove of most everything she does, so of course she resents you. She's not going to take ballet just because you and Jennifer think it would give her some grace and refinement. And she doesn't want to go to some private girls' school because you think it would expose her to a better class of people. She's her own person, but you keep trying to change her into something she's not. You make her feel inadequate and awkward, so of course she doesn't want to go to visit. So don't make it my problem, Bruce. It's yours.''

He couldn't hold Maggie's gaze, and he looked down and began picking microscopic lint from his trousers. Maggie knew from the way he compressed his mouth that she had hit a nerve, and that he didn't like being smacked in the face with the truth, but she didn't really care. He had crossed a line today, and she was angrier at him than she'd ever been.

He finally looked at her, a stiff expression around his mouth. ''*I* only want what's best for her.''

Maggie's head felt like it was going to explode from a new surge of anger, and she clenched her teeth, trying to hold it all in. She gave herself a good thirty seconds, then exclaimed, ''No, you don't. You want what's best for you.''

He gave her another unpleasant smile. ''You're a fine one to talk. From what I've seen today, you aren't exactly setting a sterling example. Cavorting around in front of her with some muscle-bound biker half your age. I didn't think you'd ever sink to that level, Margaret.''

Maggie folded her arms and tipped her head to one side, giving him a tight smile. ''And just how old is the new Mrs. Burrows? Thirty-six, if I remember correctly. And it wasn't me who abandoned my wife and kids to run off with a younger woman.''

He stared at her, and she caught the flash of guilt in his eyes before he looked away. He shoved his hands in his pockets and went to stand in front of the window. He stared out for a moment, then spoke, his voice clipped. ''Who is he?''

It took Maggie a few seconds to answer. ''Tony Parnelli.''

''What does he do?''

Figuring she owed him that, Maggie answered, ''He and his brother have a business building high-performance engines for race cars. They have the shop next door.''

Bruce shot her a startled look. ''Not Mario Parnelli.''

She studied his face. ''That's his brother. Why? Do you know him?''

Bruce broke eye contact and looked back out the window, a peculiar expression on his face.

"Do you?" she prompted.

He looked very uncomfortable. "Well—ah—well, no, I don't know him personally. But he was a client of the firm here." Bruce ran his finger along a ledge on the window, then brushed off the dust. "Are you sleeping with him?" he asked abruptly.

She considered telling him it was none of his business. Then she changed her mind. "Yes."

There was a long, strained silence, and Maggie closed her eyes and rubbed her temple, a tight feeling in her scalp. Lord, she wished he would just pick up his suit jacket, go home and leave her alone.

Bruce finally broke the silence, a tinge of bitterness in his voice. "I see. So it's just sex."

The anger that had settled down flared up again, and Maggie's pulse started to pound. "I wouldn't know. I don't have anything to compare it to," she answered, her tone cutting.

He turned and looked at her, his lips white with indignation. "And what is that supposed to mean?"

She stared right back at him. "Figure it out for yourself."

He gave her a twisted smile. "Well, you'd better have a long hard look at yourself, Margaret. Not only are you a good ten years older than he is, but you don't exactly have a lot going for you. If you think a man like that, who moves in the circles that he does, is going to be content to spend the rest of his life with you, you're in for a surprise. Do you really think you're going to fit into that crowd? You're going to be nothing but an enormous embarrassment to him—an albatross around his neck. But then," he said, his tone cold and vindictive, "that's nothing new."

Stunned by the viciousness of his attack, Maggie stared at him, a cold, cold feeling spreading through her. It was a bull's-eye hit.

The tension crackled in the ensuing silence, and she finally dragged her gaze away, her one overriding thought to get out of there. Her movements stiff and jerky, she closed the cupboard door and picked up her car keys from the counter. An albatross. He might as well have stabbed her in the back. Numbed to the bone, she lifted her chin and walked past him, her chest hurting, her face frozen. He had flattened her with one killing blow.

By the time Bruce got out to the garage, Maggie was in the car, the engine running, waiting for the big double door to fully open. He grabbed for her door handle, but she had set the door locks. Unable to even look at him, she turned her shoulders the opposite way and backed out of the garage, nearly sideswiping his maroon rental car. Yelling at her to stop, he pounded on the car roof, but Maggie ignored him.

Trembling from head to toe, her vision so blurred she couldn't see, she had to try twice to get the car into drive. Then, staring straight ahead, she gripped the wheel, thinking of nothing but escape. Clenching her jaw against the pain, she tromped on the accelerator.

One part of her brain flashed up the message that he would probably try to follow her. But Bruce always locked his car, and he always put his car keys in the right-hand pocket of his suit jacket.

Numb to the core, Maggie turned down the first alley she came to, then methodically took every alley that would take her away from home. For a split second she considered going to the office, but she knew that would be the first place Bruce would look. So she drove. She didn't know where she was going, and it didn't matter. Because she was still going to have to face herself when she got there.

Maggie spent most of the afternoon sitting on a bluff overlooking Glenmore Reservoir, staring starkly out over the glassy surface of the lake, trying to recover from Bruce's attack. His spiteful comments had been like a slap in the face. But it wasn't really the attack that had numbed her; it was the ugly revelation that had come afterward. Ever since she'd been seeing Tony on a regular basis, there had been an awful, awful feeling that would rise up to haunt her—a feeling that would gnaw away at her and leave her hollowed out inside. Only before, she hadn't known its source. But now she did. Bruce had put it into words.

When he'd told her that someday she would be nothing but an embarrassment to Tony, that awful feeling had coalesced into a hard, cold knot. Because that was what she had been afraid of all along—that someday she would be an albatross around his neck.

The age difference was a big part of it, but it was more than that. She wouldn't fit into his life. Other than Spider and Tony's family, she didn't even know what his life consisted of. They had been living in such a private little world, nothing had intruded. But she knew that someday it would.

She reconfirmed one decision, though, sitting there staring at the lake. It would never work. Never in a million years.

It was late afternoon when Maggie left the bluff and headed home. She probably wouldn't have gone back then if it hadn't been for Kelly. She felt so totally chewed up inside that she just wanted to go somewhere and hide, but she knew her daughter would be worried about her. And as much as she wanted to crawl into a hole, she couldn't do that to her.

Maggie drove down the street first to make sure Bruce's rental car wasn't parked out front; then she turned down the alley. The garage pad was also empty, and she felt a nearly incapacitating rush of relief. The thought of having to face him again made her feel almost sick.

She parked in the space beside the draped Studebaker, then shut off the ignition. She sat there for a long time, numbness weighing her down, making her reluctant to move. She didn't want to have to deal with Kelly, but she couldn't put that off, no matter how much she wanted to. And she prayed to God she wouldn't have to face Tony until tomorrow, when there was more of a chance she'd have everything under control. Releasing a tired sigh, she removed the keys from the ignition and got out of the car, shutting the door behind her. The place had never seemed less like home.

At the side door of the garage, she hit the button to close the big door, then stepped out into blinding sunlight. Feeling as if she was on remote control, she started up the walk, clutching the keys in her hand. Her face felt like wood, and in spite of the heat, she was cold right through. Once she dealt with her daughter, she was going to unplug the phone, crawl into bed and try to block everything out.

The back door was standing open, just like she'd left it, and she pulled open the screen and entered, weariness washing over her. The house was absolutely still, and Maggie experienced a twist of relief. Kelly was probably still off somewhere with Tony. Entering the kitchen, she dropped the keys into the pottery dish on the counter, then pulled her blouse out of the waistband of her slacks. There was a sealed envelope lying on the table with some writing on it, and she turned it around to read it. It was a message from Bruce, asking her to please read the letter inside. Feeling nothing at all, Maggie left it lying there.

"I was about ready to send out a search party."

Maggie's heart gave a lurch and she turned, a crazy flutter taking off in her chest. Tony was standing in the archway, his shoulder resting against the frame, his arms crossed. He had changed into jeans, and he was watching her with a steady look. Maggie's stomach promptly dropped to her shoes.

She evaded the issue. "Where's Kelly?"

"I figured it would be a good idea if she wasn't here, so I gave her and Scott twenty bucks to go in-line skating." He continued to watch her. "So where were you?"

Maggie held his gaze for a moment, then looked down, rubbing her thumb against a mark on the back of the chair. "I had some things to sort out," she said, her tone soft.

"What happened?"

She lifted one shoulder in a barely perceptible shrug.

"Don't do that, Maggie," he said, his voice dangerously quiet. "Don't clam up on me. I want to know what happened."

She managed a small, humorless smile. "He was disgusted because he caught me cavorting around with a muscle-bound biker who was half my age. And he was very upset because Kelly refused to go visit him at spring break, and he thinks it's my fault."

"Did you see the letter?"

Running her fingernail along a groove in the chair back, Maggie nodded.

"Are you going to read it?"

She finally lifted her head and looked at him, grateful she felt so dead inside. "No," she answered.

Tony stared at her, his expression grim, a hard glitter in his eyes. "I don't like your ex much," he said flatly. "And I sure as hell don't like the number he laid on you."

Feeling suddenly shaky, Maggie stuck her hands in the pockets of her slacks and hunched her shoulders. "He hasn't done anything to me."

Tony made a derisive sound. "Yeah, right. It took me about thirty seconds to figure him out. He's crowded you into a narrow little space. You're like one of those mice in the maze races you see at the fair. You follow the path and you stay within the walls, running like hell from point A to point B. Because that's what the game is all about."

His expression altered, and he gave her a twisted smile. "And I keep hoping that you're going to run down one dead end too many, and you're going see how damned senseless it all is. Then maybe you'll finally say to hell with the maze and climb out over the walls."

Maggie got this funny hot rush, one that went straight to her head, and she reached out and grasped the back of the chair to steady herself. It was as if the analogy had given her the ability to see herself more objectively. As if she was standing on the high, narrow walls of a maze, looking down. Her heart beating frantically in her chest, she stared at him, knowing every drop of color had drained from her face.

His expression grim, Tony straightened and came toward her, watching her. He stopped an arm's length from her, then hooked his thumbs in the pockets of his jeans, the muscles in his face tight. He didn't say anything for a moment, then he spoke. "Climb over those goddamned walls, Maggie," he said, challenging her with his dark, angry gaze. "Say to hell with the game and marry me."

Everything swam out of focus but him, and Maggie stared at him, her heart lurching to a stop. Marry him? Oh, God, she had never expected this. Not now. Not ever.

Her heart started to pound again, and she tightened her hold on the chair, the rushing in her head making her sway.

His gaze fixed on her, he reached out and trailed his finger down her cheek, his touch unbelievably gentle. "Marry me, Mag," he repeated, his voice gruff.

*An albatross. You'll be nothing but an albatross around his neck.* A sick feeling washed through her, and she pressed her fist against her breastbone, a deep ache forming in her chest. Feeling suddenly cornered by his closeness, she took a step back, the pain around her heart intense.

He looked away and jammed his hands in his pockets, the muscles in his jaw flexing. Then he spoke, his tone hard. "Or are you playing another game?"

Maggie folded her arms and hunched her shoulders, despair washing through her. Swallowing hard, her voice breaking a little, she answered, "It was never a game. Never. You're the best thing that ever happened to me."

He turned and looked at her, a hard glint in his eyes. "Then why don't you just say yes?"

She gestured helplessly with her hand, then looked away. It took her a while before she could answer. "Because it's wrong for you."

He grabbed her and pulled her head around, forcing her to look at him. "Don't you dare make my decisions for me, Maggie," he snapped, anger flashing in his eyes. "I'm a big boy, and I'm quite capable of making up my own damned mind about how I want to live my life. Now, I want to know how you want to live yours."

He made a disgusted sound and jerked his hand away, then went over to stand in front of the window. Maggie watched him, the pain in her chest climbing higher. She waited for it to ease just a little, then replied, "But have you really thought about the life you want to live? I'm forty-three years old, Tony. I can't have any more kids, and I'm not sure I'd want to if I could. We've been living in our own little fantasy world, but there are some realities out there we haven't even considered."

He turned, his face etched with anger. "Don't give me that crock. This isn't about reality. This is about you. You're the one who's backing away, not me. I knew—the minute I saw you standing in the living room with your face covered in paint—how I felt about you." He came toward her, his body language almost menacing. "But you'd better face a few realities yourself, Burrows. Your backing off isn't tied to any noble feelings about me or my life, it's tied to your own lack of self-esteem. I don't give a damn if you're nine years older than I am or if you can't give me kids. That's not how I measure the quality of life. It's about spending the rest of our life together, willing to take the good along with the bad. That's what this is all about."

Maggie dashed away the tears that had spilled over, then made a beseeching gesture with her hand. "Please. Just hear me out."

Resting his hands on his hips, he glared at her. "I don't want to hear your excuses, Maggie. I want to know if you're going to put it on the line and marry me."

She made another pleading gesture, but he never gave her a chance to speak. He shook his head, bitterness twisting his mouth. "Forget it. If you don't realize what this is all about, I may as well save myself a lot of grief and clear out now. I'm not going to keep putting myself through this. Because I sure as hell can't fight what I can't see."

"Tony, please—"

His face stiff, he cut her off. "Yes or no, Maggie."

There was so much pain in her chest that she couldn't answer him, and he gave her a twisted smile. "Fine. If you ever make up your mind, let me know." Slapping his leg, he turned to go. "I'm outta here."

Maggie covered her face with her hands, a sob tearing loose when she heard the door slam.

Nothing had ever sounded so final.

## Chapter 12

Maggie never slept at all that night. By morning, she was so pale, her face so puffy and swollen, that she actually looked ill. And Kelly never questioned her explanation when she said she wasn't feeling well.

She let her daughter blow off steam about what a jerk her father had been, and somehow managed to keep her emotions in check when she rattled on about how terrific Tony was and how he'd driven her and Scott to Prince's Island to go skating. Maggie managed to keep everything in check until Kelly asked if she could go to the Drumheller Badlands with Scott and his parents. And then she really had to fight to keep up her front. It wasn't that she didn't want Kelly to go; she did. With Kelly gone for the day, she wouldn't have to keep pretending that nothing was wrong.

After Kelly left, Maggie went downstairs and huddled in the corner of the sofa in the family room, her throat aching as she stared blindly into the semidarkness. She couldn't even bear to think about Tony. But she did think about how long it would be before she stopped hurting.

She was at least able to function the next morning. Granted, she looked like hell, but an awful numbness had set in, and she felt oddly disconnected, almost as if she were in someone else's body. Maggie was never sure how, but she also managed to function at work, although Frank kept giving her funny looks. And she saved herself a lot of heartache by walking the long way home.

But the minute she started up her back walk, her throat got tight and her eyes started to fill up, and she felt so raw inside that she wasn't sure she could make it into the house. Dropping her purse and keys in the hallway, she went straight to the bathroom and locked herself in, her subsequent emotional purge just about turning her inside out.

By the time Kelly came home, she had more or less pulled herself together. She was in the kitchen making potato salad—with the blind pulled down so she couldn't see next door—when the back door flew open. Storming into the kitchen, Kelly threw her backpack across the room, then turned to face her mother, her face stark white. "What's going on?" she nearly shouted. "I just stopped in at Tony's, and he's leaving town tonight. He would barely talk to me, and Spider said he's going to the States instead of Mario, and he won't be back for at least six weeks." Tears welled up in the teenager's eyes and her mouth started to tremble. "What did you do to him?" she demanded. "I asked him what was wrong, and he wouldn't even look at me. He said I'd have to ask you."

It was a double blow for Maggie—her daughter's obvious distress, plus the news that Tony was leaving. Except the second one was much worse. A hundred times worse. Knowing her own face had gone pale, she went to touch Kelly, but the girl dodged away from her hand. "Don't! Don't try to make things all right. Because they aren't. You did something, didn't you?"

Feeling as if her heart had collapsed, Maggie stared at her daughter, not knowing what to say.

Tears were streaming down Kelly's face when she demanded, "Didn't you?"

Her own vision blurring, Maggie swallowed hard, then nodded.

Her daughter gave her one scathing look, then turned and snatched her backpack off the floor. "I really think I hate you." Shoving a chair aside, she ran out of the room, and Maggie heard her sobbing as she started down the basement stairs.

Her throat so tight she couldn't swallow, Maggie went to stand at the window overlooking the backyard. Tightly folding her arms to compress the pain in her chest, she stood staring out, unable to see. Just like that, she had lost them both.

Over the next few days, Kelly pretty much stopped speaking to her, and Maggie pretty much stopped eating. It was a grim, silent household, and Maggie went to work and came home feeling like death inside. She had received a couriered letter from Bruce, which she threw unopened on top of the fridge, along with the one he had left on the table, also unopened.

After the second letter arrived, Maggie turned off the answering machine, knowing he would likely follow up with a phone call. She didn't even want to hear the sound of his voice. She would have disconnected the phone as well, but she didn't want to do that to Kelly, since most of the calls were for her.

And Maggie knew with an awful certainty that the one call that would mean anything to her would never come. Because she had seen him leave. After Kelly had stormed off downstairs Monday evening, Maggie had gone into the living room and watched out the window until nine o'clock, when the car transport had pulled up in front of the shop. She'd watched Spider load a car from one of the bays, and she'd watched as Tony tossed a duffel into the cab, then climbed up into the driver's seat of the eighteen wheeler. And then she had watched him drive away, taking her last piece of hope with him.

Thursday night after work Maggie went for groceries, feeling so listless that even pushing the grocery cart was an effort. By the time she got home, she was so drained she just wanted to put her head down on the steering wheel and not move for twelve straight hours. Normally Kelly would have brought in the groceries, but Maggie carried them in herself. She couldn't face another one of Kelly's silent rebukes tonight.

She heard the phone ring as she came up the deck steps with the last three bags. She had left the screen door propped partially open, and she shouldered her way in. Kelly was standing in the kitchen with the phone in her hand. She didn't look up as she held out the receiver. "It's Dad."

Hurt by the slight, Maggie set the groceries on the counter. The very last thing she wanted right now was to talk to Bruce. "Tell him I'll call him back."

Kelly dropped the receiver on the counter, then walked away. "Tell him yourself."

Maggie closed her eyes, wishing right then that she could find a deep hole for herself. She toyed with the idea of just ignoring him until he got tired and hung up, but she knew he'd call back. Heaving a sigh, she picked up the receiver. She might have to talk to him, but she didn't have to be nice about it.

She opened the cupboard door and started putting away groceries. "What do you want?"

There was a brief silence, as if her sharpness had caught him off guard. "I was wondering if you got my letters."

Maggie jammed a box of salt into the cupboard. "Yes. I got them."

"I felt I owed you an explanation."

Maggie stuffed three jars of spices beside the salt. "You gave me an explanation, Bruce," she said, feeling uncharitable. "It had something to do with me being an albatross."

There was a hesitation, then he spoke again, a gruff tone in his voice. "I meant in the letters, Margaret."

Suddenly close to tears and not even sure why, Maggie started yanking items out of the bag and stacking them on the counter. "I wouldn't know. I didn't read them." She emptied the bag and threw it on the table. "So if that's all—"

"Margaret! Wait!" Then the tone of his voice changed. "Please."

Maggie leaned back against the counter and closed her eyes, rubbing at the dull ache between her eyes. If she cried one more tear, she was going to evaporate. Taking a deep, shaky breath, her tone unbearably weary, she asked, "What do you want, Bruce?"

It was three full seconds before he answered, and his voice was very quiet when he did. "I was very unfair to you, Margaret." There was another long pause, then he continued, "I never thought it would bother me if I saw you with another man, but it was—was quite unsettling, and I reacted badly. And I suppose that was the first time I had some idea of how you must have felt when I married Jennifer. And whether you know it or not, I've always felt very guilty about that." Maggie heard him try to clear his throat, and for some reason her own got unbearably tight, and she rubbed the ache again.

"Maybe that's why I've been so—so intense with Shawn and the girls—because I was trying to compensate. But the reason doesn't matter." He took an unsteady breath, then continued, "But my worst crime is what I've done to you. You were an excellent mother and you were a good wife, and I said some things on Saturday that weren't even remotely true. You were never an embarrassment, Margaret. And you were never an albatross."

Maggie wiped away the tears that had slipped out, a huge wad of emotion clogging her chest. She wondered if he had any idea what it meant to her to hear that.

"After I thought it over, I realized I was being . . . I don't know. Sour grapes, maybe. I suppose I was a little jealous— which is rather silly, considering the circumstances. But I've really thought about it the past few days, and I sincerely want you to be happy, Margaret. And I'm going to try very hard to be less managing with the kids. You've always been more than fair with me. It's time I was equally fair with you."

Maggie looked up at the ceiling, trying to will away the tears, will away an ache in her chest the size of Kansas. It was as if he had removed an old, painful weight from her shoulders, and she experienced a rush of real gratitude toward the father of her children. She blinked several times, then swallowed hard. "I'm glad you called," she said, trying very hard to keep her voice from breaking. "I don't want bad feelings between us. I really don't."

"I'm sorry. I didn't mean to make you cry."

Maggie managed a shaky laugh. "This isn't bad crying, Bruce. This is good crying."

There was another brief pause, then he spoke again. "I hope you'll read the letters, Margaret. They were written with the very best of intentions."

The cramp finally let go in her throat, and her voice was steady when she answered, "I will. I promise."

"Could you put Kelly Lynn back on? I wanted to speak to you before I spoke to her."

"Just hang on." Maggie was about to lay the phone down, then she put it back to her ear. "Bruce?"

"Yes?"

She looked at the ceiling, her eyes filling up again. "Take care."

His voice was very gruff when he responded, "You, too, Margaret. Take very good care."

Maggie lay the receiver down, then went to the landing and called for Kelly to pick up the phone downstairs. She went back and lifted up the receiver, listening until she heard her daughter's voice. Then she hung up the phone, turned and went into bathroom, locking herself in. This time it wasn't so much an emotional purge, it was more of an emotional commemoration.

Things were a little easier after Bruce's phone call. Not much, but a little. They were also a little easier with Kelly. She didn't disclose what her father had said, and she still didn't speak to Maggie unless she had to. But she was less hostile, more thoughtful—as if she was working through something in her mind.

For Maggie, it was as if Bruce's call had unlocked some old, emotional shackles. And she finally realized that Tony was right. She was like a mouse caught in a maze, always playing the game, always doing what was expected of her. More than anything she wanted to climb over that wall, but she didn't know how. She didn't even know if she could. Because Tony was right about that, too: it boiled down to her own lack of self-esteem. She was a good employee, and she had tried her best to be a good daughter, wife, mother. But she didn't know who or what *she* was. And that was a hard thing to deal with, knowing she had lost Tony because she was afraid to climb over the wall, afraid to say to hell with the game and be her *own* person.

She got through Saturday and most of Sunday, but by Sunday evening she was feeling pretty damned lonely.

She'd been working in her home office, but by nine o'clock she'd developed a blinding headache, and she went into the kitchen to get some over-the-counter medication she kept in the cupboard with her vitamin pills. Kelly had gone to a movie, and the house was uncommonly quiet. Far too quiet. With the two pills in her hand, she got a clean glass out of the dishwasher, then turned on the tap, holding her finger under it while waiting for it to get cold. Without thinking, she glanced out the window, and she got such a numbing shock that it drained the blood out of her face.

There was a moving truck backed up at right angles to the stairs, and Spider, one of Tony's brothers, a brother-in-law and two other men were lugging Tony's furniture down the stairs and loading it into the back of the truck.

The reality nearly brought her to her knees. He was really leaving—not just for six weeks, but for good.

If there was ever an ultimate devastation, this was it. The shock sent a crazy kind of panic through her, stripping away any lingering hope she might have had, and she turned blindly away from the window, litanies of denial racing around in her head. He couldn't leave. He couldn't.

But he could. And he was.

A wrenching sense of loss piled in on her, and she stumbled into a chair at the end of the table, put her elbows on the wooden surface and covered her face with her hands.

He was never coming back.

Sobs broke from her—great sobs that came from so deep within her that her whole body shook, and Maggie let it all go. The pain, the sense of loss, but mostly the hope.

Once she started, she couldn't stop. She didn't even try. It was just too much, the proverbial last straw. It was the end of everything.

A single sound penetrated—the sound of the screen door closing. Maggie tried to stop, but trying to stop that kind of crying was a little like trying to stop a fast-moving freight train—there was just too much momentum built up.

"Mom! What's wrong?"

Maggie heard Kelly go to the sink and shut off the running water, then cross the room and kneel by her, brushing her hair back. "Come on, Mom," she prodded. "Tell me what's wrong."

"I need a tissue," Maggie managed to say in a choked voice.

Kelly got up and went to the counter, collecting the box of tissues. She set it on the table, pulled one out and pressed it against Maggie's hand.

Knowing her face was pretty much a mess, Maggie took it, blew her nose and wiped her eyes, random sobs still shuddering loose. Kelly got up again and went to the sink, coming back with a glass of very cold water. "Here," she said softly. "Drink this."

Maggie almost started crying all over again. It was what she used to do when the kids were small, when they got crying so hard they couldn't stop. And now her daughter was doing it for her.

Kelly pressed the glass against her hand. "Come on, Mom," she coaxed.

Regaining a tiny modicum of control, Maggie took the glass and tried to drink, though her throat cramped up and new tears spilled over. She managed to get most of it down, though, and it did help.

She set the glass aside and pulled two more tissues from the box, then wiped her eyes and nose again, her lips puffy, her throat raw.

Kelly pulled a chair around the corner of the table and sat down. "Are you going to talk to me?"

Maggie looked at her, her eyes filling up again. She dropped her gaze and folded the tissues, taking a deep, shuddering breath. "I've been so stupid," she whispered.

"Is this about Dad or about Tony?"

Maggie couldn't quite bring herself to confront the truth, so she skirted it. "It's not about your dad. He was actually was very nice when he called."

Resting her arms on her thighs, Kelly began rubbing Maggie's hand. "He told me he had said some pretty awful things to you."

Maggie managed a wobbly smile. "Well, I said some pretty awful things to him, too."

Shifting in her chair, Kelly propped both elbows on the table, then rested her chin in her hands, her gaze fixed on her mother. "I know I'm only fifteen, Mom," she said quietly, "but I'm not exactly stupid. You can tell me, you know."

Unable to hold her daughter's gaze, Maggie refolded the damp tissues. "It really bothered me that I was so much older than Tony, and that scared me, I guess." Her eyes filled up again, and she quickly wiped them, then swallowed hard. "And I guess I couldn't understand why somebody like him could be remotely interested in someone like me."

"So you blew it."

Maggie tried to smile. "Yeah," she whispered, "I blew it."

"And you're feeling really bad."

Maggie locked her jaw against the renewed ache in her throat and nodded.

"Maybe you could just talk to Tony."

The ache getting worse, Maggie looked away and shook her head. It took her a while before she could answer. "He's not going to give me another chance," she said, her voice breaking. "I've backed away one time too many." She took a deep breath. "And there's a van next door. He's moving out."

Alarm flitted across Kelly's face and she jumped up and went to the window. She stood there for the longest time, as if she couldn't believe what she was seeing. Then she came back and knelt down by Maggie, slipping her arms around her waist. There were tears in her voice when she whispered, "I'm really sorry, Mom."

Another sob threatening, Maggie hugged her daughter, her voice so thick she could barely answer. "So am I, sweetie. So am I."

It was as if Maggie's admitting she had made a terrible mistake was all Kelly needed to hear and, overnight, her attitude changed. They didn't talk about Tony anymore, but they did talk about Bruce, and if nothing else, some good came out of that.

And it was as if that one wrenching breakdown dulled Maggie's emotional state. She still had trouble sleeping and eating, but she was able to get through each day, simply by putting one foot in front of the other. But she did begin to wonder if she would ever laugh again.

Frank was still giving her funny looks at work, but he didn't say anything. On Wednesday afternoon, however, he went out for coffee and came back with a big bouquet of yellow roses from the discount florist down the street. The buds were a little wilted, and some of the leaves had started to wither, but it was the thought that counted, and it was all Maggie could do to keep from shedding more tears. She had picked off the wilted leaves and was arranging the flowers in the cheap plastic vase when Stevie showed up looking fit, tanned and gorgeous.

Closing the door, she looked impressed when she saw the roses. "Ooh, yellow roses. And what secrets have you been keeping from me, Mary Margaret?" She set the briefcase she was carrying down on Maggie's desk, then reached past her friend and caressed one still-perfect bud.

Maggie stuck in another bud amidst the fern and baby's breath. "Don't get too excited. They're from Frank."

Stevie sat down on the edge of Maggie's desk and folded her arms, her gaze thoughtful as she studied her face. Finally she spoke, her voice very quiet. "You look like hell, M and M. What's the matter?"

A huge lump forming in her throat, Maggie shook her head.

Stevie didn't say anything. She just continued to watch Maggie, then got up, picked up her briefcase and started toward Frank's office. "Hey, Frank. You out-of-shape, cholesterol-saturated hunk, you. I brought you the spa books." She pushed opened his door just as another bomb blast sounded on his computer.

Frank yelled at her. "Damn it! You got me killed, and I was on level eleven."

"Well, Frank, dead is dead, whether you're on level eleven or not. Now," she said, as if getting ready to negotiate, "I won't tell your clients you play computer games on their time if you let me kidnap Mags.''

"Hell, take her. Just leave me alone."

Stevie reappeared by Maggie's desk without the briefcase. She reached past her and shut off the computer, picked up Maggie's handbag, then latched on to her wrist. "Come on, Mary Margaret. Auntie Stevie is taking you away from all this."

Maggie looked dumbly at her computer. "You shut it off," she said, stating the obvious, "and I had a file open."

"I know you, Maggie. You would have saved it three times before you got up." She started toward the door, tugging Maggie behind her. "Don't drag your heels, M and M. You're coming with me."

"I can't—"

Stevie gave her another firm tug. "Yes, you can. And you are. I'll get Hans to carry you out of here if I have to." Hans was one of Stevie's employees. He stood about 6'4", had muscles on his muscles and arms like tree trunks. Maggie experienced an actual flicker of amusement. It would be no contest. She'd once seen Hans hold up the back end of Stevie's car so another employee could change the tire.

Well aware of the fact that Stevie didn't know what the word *no* meant, Maggie finally relented. Who knew? Maybe La Goddess could make her laugh.

Stevie took full control. Without being actually sure how she got there, Maggie found herself seated in one of the window tables in the elegant little café a block away. It had a real French waiter, real linen tablecloths, and it served the best lemonade in the entire world.

With two very large glasses between them, Stevie planted her elbows on the tablecloth and laced her immaculately manicured hands together under her chin. She stared at Maggie, a no-nonsense look in her eyes. "Okay, Mary Margaret. Give. You're the most pathetic-looking thing I've ever seen."

Maggie looked out the window and sipped lemonade through a straw.

Stevie heaved a sigh. "Look," she said, sounding bossy. "I'm not going to be nice to you. I know that if I say one nice thing, you're going to burst into tears. And I'd say you've cried too many already. So I'm just going to bully you, be nasty and say rude things.''

A hint of a smile surfacing, Maggie finally looked at her friend. Which was a mistake, because there was real, honest compassion in Stevie's eyes. Maggie's throat got tight, and she abruptly looked away again, continuing to sip the ice-cold drink until the contraction eased. Once she thought she had things under control, she set down the glass, hooked her elbows on the table and started to talk.

Stevie barely said anything. Once or twice she prompted Maggie with questions, but mostly she just listened. And until Maggie got started, she didn't realize how badly she needed that. She told Stevie everything—about how she had shied away from Tony because of the age difference, except it wasn't the age difference at all, and about the scene with Bruce and the final one with Tony, when he'd made the comment about mice in a maze and her own lack of self-esteem. The only time her voice nearly gave out was when she told Stevie about Tony moving out.

When she finally finished, there was a long silence; then Stevie pushed aside her glass. ''I'm going to tell you my big theory. Self-esteem isn't really about self-esteem. It's about power. It's about taking control.'' Resting her arms on the table, she took a deep breath. ''People think a health spa is about egos and getting beautiful, and for some people—the shallow ones—that's what it is. But for some of us, it's about taking control of our lives. I used to weigh a ton, I was unhappy in my job and my life was pretty much a mess. I had handed control over to everyone else in my life—my parents, my boss, my boyfriend. And I was miserable.''

She looked up at Maggie, her gaze serious. ''I want you to do something for me, Maggie. I want you to go on a program I'll design for you. For one month. I *know,* from what I went through myself, that getting fit and healthy is the first step to recovery. It won't work if you're doing it because you want people to start noticing you, or if you're doing it so you'll have great buns and thighs. But it'll work if you're doing it to get some control back in your life.''

Stevie frowned and traced her finger around the base of her glass, then met Maggie's gaze again. "I could sit here and tell you to try to patch things up with Tony, but he's right. And you know he's right, so leave him out of this. Do it for yourself. I'll guarantee you—if you go into a fitness program with the right attitude, even after two weeks you're going to start having a whole different attitude about yourself. You're going to start feeling the physical power. And when that happens, you're going to start tapping into the psychological power. You're going to start feeling better and looking better, and pretty soon you're going to start looking around and saying, gee, if I've accomplished all this, what else can I do? I've seen it happen a thousand times, and that's why I love what I do."

Compassion warming her gaze, she reached across the table and squeezed Maggie's hand. "I know how you feel, Maggie," she said, her tone soft with kindness. "I've been there. And I know you just want to crawl in a hole and die, but you can't. You need to do something constructive right now, and believe me, getting fit is the most constructive thing you can do for yourself."

Maggie stared at her friend, a whole new respect dawning. It made sense; even to her, it made sense. Folding her hands under her chin, she looked out the window, a terrible rush of unhappiness making her eyes sting. Too bad it was a week and a half too late.

She waited for the feeling to ease, then looked back at Stevie, a wry smile appearing. "Are you going to make me wear one of those awful, slinky leotards?"

Stevie grinned. "Even I don't wear those things when I'm working out. They're strictly marketing." Giving a pleased little wriggle, she stood up and went back to being bossy. "Come on, Mary Margaret. We're going shopping for some good cross-trainers. If nothing else, you've *got* to have good shoes."

For the second time that afternoon, Maggie experienced a twist of real amusement. She should have known that Stevie would want to go shopping.

* * *

After the first two days on Stevie's program, Maggie didn't want to crawl into a hole. She just wanted to die. Every muscle in her body hurt, her abdomen felt as if a tank had driven over it and she could barely lift her arms over her head. The only good thing to come out of all the agony was that she slept like the dead at night.

After a week on the program and two sessions with Stevie's masseuse, the soreness disappeared, and Maggie was starting to get the hang of lifting weights. Stevie rode her like a drill sergeant, making sure she did each exercise with military preciseness. Proper form, proper body positions. Stevie didn't allow any sloppiness in her establishment.

After two weeks, Maggie started doing a run-walk routine in the morning before she went to work, and she started staying later at the spa. The morning-run thing she did for herself, because it gave her more energy during the day. The reason she stayed later in the evenings was because she felt so damned lost at night and so alone. She had one particularly bad night, after Kelly told her Spider had moved into the apartment over the shop. That was the night she started writing letters to Tony—ones she knew she would never send, but where she told him how much she regretted the mistakes she'd made with him and how right he'd been. She tried to explain herself in those letters. And in writing them, she often explained things to herself. It helped a bit, feeling as if she was somehow communicating with him, but those last couple of hours before she went to bed were the absolute worst. And if rank unhappiness moved in, it was usually then.

She noticed right away that she was sleeping better. Except she was plagued with one recurring dream, of her running through a maze, looking for a way out.

By the beginning of the fourth week, she started noticing something else—the fit of her clothes. Which surprised her, because she was at least eating again. When she finally got on the scale, she was astounded to discover that she had lost twelve pounds.

But the most astounding thing happened to her midway through that fourth week. She was on the Stair Master, and twenty minutes into the exercise, with sweat rolling off her, she got this incredible, amazing rush. It was as if she'd just tapped into a major energy source. Feeling as if she had the strength to go forever, she set the difficulty level higher and really went for it, the unbelievable surge of raw energy pumping through her. Damn it, if she could do this, she could do anything she wanted.

Stevie came over and handed her a dry towel, a knowing smirk on her face. "I told you," she said.

Maggie felt like laughing. "Get out of my way, or so help me, I'll run right over you."

The very next day, Maggie signed up for diving lessons. She'd been a half-decent diver when she was in high school, and she darned well wanted to do it again. There was something so freeing about soaring up, then arching over and arrowing down into the water, the whole wonderful flight controlled by your own strength. She had never considered doing it again, because she would have had to be in half-decent shape. But by September, when the course started, she would be in good-enough physical shape. She felt like dancing and throwing her arms in the air when she came out of that registration office. Stevie was right. She had the power! And God, it felt wonderful!

That sense started to deteriorate badly at the beginning of the sixth week. And it had nothing to do with the program or what she was doing in her life. It had to do with Tony Parnelli.

With increasing frequency, Maggie found herself standing in front of the living room window, her stomach in knots, watching for some sign that he was back, regret and loneliness settling on her like some shapeless weight. The loneliness was bad enough. But the regret? God, she couldn't even measure it.

One night it was particularly bad. She felt as if all her old mistakes were crowding in on her, and she spent hours pacing around the house, a terrible frustration building up in her chest. Deciding in a fit of desperation that she needed to do something decisive to cut those ties to the past, she marched into her bedroom, tore everything out of her closet that represented her old life and tossed it on the bed.

It didn't matter that it was past midnight; it all went. Tidy little suits, drab-colored skirts and slacks, uptight blouses, practical shoes—anything that represented what she did not want to be anymore she got rid of. She stuffed the whole mess into two large orange garbage bags, then marched the works out to her car and drove it all to the nearest charity drop box. She cried all the way home, experiencing a weird kind of relief, as if she'd just got rid of every drab, dull thing in her whole life. It was something she should have done years ago.

The very next day, she transferred money from her savings account—the one for her old age. Then she picked up Stevie after work, dusted off a credit card that she rarely used and went shopping. Frank nearly fainted when she showed up for work the next morning.

It helped. It really did. At least as far as her rebirth was concerned. But it didn't help to heal the gaping hole in her heart.

By the end of eight weeks, she had a new wardrobe, a trimmer body, a very much slimmer savings account, and she was really beginning to feel good about herself. Except she couldn't stay away from the living room window, hoping to catch one more glimpse of Tony. It finally hit her, after she'd stared out the window for nearly two hours one Friday night, what her vigil was all about. It wasn't about getting one more glimpse of him; it was about getting one more chance.

That realization shook her—really shook her—and it also scared her to death. Because another realization came hard on the heels of the first. If she really wanted it to happen, she was going to have to make it happen.

Her heart started hammering and her hands turned clammy, and she had such a wild flutter in her chest that she could feel it all the way down to the soles of her feet. It was up to her. Nobody else. Just her.

Turning from the window, she stared blindly at the opposite wall, her heart trying to escape from her chest. It was up to her.

Without giving herself time to reconsider, she turned and headed for the front door.

Leaving the door ajar, she went down her recently painted steps and ran across the yard, the crazy clamor in her chest getting worse when she saw that one big bay door of the shop was open. Feeling shaky from the inside out, she entered the brightly lighted area, hope warring with dread.

Spider was working on something he had clamped in a vise, and he looked up when her heel scraped against some scrap metal on the floor. He stared at her, pure distaste in his eyes, then gave a disgusted snort and turned back to the workbench. The frenzy inside her abruptly contracted into one awful, hollow knot. With fear caught in her throat, Maggie clenched her fingers and took a very deep breath. "I need to know where Tony is."

Spider slammed one screwdriver down and picked up another. "I ain't tellin' you nothin'," he growled. "You sliced him up pretty good last time, lady, and I ain't gonna help you do it again."

Going over to the bench where he was working, Maggie fingered a bubble-packed set of spark plugs, then folded her arms. She hesitated for a minute, then went on sheer instinct. And instinct told her Spider needed an explanation. Her tone was not quite even when she spoke. "I'm nine years older than he is, Spider. I can't have any more kids, and I was so sure he'd regret that someday."

He turned his head, giving her a hard, assessing look. "You gonna cry?" he demanded, in much the same tone he'd use if he was asking if she was a carrier of typhoid fever.

Maggie returned his look. "No, I'm not going to cry."

He picked up a small socket wrench and loosened a nut. "If there's anything I hate, it's a bawlin' woman."

Maggie experienced a tug of humor. It was a darned good thing he hadn't been around her the past few weeks. Spider removed the nut and bolt and threw them into a can filled with solvent. "You can't have any more kids, huh?"

"No." Maggie ran her thumb along the seal in the pack of spark plugs, then folded her arms again. "I'm not sure I'd want to start all over even if I could."

Spider loosened two more nuts. "Makes sense, under the circumstances." He stripped those out and tossed them in the container, then started to disassemble what seemed to be an oil-covered electrical motor. He spoke again, his tone just a little too innocent. "So why ain't you been over sooner? You ain't exactly a long way away."

Maggie looked across the shop, not wanting to recall how she'd felt the day they'd moved Tony's things out. Once she was sure her voice wasn't going to give out on her, she answered, "I knew he'd left town for a few weeks. And I knew he'd moved out." She had to wait a minute before she could continue. "I thought he might show up here," she said, her voice wavering a little, "but I haven't seen him around."

"Ain't been around."

Maggie studied the mechanic's face. "Is he back?"

"Yep. Been back a week or so." He gave her a steady look. "Heard he's plannin' on moving to the States."

Experiencing an awful sinking sensation, Maggie tightened her arms and looked away. "I see," she said very quietly. She stared out into the gray twilight, her heart absolutely hollow. That was it then; she had burnt all her bridges.

"Ain't seen him, ain't talked to him, but—" he paused to wipe the motor with an oily rag "—I expect he'll turn up at the Blue Hornet tonight. Some of us are headin' over for a couple of beers and a little blues."

Her heart suddenly pounding, Maggie fixed her gaze on the mechanic. "Spider?"

He looked at her with that same steady look.

She stared at him and swallowed hard, her heart climbing higher. "Are you telling me where he's going to be?"

Spider studied her for a moment, then a faint glint appeared in his eyes. "'Spect I am."

A thousand emotions breaking loose in her, Maggie reached up and kissed him on the cheek, not caring a damn if she got grease all over her. "Thanks, Spider," she whispered, gratitude cramping up her throat. Maybe she had one more chance, after all.

The place was packed, and Maggie had to scrunch up her shoulders to wedge herself through the crowd standing by the bar. She could barely breathe, but she didn't know if it was from the thick layer of smoke or from the panic in her chest. After she'd left Spider, she'd gone straight home, but the moment she stepped through the door, a frantic kind of terror had rolled over her. She had done circuits around the house, trying to outrun it, but it had dogged her every step. She was scared out of her mind. During one single burst of courage, she had called a cab, knowing she would never get out of the alley if she drove herself.

And now she was here, her heart the size of a basketball and her nerves in shreds. She was still scared to death to face him. After what had happened the last time, she knew she had about one chance in a million, but it was that one chance that kept her from heading back out the door.

She had done her hair, put on some new clothes, fixed her makeup—but it didn't help a bit. She still had this huge wad of dread bouncing around in her chest.

Her hands clammy and her throat tight, she skirted the perimeter of the room, looking for someone—anyone—who might be with Tony. But after two careful circuits and several heart-stopping false alarms, Maggie knew he wasn't there, and she began to truly feel like a mouse in a maze.

Aware that she was beginning to get peculiar looks from the bouncer standing by the door, she made one final tack. Squeezing through the crowd of people standing just outside the short hallway leading to a fire exit, she made her way into the pool room, her insides twisting into knots. *Let him be here,* she prayed silently. *Please, let him be here.*

That room was crowded as well, and it took some time to get through the congestion by the door, but once she had, the room thinned out.

The first person she spotted was Spider. He was standing at the far right-hand side of the room, the butt of his cue resting on the floor, his hands wrapped around the tapered end. With her heart wedged in her throat, she scanned that end of the room, her fear climbing higher. Unable to spot Tony, she scanned the room again, her heart dropping abruptly to her shoes. He wasn't there. The tightness in her chest got worse, and her throat closed up. God, he wasn't there.

Spider glanced toward the door and saw her, his expression bland. Attempting a smile, Maggie held out her hands and shrugged, not sure she could keep up any kind of a front. He narrowed his eyes, as if assessing her; then he stepped back and made a motion with his head, directing her gaze.

Maggie went so weak her heart nearly stopped altogether. Tony was crouched down on the far side of the table, a long, thin aluminum case on the floor before him, and he was assembling a custom-made cue. He stood, handed the case to one of the men standing behind them, then tested the weight of the stick. He grinned and said something to Spider, then leaned over the table to line up a shot.

Grounded by indecision, Maggie stared at him, afraid to stay, even more afraid to go. Anxiety made her palms itch, and she glanced at Spider, her expression stark. He grinned again and motioned her over with a jerk of his head.

Certain she was damned no matter what she did, she turned right and slipped between two tables, feeling as if there was an avalanche happening in her stomach. Deliberately staying out of Tony's field of view, she went over to where Spider was standing, her heart pounding.

She opened her mouth to speak to him, but he shook his head, put his finger to his lips and shoved the cue into her hand. Then he gave her a thumbs-up sign.

Maggie knew what he was doing: he was setting Tony up. And she didn't have a clue what to do. But before she got a chance to decide, Tony spoke. "Okay, Spider," he said, slapping a twenty-dollar bill on the wooden rim of the table. "Now we get serious. This cue is a honey, and I'm gonna clean you out."

Spider went over to the table and put some coins in the slot, releasing the balls Tony had sunk. Setting the balls and the rack on the table, he gave Tony a sly smile over his shoulder. "Since we're playing for hard, cold cash, I hired me a ringer."

Grinning at Spider's little joke, Tony turned and reached for a bottle of beer sitting on the side table, his expression going perfectly still when he saw Maggie standing there. He didn't say anything; then his face hardened and he turned away. He took a long pull on the beer, set it back on the table, then turned back, his jaw rigid, his eyes like ice. "Fine," he said, his tone flat. He picked up a cube from the edge of the table and chalked his cue; then he looked at her, not a trace of expression in his eyes. "Put your money on the table. Best two out of three."

A nasty little flutter took off in Maggie's throat, and she felt the blood rush to her middle. It got unnaturally quiet in their corner, and she tried to swallow the awful feeling climbing up inside her. Still gripping the cue, she opened her handbag, took a twenty-dollar bill out of her wallet, then zipped her bag. Without looking at Tony, she pulled her purse strap off her shoulder, then set the bag beside the bottle of beer.

Turning back to the table, she placed the bill beside the one Tony had laid down. Knowing he would never talk to her, knowing this was the one and only chance she was going to get, she said a silent prayer, then wiggled her grandmother's wedding ring off her finger. Hoping everyone watching would think it was something she normally did, she placed it very carefully in the center of the paper money. Steeling herself, she looked at Tony, hoping he would see it for what it was. He looked from the ring to her, his jaw rock hard, not a trace of forgiveness in his eyes.

He stared at her for a good ten seconds, then spoke, his tone like steel. "Call it."

Dread building within her, she held his gaze, her heart hammering. "My win."

He gave a cold, insolent smile, and Maggie knew. If he won, the game was truly over. And she'd lose far more than twenty dollars and a gold ring.

And she knew with sickening clarity that the game was over anyway.

That same contemptuous smile on his face, he continued to stare at her. "Your break."

Trying to close down inside, trying not to think at all, Maggie bent over, bridged her hand on the table and lined up her shot, counting on nothing but experience to get her through.

It was a bad break. And Maggie was a long way from championship form. She was shaking so badly inside that she couldn't stay focused, and she badly misjudged a bank shot.

But what killed her was that it became increasingly clear that Tony was playing a focused, cutthroat game, and he was doing his damnedest to annihilate her.

The first game was close. But it was his win.

In the second, she didn't have a chance. She was so sick inside, so close to tears, that she could barely see, and she completely blew her first shot.

Chalking the end of his cue, he gave her a long, level look, his face set; then he bent down, his voice curt. "Red ball in the corner pocket." And without another glance at her, he ran the table with single-minded thoroughness, making one impossible shot after another. Having run all the solids, he spoke, his voice slicing through the silence. "Eight ball in the side pocket."

With a sharp report of white against black, the black ball disappeared in the side well. And it was over.

Feeling like she was dying inside, Maggie forced a smile, then placed her cue on the table. "Good game." Without looking at anyone, she went over and picked up her purse. Turning to leave, she touched Spider on the arm, her throat too tight, too clogged with tears to speak. Determined to keep her dignity intact, she walked away from the table, her spine ramrod straight. All she had to do was keep it together until she got to the exit door.

But the minute she turned down the short hallway, the awful pressure in her chest overrode her determination, and her vision blurred. A sob wedged in her throat as blind panic gripped her. Out. She had to get out. She had to get out right now.

She had her hand on the safety bar of the door when she was caught from behind, whirled around and shoved back against the wall. And suddenly, she was face-to-face with a furious Tony Parnelli.

Clenching her teeth to hold back the tears, she closed her eyes and turned her head away, so destroyed that she couldn't meet his gaze. Grasping her by the jaw, he forced her face up, and for one split second, she thought he was going to strangle her.

His eyes flashing with anger, he pressed her back against the wall, so furious that his voice shook. "For two cents I'd strangle you right here, Burrows. Where the hell do you get off pulling a damned stunt like that? The rest of my life is not going to be based on some damned joke, and it isn't going to depend on some stupid challenge."

Tears slipping down her face, Maggie tried to twist away, but he thrust her head up, his face inches from hers. "There was no bloody way I was going to let you win. No bloody way. Because I'm not going to let some damned game determine the rest of my life." His breathing rapid, he stared at her, as if trying to get his fury under control. "Damn it, Maggie. You drive me crazy." Then, with a rough exhalation of air, he clenched his eyes shut and hauled her into his arms, jerking her head against his shoulder. "God," he whispered hoarsely, "I'd just about given up on you. And this time I'm not letting you go."

The sobs broke loose, and Maggie wound her arms around his neck and held on for dear life, a crazy kind of relief rushing through her. "Marry me," she murmured brokenly. "I want you to marry me." Clutching his head, she tightened her hold, tears slipping down her face. "I need you in my life. I don't want to lose you."

Tightening his own grasp, he whispered against her hair, his voice ragged, "There's isn't a chance in hell you're going to lose me. No damned way." He ran his hand up her back, then hugged her hard. "You're mine, Burrows. I just wish it hadn't taken you so damned long to figure that out."

Her bedroom was dark, but the sky was starting to lighten, and Maggie shifted her head on Tony's shoulder and smiled, slowly caressing his chest. It was a miracle she could move at all. She felt as if she'd been through a nuclear meltdown.

Tony tightened his arm, giving her a little hug. "Are you smiling, Tink?"

She smiled again and gave him a light pinch. "Yes, I am."

Running his hand up her arm, he gave her another hug. "You're really going to marry me?"

Maggie closed her eyes and hugged him back, pure happiness making her eyes fill up. "Oh yes, I am."

Tony rubbed her shoulder again, and she felt him smile. When he spoke next, his tone was serious. "Are your other kids going to have a problem with that?"

"I don't know." She sighed and ran her hand up his rib cage, trying to reassure him. "Haley won't, but Shawn might. At first. It takes him a little while to work things through."

It took Tony a few minutes to consider that; then he spoke again, his voice heavy with reluctance. "We can wait, if it's going to be a problem."

Raising up on one elbow, she gazed down at him, his face indistinct in the semidarkness. "I don't want to wait," she said softly. "I don't want to waste another day."

His expression sober, Tony reached up and tucked back a strand of her hair. "And I don't want to cause problems with your kids."

Cupping his face, she leaned down and kissed him, loving him so much her chest felt as if it might split wide open. She lifted her head and gazed down at him. "It'll all work out," she whispered softly. "I know it will. All it's going to take is some time."

Tony released a sigh. "God, I hope so." He touched her hair again, then smiled. "You're looking pretty good there, Burrows. You nearly blew me out of the water when you sashayed up to that pool table."

Smiling down at him through the heavy twilight, she pinched his lips together. "Then it wasn't me. I couldn't sashay if my life depended on it." She ran her fingertip along his bottom lip, then met his gaze, her own expression serious. "I want to tell you about that—about my reformation."

He reached up and caressed her jaw with his knuckles. "So tell me," he said, his tone gentle.

The room had lightened considerably by the time she finished telling him everything—all that she had learned about herself. Stroking his face with the back of her hand, she looked directly into his eyes. "I wanted you know," she said, her voice a little husky, "so you won't always be wondering if I'm going to bolt. I want you to know that I don't have a single doubt about us. I don't care if I'm nine years older. I love you, no matter what.''

Catching her by the back of the head, he drew her down, his mouth soft and warm and unbearably gentle against hers. "Then we're home free, Maggie,'' he whispered against her lips. "We're damned well home free.'' Then she felt him smile. "This is much better than the garage.''

She gave him a sharp poke and pulled away, narrowing her eyes. "Now who's pushing his luck?''

Running his hand up her back, he glanced at the clock on her bedside table, then looked at her, his smile a little off center. "According to the clock, I am.'' Using both hands, he brushed her hair back, smoothing his thumbs across her cheekbones. "It's quarter to five, babe,'' he said, his voice low with regret. "I'd better clear out.''

Not quite able to hold his gaze, Maggie ran her finger back and forth across his bottom lip. "Since I threw out most of my clothes,'' she said, her voice uneven, "half my closet is empty. And since you don't have a place to live—'' taking a breath, she met his gaze "—do you want to move in?''

There was a sudden glimmer of raw emotion in his eyes, and he abruptly looked away. Maggie saw him try to swallow. He waited a moment, then looked back at her. "You have no idea,'' he said, his voice very strained, "how much I want to do exactly that.''

Her own throat closing up a little, she touched his cheek. "Then come home,'' she whispered.

Tony shut his eyes and the muscles along his jaw contracted. He swallowed again, then released his breath. It was a long while before he spoke. "What about Kelly?''

"She'll be fine.'' Maggie smiled softly and stroked his cheek. "In fact, she'll be thrilled.'' She leaned down and kissed him. "I don't want to miss one more day with you,'' she whispered against his mouth.

"Ah, God, Maggie,'' he said, wrapping her in a fierce embrace. "I love you so damned much.''

Tears burning her eyes, Maggie hugged him back, feelings for him welling up inside her. This was right. They had both come home.

# Epilogue

It was cold and damp, and Maggie sat a row below Tony in the old wooden bleachers, huddled in the shelter of his body. He was hunched over her, his arms looped around her, his chin resting on the top of her head. He chuckled and gave her a hug. "Having fun, Tink?"

She put her arms over his, hugging his warmth. "This is insane. We're going to freeze."

"Nah," he said, giving her another hug. "We're going to have fun."

Maggie smiled to herself and snuggled closer. It was the end of April. And here they were, sitting on a wobbly set of bleachers at a go-cart track, waiting for the first outdoor race of the season to begin. And they were here, freezing their butts off, because her daughter—her baby—was about to get into one of those things, zip around the track, dodge through all the traffic and hopefully not get in a wreck.

And it was all Tony's fault. And Mario's. And half the Parnelli clan's. They had all encouraged Kelly, and Mario and Tony, God forbid, were convinced she was going to make one hell of race-car driver. Go-carts were her start—next year it was going to be stock cars. They had it all planned. And they were

all here—all the Parnellis, except Tony's grandmother—
waiting for their new step-daughter/granddaughter/niece/
cousin to do them all proud and bring home the checkered
flag. Kelly, needless to say, was having the time of her life.

Maggie looked across the track to the pits, emotion making
her throat close up a little. Her son was standing beside Mario
Senior, right in the thick of things, and Shawn was laughing at
something the older man had said. Lucky. God, she was so
lucky.

Shawn and Haley had both written their last final exam a
few days ago, and they were both home for the summer. Just
before Christmas, Spider and Jeanne had bought a little house
around the corner from the shop, so Tony had fixed up his old
apartment for her two oldest, and that had been a godsend.

Her son had been pretty reserved about her marrying Tony.
It had taken him awhile to adjust—and the apartment had
been the first step. But then Mario Senior had taken him under his wing, and in no time at all, they were thicker than
thieves. And in no time at all, Shawn had been absorbed into
the Parnelli brood. Mario Senior had even given him a summer job, working with a raft of other Parnelli cousins and un-
cles. The older man had plans. Everybody had plans, usually
cooked up behind Maggie's back and in Italian. About two
months after she and Tony were married, she had given up and
thrown her Spanish tapes into a drawer. She was now taking
Italian. It seemed like the smart thing to do.

Trying not to shiver, Maggie let her gaze sweep over the
crowd, another smile surfacing when she spotted a tall blonde.
La Goddess and Le God had crossed the track and were in-
specting Kelly's go-cart. Stevie had designed Kelly's racing suit,
and it was spectacular, to say the least. Stevie and Mitch had
pretty much been adopted by Rosa Parnelli as well. Tony and
Mitch played handball twice a week, and the four of them often went running together in the morning. Maggie was so
proud of herself. She could keep up, and run and talk at the
same time without collapsing from oxygen starvation.

Haley appeared at the bottom of the bleachers, a tray of hot
dogs and cups of coffee in her hand, a screaming-neon yel-
low-green beret yanked down over her ears. She grinned at

them, then clambered up, her screaming yellow scarf trailing on the weathered seats. Plunking herself down beside Tony, she passed her mother a hot dog and a cup of coffee, then gave Tony a poke in the ribs. "So, Dada," she teased, "are you going to set me up with that gorgeous cousin of yours?"

Tony took a bite of the hot dog Maggie offered him, then cuddled her closer. Maggie could tell he was grinning. "Not in this lifetime, chickie. I'm not letting you near any damned Italian."

"Ah, come on, Pa. My life's a drag. And he's pretty darned cute."

"He's pretty darned bad," Tony retorted.

Haley's tone was very dry. "Coming from such an angel."

"I am. Ask your mother."

Hanging over Tony's arm, Haley checked with her mother. "Is he?"

"Umm," answered Maggie around a mouthful of hotdog, almost choking.

"Yeah. Right."

Tightening his arms around her, Tony leaned down, putting his face against hers. "Hey, Toots. Are you having fun yet?"

Maggie grinned. "Just be nice about it when you thaw me out, okay?"

He gave her another squeeze. "I think I want to thaw you out right now," he murmured against her ear.

She grinned again and gave his arm a little hug. "Later."

Kelly won the race, well ahead of the pack. The whole Parnelli family carried on as if she'd won the Indy 500. Which, in many ways, wasn't out of line. After all, she had brought home the checkered flag.

Maggie grinned. But then, so had she.

*     *     *     *     *

# INTIMATE MOMENTS®
## *Silhouette*

# COMING NEXT MONTH

## MILLION DOLLAR SWEEPSTAKES
## AND EXTRA BONUS PRIZE DRAWING

No purchase necessary. To enter the sweepstakes, follow the directions published and complete and mail your Official Entry Form. If your Official Entry Form is missing, or you wish to obtain an additional one (limit: one Official Entry Form per request, one request per outer mailing envelope) send a separate, stamped, self-addressed #10 envelope (4 1/8" x 9 1/2") via first class mail to: Million Dollar Sweepstakes and Extra Bonus Prize Drawing Entry Form, P.O. Box 1867, Buffalo, NY 14269-1867. Request must be received no later than January 15, 1998. For eligibility into the sweepstakes, entries must be received no later than March 31, 1998. No liability is assumed for printing errors, lost, late, non-delivered or misdirected entries. Odds of winning are determined by the number of eligible entries distributed and received.

Sweepstakes open to residents of the U.S. (except Puerto Rico), Canada and Europe who are 18 years of age or older. All applicable laws and regulations apply. Sweepstakes offer void wherever prohibited by law. Values of all prizes are in U.S. currency. This sweepstakes is presented by Torstar Corp., its subsidiaries and affiliates, in conjunction with book, merchandise and/or product offerings. For a copy of the Official Rules governing this sweepstakes, send a self-addressed, stamped envelope (WA residents need not affix return postage) to: MILLION DOLLAR SWEEP-STAKES AND EXTRA BONUS PRIZE DRAWING Rules, P.O. Box 4470, Blair, NE 68009-4470, USA.

SWP-ME96

# As seen on TV!
## *Free Gift Offer*

With a Free Gift proof-of-purchase from any Silhouette® book,
you can receive a beautiful cubic zirconia pendant.

This gorgeous marquise-shaped stone is a genuine cubic
zirconia—accented by an 18" gold tone necklace.
(Approximate retail value $19.95)

## Send for yours today...
### compliments of ▼ *Silhouette*®
™

To receive your free gift, a cubic zirconia pendant, send us one original proof-of-purchase, photocopies not accepted, from the back of any Silhouette Romance™, Silhouette Desire®, Silhouette Special Edition®, Silhouette Intimate Moments® or Silhouette Shadows™ title available in February, March or April at your favorite retail outlet, together with the Free Gift Certificate, plus a check or money order for $1.75 U.S./$2.25 CAN. (do not send cash) to cover postage and handling, payable to Silhouette Free Gift Offer. We will send you the specified gift. Allow 6 to 8 weeks for delivery. Offer good until April 30, 1996 or while quantities last. Offer valid in the U.S. and Canada only.

## *Free Gift Certificate*

Name: _____

Address: _____

City: _____ State/Province: _____ Zip/Postal Code: _____

Mail this certificate, one proof-of-purchase and a check or money order for postage and handling to: SILHOUETTE FREE GIFT OFFER 1996. In the U.S.: 3010 Walden Avenue, P.O. Box 9057, Buffalo NY 14269-9057. In Canada: P.O. Box 622, Fort Erie,

---

**FREE GIFT OFFER**                                    079-KBZ-R
ONE PROOF-OF-PURCHASE
To collect your fabulous FREE GIFT, a cubic zirconia pendant, you must include this
original proof-of-purchase for each gift with the properly completed Free Gift Certificate.

---

079-KBZ-R

## Assignment: R♥MANCE

by
**Cathryn Clare**

The Cotter brothers—two private detectives and an FBI agent—go wherever danger leads them...except in matters of the heart!

But now they've just gotten the toughest assignments of their lives....

Wiley Cotter has...
*THE WEDDING ASSIGNMENT:* March 1996
Intimate Moments #702

Sam Cotter takes on...
*THE HONEYMOON ASSIGNMENT:* May 1996
Intimate Moments #714

Jack Cotter is surprised by...
*THE BABY ASSIGNMENT:* July 1996
Intimate Moments #726

From Cathryn Clare—and only where
Silhouette Books are sold!

CCAR1

# Alicia Scott's

## Elizabeth, Mitch, Cagney, Garret and Jake:

Four brothers and a sister—though miles separated them, they would always be a family.

Don't miss a single, suspenseful—sexy—tale in Alicia Scott's family-based series, which features four rugged, untamable brothers and their spitfire sister:

THE QUIET ONE...IM #701, March 1996

THE ONE WORTH WAITING FOR...IM #713, May 1996

THE ONE WHO ALMOST GOT AWAY...IM #723, July 1996

---

"The Guiness Gang," found only in—

▼INTIMATE MOMENTS®
™ Silhouette®

"Motherhood is full of love, laughter and sweet surprises. Silhouette's collection is every bit as much fun!"
—Bestselling author **Ann Major**

This May, treat yourself to...

# WANTED:

# MOTHER

Silhouette's annual tribute to motherhood takes a new twist in '96 as three sexy single men prepare for fatherhood—and saying "I Do!" This collection makes the perfect gift, not just for moms but for all romance fiction lovers! Written by these captivating authors:

## Annette Broadrick
## Ginna Gray
## Raye Morgan

BOOKS

THE GREATEST GIFT

"The Mother's Day anthology from Silhouette is the highlight of any romance lover's spring!"
—Award-winning author **Dallas Schulze**

Silhouette®

TM

MD96

**SILHOUETTE®**

***Desire®***

**CELEBRATION 1000**

## is on its way
## in April, May and June 1996!

Join us for the celebration of Desire's 1000th book!
We'll have

- Book #1000, *Man of Ice* by Diana Palmer in May!

- Best-loved miniseries such as **Hawk's Way** by Joan Johnston, and **Daughters of Texas** by Annette Broadrick

- Fabulous new writers in our Debut author program, where you can collect **double** Pages and Privileges Proofs of Purchase

Plus you can enter our exciting Sweepstakes for a chance to win a beautiful piece of original Silhouette Desire cover art or one of many autographed Silhouette Desire books!

**SILHOUETTE DESIRE'S CELEBRATION 1000**
   ...because the best is yet to come!

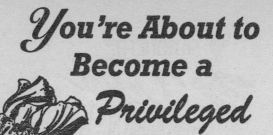

# You're About to Become a *Privileged Woman*

**Reap the rewards of fabulous free gifts and benefits with proofs-of-purchase from Silhouette and Harlequin books**

# Pages & Privileges™

It's our way of thanking you for buying our books at your favorite retail stores.

**Harlequin and Silhouette— the most privileged readers in the world!**

For more information about Harlequin and Silhouette's PAGES & PRIVILEGES program call the Pages & Privileges Benefits Desk: 1-503-794-2499

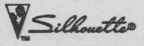

SIM-PP122